NEVER THERE

Nicole Loughan

Little Spot for Stories
Mason, MI

Never There
Copyright © 2024 by Nicole Loughin

ISBN: 979-8-9902483-1-1

Published by
Little Spot for Stories
Mason, MI

Cover Design by Eric Labacz, LabaczDesigns.com

To my own great big farm family and the loved ones that we lost too soon, Dad, David, and Duane. The warmth of the farm and the people who built it will live forever in my heart.

CHAPTER ONE

REMEMBER BACK IN THE EIGHTIES, getting home from school and eating Jiffy peanut butter with a spoon or watching Ed McMahon running up to houses with big checks and balloons to announce winners of the Publishers Clearing House? If you remember that, then we have two things in common: our memories are the same, and we are both completely wrong. Neither of these things ever happened. Jif has always been Jif and never Jiffy, and Ed McMahon never touched a Clearing House check or surprised a prize winner.

You might share another memory, a strong one, of visiting a farm when you were a kid. It was called Pendleton Farms. It was a huge property out in the country with rolling hills, a silo, and a big blue barn. You might even remember feeding a baby goat or petting a giant rabbit. You might remember the way the spring sunshine warmed you while you played in the hay. You might recall passing a sign on your way to that scenic farm that declared, "Welcome to Cedar Rapids."

If you remember all of this, just like me and my entire third-grade class, you are wrong again. Our parents assured us, and the lack of any photographic evidence proved it, it was a place that existed only in our minds.

I didn't have words for the phenomenon when it happened, but I've since learned that many people are plagued by false memories, or perhaps memories that were real and denied by the powers that be, for reasons unbeknownst to us. This phenomenon is known as the Mandela Effect. Discovered after a group of people gathered for a panel and recalled their memories of the funeral of Nelson Mandela, they described the ceremonies and people who attended the service, the speech of his widow. All recounted the same thing, only to learn that what they thought they had seen had never happened. Mandela was still alive. Some theorize these memories are from an alternate reality, and others think the effect is more straightforward: simply a confused memory, mistaking one thing for another.

Whatever the cause, my third-grade class experienced it. By the time we graduated from high school, Pendleton Farms and Cedar Rapids had become an ongoing joke, a shared memory we all had of a place we had never been. That memory is what made it all the more astonishing when I got a call one week before my high school reunion from Tammy Davis, a friend I hadn't talked to in a long time.

"Michelle, this is Tammy, guess where I'm heading, Cedar Rapids, baby!"

The message was shocking. Shocking because it came so late at night. Shocking because it came to me. And most shocking of all, when the call ended, just like Cedar Rapids, Tammy disappeared.

WHEN I WOKE TO THE MESSAGE, I was surprised. I hadn't talked to Tammy in years. I dialed the last number I had for her and was disappointed to find it had been disconnected.

I called another mutual friend from back in the old days, Missy Stacky.

"Hey girl! Can't wait to see you next week!"

"Me too," I squealed at her and jumped up and down, just like I did when we were in school having a chat about the gossip of the day. Though back in 1999 I was in the kitchen of my grandparents' farmhouse, and today, ten years later, I was tucked into a fifth-floor walk-up in Chicago with flimsy walls and thin floors. My neighbors were quick to remind me that my every move could be heard and banged on walls every time the floor squeaked.

"Shut up, 525!" bellowed from below me.

I gave an extra stomp to shut them up, feeling mighty proud of myself for my petulance. A round of aggressive pounding followed my mini act of defiance. It was frightening enough for me to latch the chain lock on my door and take a cautious step back to my little kitchen table.

"Was that person yelling at you?" Missy said.

"You can hear that?" I said embarrassed.

"Goodness yes, is that person in your apartment?"

"No, just thin walls. Anyway, I'm calling because I got this really weird message last night. It was Tammy, and she said she was heading to Cedar Rapids."

"Cedar Rapids?" she laughed. "Gosh, I haven't thought of that place in ages."

"So, she didn't call you?"

"Nope, but you were always the one obsessed with finding it, so maybe she thought you would want to know."

"Hmm, I bet Corey will know more; he still lives in town. They talk more than the rest of us. And… on that note, I thought maybe we'd all get together at The Alpine next week, like old times."

"Well, I'd love a basket of nachos and a rum and Coke, so I'll be there, but if Tammy pulls a Tammy, I'm out."

"She's not that bad, and I don't even know if she'll come. I haven't talked to her in ages."

"It's not me you have to worry about; it's Jen. She's not going out much these days. The baby isn't even here, and it's already her excuse to get out of everything. Baby this and baby that."

"I know. I'll call her."

After we hung up, I dialed Jen. It went straight to voicemail; I hated it when people had their tape set to pick up on the first ring.

"Hey Jen, it's Michelle. I got a weird call last night. It was Tammy. She said she was headed to Cedar Rapids; remember that farm trip in third grade? Anyway, wondered if she called you…maybe we could all get together. Your mom sent me the invite to the shower. I'll be there. I'm heading your way this weekend. I can't wait to see you. Talk to you soon. Kisses."

That left Corey. I still talked to Corey every now and again. His proximity to my cousin John meant he occasionally called to let me know a lamb had gotten out or one of John's chickens wandered over the property line. Outside of the antics of livestock we didn't find much to talk about anymore. I assumed it was the distance because whenever we got together it felt like old times.

He picked up on the third ring, "Hey Corey, it's

Michelle."

"Mmmm," he mumbled. Then he yawned. He sounded like he'd been asleep. I checked my watch: 8 a.m., not that early on farm time.

"Hey, um sorry to bother you."

"It's not my goat," he mumbled.

"I'm not calling about a goat. I'm calling about Tammy."

"Tammy?" he perked up.

"Yeah, she called me last night."

"You? Why would she call you?"

"Well, we were good friends once you know."

"Yeah," he coughed. "But when was the last time she wanted to talk to you?"

"I'm delightful, Corey; people want to talk to me often, but that is beside the point. She called and said she was going to Cedar Rapids."

"Cedar Rapids? The fake place?"

"That's why I'm calling. Do you know what she's talking about?"

"Oh, shit. Well, she's got some things going on, and uh, well, let me make some calls."

"What's she got going on?"

"I don't know if she'd want me to tell you about it. Because you will tell Missy, and Missy will tell Jenny, and then it will just be all these people in her business that she doesn't want in her business."

"Well, can you check on her and tell her I'm glad she called? I want us all to get together. Next week at The Alpine. Are you in?" I asked.

"Uh, yeah, I'll make something work; my cousin is coming into town too, so I'll be pulled in a few directions. Are you going to come to town early for the fair? Your grandmother keeps asking me to work a shift to sell milk at her barn stand."

"Why are you talking to my grandmother?"

"I always talk to your grandmother."

"I'll ask you more about that later. The short answer is, yes, I'll be there. I'm leaving early. My boss doesn't want me to go, but I'm doing it this time. I'll be there for sure. By the way...what are they paying you to work in the milk barn?"

"A gallon of chocolate milk."

"Good, that's what I get."

"Anyway, I'll make some calls. I'll talk to you later in the week. Pick a night and let me know."

"Oh, wait, any chance you can pick me up at the train station in Battle Creek on Saturday and take me to grandma's house?"

"Normally yes, Saturday no. You're going to have to call your grandmother."

"She already said she'd pick me up. I just didn't want to bother her. I'm trying to stay out of her way. She's so busy with everybody at her house and making meals for the whole family all the time. And Grandpa's not getting around so well and all that. So, I'm planning to stay out at the camper."

"The camper is awesome. I'll visit out there, and we can get in some time on the boat."

"You got it."

I hung up the phone and listened to see if my neighbor had calmed down, or if there was any continued threat of a reprisal from my stomping.

Talking to Corey was enough to paint a picture of home in my mind. He was probably in his apartment above the garage at his parents' house, with the big window that looked out over the field. It was early, so the sun would be up casting a golden blanket of light over the corn. It wouldn't be high yet, but if it was doing well, it would be knee high, like the old saying, knee-high by July.

I longed to run along the lane that separated my family farm from his family property. Back home I had wide-open spaces. The world felt boundless when I ran from one field to the next. I could run past the soybean field my father had sown, to the cornfield my grandfather had sown, straight through to my uncle's cow patch, and then on to Corey's family plot with acres of corn on one side and a horse pasture on the other. The horse would run with me sometimes, and I would run until I hit the woods. Their pasture stretched as far as the eye could see.

In Chicago, I had one small square of earth to call my

own, and it was situated above four other people's square of earth. I owned, or rather, rented air space. It was a small apartment with gray walls and beige vinyl flooring. The room was cheered somewhat with a yellow fridge and stove which matched a yellow sofa I'd picked up off the curb when I got to town. The couch was quaint in its way, with a multi-colored mailbox and bird print.

My little place wasn't quite a studio as it did have a small bedroom, just large enough to fit a full-size mattress. It sat on the floor, and I could lie to myself and pretend that with my mattress on the floor I had higher ceilings, which would help ward off the claustrophobia from lack of windows. The reality was I couldn't afford a headboard or a bed frame.

I should have money, but I don't. I graduated from college with a degree in journalism that promised an anticipated income that never came. When I graduated, I set off to make my mark in the world. I was going to be like Woodward and Bernstein, the journalists who took down Nixon with their tenacious sleuthing or go undercover to expose wrongs using long form exposés like Gloria Steinem did when she went undercover at Playboy. It wasn't long after I graduated that I learned journalism was in the final throes of a death spiral. When I entered my first newsroom, I was taking over the beat of great journalists who came before me. They enjoyed the golden age; they were unionized, well-paid journalists who, just as I graduated, had been given early retirement and shown the door. I didn't feel too bad for them when I learned they were paid a living wage, had health care, and earned a pension. I was forced to work for half the pay, had to do twice the amount of work, and benefits were on offer only if I could afford them, which I could not.

On top of the lousy pay and terrible hours I also couldn't do investigative journalism. The artform was all but dead. With budget cuts, I would never get a month to work on a story, or a week, or even more than a day.

I was tasked to write five stories a week, and I had to do it in a cube surrounded by three other empty cubes. Those cubicles used to be occupied by other writers, copy editors, and developmental editors. I could walk down the hall and find other groupings of cubes that were mostly empty. My office had a lone sports reporter in his empty cluster, or I could go even one more row over and talk to the middle-aged goth woman who did government updates, obituaries, and classified ads, but she wasn't very friendly since she'd been forced to take on those other departments. Her heart was really only in obits.

I had one editor, Bill, who barely had time to read my work though somehow found time to pace around the office at deadline time. He wanted my stories to be perfect the first time, every time, but I was more like a half-the-time sort of lady. Whenever he had to make an edit, I swear he circled the mistakes so loudly I could hear it through three empty cube walls.

He was a decent editor but a terrible boss. In an unguarded moment in the coffee room, he told me about the before times, when he just edited stories. His eyes lit up when he told me about all that I had missed, a lively newsroom filled with crosstalk from writers, photographers, and editors, many putting their heads together to cover a big story as a team. He said you could feel the excitement in the air in those days.

"You missed the glory days," he said and hung his head. "Now, I have to write, and manage people, and layout pages. I used to just edit. I used to be a thinker."

I swear a tear slid into his coffee. I wasn't sure if it was a tear or sweat rolling off his balding head, but something definitely emanated from him and rolled into his coffee. I gave him a sad pat on the back, and he walked away shaking his head as if he had forgotten he was even talking to me.

On my way to work that morning, I felt a sense of dread. I had to finish two stories in advance for next week and one more to finish the week I was in. I usually finish one article per day, but I was going to need to knock out three so that my boss would keep his cool while I snuck away for a whole week.

He was waiting for me by the door. "Are you going to get all three of those in today?" he snapped.

"Good morning, Bill." I said, pushing past him and past the reception desk which didn't even have a chair behind it, as the company had long abandoned having a receptionist.

"Good morning to you, Michelle." He corrected his manners, then just as easily went back to his rushed state. "What's the status? You can't leave without giving me a story for the school section and the city council wrap up."

"I know, Bill. I was thinking of my angle for the school story on the way over. I'm on it."

"If you can write three stories in one day, you can write more than one a day and take a few more off my plate, you know."

I rolled my eyes. My predecessor averaged one and a half stories per week. I walked away from Bill to my cube without conversation and noticed he was still standing by the door, probably waiting for the sportswriter to come through to make sure he would meet his deadlines too.

It was a bad time for the paper, and with more cuts looming over us from corporate and talk of the internet getting more and more popular with our advertisers, every moment seemed like a scramble to keep my job. I knew it was a bad time to leave Bill, but I had to. I needed a getaway. I needed to push away the boundaries of my 396-square foot apartment and be in wide-open spaces. While I typed away in my cube, I pictured running through the pasture at Corey's grandparents' house and spinning like I was Maria in the *Sound of Music*.

I had finished two out of three stories, and it was almost five o-clock.

"Two down, one to go," I whispered to myself. I was a deadline writer; I could do this. I got my head out of the hills and back to the keyboard just as Bill popped up over my cube like a shark. "You're not going to finish the council story. I knew it!"

"I'm on it, Bill. I won't leave till it's done."

"Do you really need to take your whole week of vacation all at one time? Break it up; you can take three days next week and then two days another time. You're tying up all your days with one trip."

"I need to go, Bill. I haven't had a vacation in six months, and I haven't seen my family in over a year. And I'm entitled to one more week of vacation in addition to this one."

"Don't remind me. Well don't you go planning to take

that one all at once. This is killing me."

"Bill, I'll take it when I take it. Calm down so I can write."

I typed away, hacking out a mundane story with poor transitions. I would normally have smoothed those out, but it was hard to think with Bill pacing in front of my cube. Just before six I shouted over the wall. "It's done. I'm going home."

He pounced; without saying a word he ran down to his office and pulled up the story and printed it. I heard a furious scribble from his desk and quickened my pace to leave.

Just as I opened the door, I heard a shout from his office but pushed on through without looking back. Bill was going to have to make his own edits on this one.

I was out of the building and checked behind me several times as I hustled home. My heart was pounding so hard I felt like I was running from a slasher. But it was just the threat of my work stalking me. If Bill was following me, he was doing it at the pace of Jason Voorhees. It's not like he could make me go back, but I didn't want to argue. I scurried home, and when I was finally in the safety of my apartment, I threw the lock on the door, grabbed my phone off the receiver, and made my way to my bedroom. I opened my suitcase and set it on the ground in front of my dresser, sorting through my clothes while I dialed Grandma.

"Emm, hello," Grandma said. She always cleared her throat before she said hello. It was an old trick she learned when she worked as a telephone operator to make sure the line had time to connect before she talked."

"Hi Grandma, it's Michelle."

"Oh," she exclaimed with excitement. "Tomorrow is the big day. I can't believe it's tomorrow. We haven't seen you for ages."

"It's going to be great. I'm really looking forward to seeing you. Are you sure Skeeter or somebody can't come and get me? I don't want you to have to drive so far or ruin your plans." My real worry is Grandma was driving slower every time I saw her, and her reaction times weren't quite what they used to be.

"Nonsense, you are my plans."

We chatted about the milk barn and the best way to pack for a Michigan summer, which was exactly the same as a Chicago summer, before Grandma came around to the question that I knew she wanted to ask. The words that she used were, "How are things," but what she meant was, "Do you have a boyfriend yet? Do you have any money? Is that job going anywhere? How long do you plan to live in squalor?"

"Things are…fine," I said.

Hmm she replied. Which meant that was not the end of that discussion. She would ask me how "things" were again when she had me trapped in her Buick for an hour and a half long car ride.

"Okay Grandma, gotta finish packing. I love you, bye!"

And I clicked off the phone before she could say anything more. No need to have the discussion about "things" twice.

I had just set the phone down on the bed so I could free my hands for folding when it rang again.

"Emm, Hello," I uttered, involuntarily emulating the way Grandma answered the phone.

"Uh, Michelle?" It was Corey.

"Yes, it's me; sorry I just got off a call with Grandma."

"Yeah, you did that throat clearing thing she does; it threw me off. Oh, well I don't want to freak you out or anything, but nobody has heard from Tammy since yesterday. She never came home last night, and she didn't show up for her shift at work today. What exactly did she say when she called?"

"She just said she was going to Cedar Rapids."

"Did she sound scared or upset?"

"No, she sounded really happy."

"And Missy and Jenny didn't hear from her?"

"Missy said no, and I just left a message for Jenny."

"It's weird that she called you and not me. No offense, but I talk to her pretty regularly, and I know you guys don't talk anymore. Why do you think she called you?"

"Sorry, Corey, I don't know why she would call me. Truth be told, I didn't know she had my home phone number."

"Okay, well if you hear from her again can you call me? Her mom is getting a little worried."

"I'll let you know. I'm leaving in the morning, but I can call back home and check my messages."

"Let's plan to meet up tomorrow night. I'll pick you up at your grandparent's house around seven if that works for you."

"I'll see you then."

I walked back to my kitchen and looked at the machine as I replayed the message; it said it was left at 3:16 a.m. "Michelle, this is Tammy, guess where I'm heading? Cedar Rapids baby!"

CHAPTER TWO

IT WAS A QUIET THREE-HOUR train ride back to Michigan; Tammy was on my mind. She was always a ball of energy, and she stood out wherever she went. She had red hair and freckles when we were kids but had dyed her hair black when she got older. You couldn't miss her. She had so much energy that sometimes it was too much. When she did what we called "pulling a Tammy," she turned from exciting to scary. Some of her greatest hits were picking fights with waitstaff, yelling obscenities across crowded restaurants, and telling strangers to mind their own business when they looked at her for her wild behavior. I wondered if she was having a "Tammy" moment when she called and was still in it someplace.

I was coming in through Battle Creek, the Cereal City, the place where Kellogg had been headquartered for approaching a century after the invention of the Cornflake, conceived as a cure for masturbation. It was a town that was not big but not small either. It was also once very prosperous with abundant manufacturing and a high per capita income, but the manufacturing sector was in decline, and it had led to the city slowly wearing away, exposing some of its rough edges.

The train let out at a little station just outside of town, and I saw my grandmother's oversized burgundy Buick parked at a restaurant across from the station.

I ran up to her car and found her waiting inside, fiddling with the radio. I gave her a little knock, and she startled. But a smile spread across her face when she saw me, and she reached up to her dash to hit the button to pop the trunk.

I tossed my bag in the back and bounded up to the passenger's seat. We leaned together to give a side hug in the car; I was a full foot taller than my petite grandmother, and I outweighed her by the heft of a husky kindergartener. She always felt small in my embrace, and I made sure my hugs were gentle and small to match her size.

My grandmother was descended from Quakers, who

don't believe in violence or confrontation. That doesn't mean they don't confront people; what they do is ask pointed questions wrapped in the genteel veneer that befitted a proper Quaker. She wasted no time in non-confrontationally confronting me about my mess of a life. As soon as we passed Tony the Tiger, on a billboard, waving goodbye and urging us to make a return visit to the city of Battle Creek, she cleared her throat, "Emm, how are things?"

"Things are good." *You're going to have to do better than that, Grandma.*

"Good with that job? Cause last I heard you still didn't have any health benefits. And that is very important when you are an adult."

She left the question open-ended, and to say yes would be a baldfaced lie, not very Quaker of her to trap me in this question.

"No," I sighed. "Things are not going so well at that job."

"So, you've been there for a few years now. How long are you going to keep at it?"

"I need more clips to get into a better paper. I need a big story, and I haven't had one yet. It's hard to really dig into something because we are so short staffed. I just need some time to get better; then, hopefully, I'll find something else."

She slowed the car and pulled over to the side of the highway, positioning herself on the shoulder of the road but not all the way off the street.

"Hand me my purse back there?" she pointed to the back seat. I reached back and grabbed it for her. She rifled through it slowly while cars whizzed past us; one even gave a honk, but she didn't move one bit faster.

"Grandma, we shouldn't be on the side of the road. What are you looking for? I can help you."

"Distracted driving is as bad as drunk driving. They can wait," she said, staying buried in her bag. Then she mumbled, "People are in too big a hurry these days."

Another car whizzed by, and grandma slowly pulled an article out of her purse. I noticed she pulled it from a roll of other articles held together by a paperclip. She slowly passed it over to me.

"Are all of the articles in that stack for me?"

She didn't say anything, which was a resounding yes in Grandma World.

"So do you want to hand them all over to me at once so we can get it all out of the way?"

"No," she said pointing to the headline of the article now in my possession.

The headline read, "Journalism is dead. Comms degrees listed as most regretted in the country."

She pulled away slowly, leaving her blinker on to signal entry to the road for almost a full five minutes. It gave me time to read through the article, which was pretty well summed up by the headline. I found it ironic that an article about the death of newspapers was written by a journalist in a newspaper.

"So, is there really a better job to be had?" she asked.

I had to think to answer that truthfully. "I don't know Grandma, but I don't know what else to do. I've applied to every newspaper from here to Nebraska, and I got the one job that called me back."

"Maybe there's something else you can do. Do you have any savings, so you could spend some time trying something new?"

"Well, I have 280 dollars, and after two more paychecks, my student loans, my rent and my bills, I'll have 210 dollars."

"Well at that pace you'll be out of money in just a few months."

"Twice a year I have a three-paycheck month, so there's that. And you usually send me a hundred bucks on my birthday, so that month I live like a king. Name brand macaroni and everything."

"Maybe you could use some budgeting help."

"I don't think budgeting is my issue; my income doesn't even hit a grand some months, Grandma."

"Oh, my, that is difficult to budget. Well, are you meeting any people?"

Men, she means have I met any men.

"With 280 bucks to my name I don't go out all that much."

"Oh dear."

"It's okay, Grandma. I'm still figuring some stuff out."

By the time my grandmother was my age she already had five children, 200 acres of land, 100 head of cattle, and two big Ford trucks. I didn't need reminding that I had no acres of land, zero cattle, and I wasn't even one-truck rich.

"If you want to come home and try something else, we will be here for you," she said. "I can't help a vast deal financially…it's just so sad because I think if your parents were alive things would have been different." She started to tear up. Their death was harder for her than it was for me. The accident happened when I was so young, I could barely remember them. They only existed in snippets of my memory. In fact, I wondered if the memories I had of them now were even memories at all or just what I remembered from stories I heard about them.

I still talked to them sometimes like they were there, sort of like a prayer and mostly to my dad. I had a book full of pictures that my grandmother had made for me to help me remember them. Seeing myself in my dad's arms standing in front of his cornfield or in front of his truck filled me with comfort. I could still remember the feeling of being safe with Dad though I didn't quite remember why anymore. When I was having trouble with relationships I talked to Mom, which seemed like something a mom would have helped with, and whenever I was in danger I prayed to Dad, and he always answered.

The extent of his answers varied but the most glaring example happened in high school. On my way home from school on a narrow country thoroughfare, I was forced off the road by a Dodge Ram pick-up. I rolled my colossal Chrysler Fifth Avenue down a hill and into a tree. As a reckless teenager, I had ignored safety measures like seatbelts and was driving with my left foot wedged under my buttocks, which is why I was so slow to brake. I covered my head with my arms and, in the first of three car flips down the hill I felt my arms hit the ceiling, and I prayed, "I'm going to need some help on this one, Dad."

The car flipped two more times, and my arms hit the ceiling twice more before the spinning ultimately ended with my whole body sprawled on the ceiling of the overturned car. I slowly crawled out of my broken driver's side window, seconds before the car collapsed onto itself. My loose CDs and fast-food wrappers were strewn all around the wreck, and somehow I stayed in the car the whole time and walked, or rather crawled away, completely unharmed.

When the police came, they congratulated me on wearing my seatbelt, saying if I hadn't, I would have been a goner, thrown from the car like all the other debris. As I was not a goner, I could only attribute that miracle to my dad. A miracle I kept to myself to avoid a ticket and the wrath of my grandma for my carelessness.

"What are you thinking?" Grandma asked. I must have been smiling about how I avoided that ticket. It had triggered her senses.

"I was just thinking how lucky I am to have so much loving family."

"We love you. But things would have been different if your parents had lived. We could have helped more. We're farmers, so we're land rich and cash poor. I wish we could have given you more, but it was just so much to raise little kids at our age."

"I know. I don't need more."

We went quiet; this conversation was getting too serious for both of us, so Grandma turned up the AM radio where the Farmer's Almanac was being read by a monotone speaker. It was as good as a bedtime story for me, and I nodded off.

When I woke, the unmistakable smell of cow manure hit my nostrils. It was a sour burn, horrible, but it let me know I was home. Within a few moments I was acclimated, and the smell was imperceptible. I stepped out of the car and found Grandma trying to lift my bag out of the back. I ran to help her, hefting it out of her hands.

"You were always so strong," she said.

"Maybe I can move furniture for my next career," I replied.

She shook her head at me and started for the house. Grandma always got where she was going, but she moved at a sloth's pace. I would usually zip ahead of her and end up holding a door open long enough for multiple small talk exchanges, making it awkward for all involved.

Standing at the back door, I surveyed the farm, just as expansive, maybe even more, than I remembered. I dropped my bag by the door and turned to the field.

"I'll be right back," I said.

I ran up the big hill at the back of the house, the one where all of us kids did our sledding when we were young. I got to the top of the hill, dubbed Mount Moo, and twirled around, letting my blouse billow up around me. After several twirls I didn't feel much like walking down the hill like a normal person, so I lay on my side and rolled, safe from the usual cow crap as they had moved to the other pasture earlier in the season. When I got to the bottom my Uncle Skeeter's giant hulking form was looming over me, blocking out the sun. I covered my eyes and could just make out his face. He was smiling and chewing on a length of straw.

"Whatcha doing?"

"Maria'ing."

"Like *Sound O' Music*."

"Precisely."

"I respect that."

He helped me up, and we walked to the house.

"How are things?" Skeeter asked.

"I already talked to Grandma about things. How are things with you?" I asked.

"Well, I've had a string of good luck lately."

"You always have a string of good luck, Skeeter."

"Well, more luck than usual. I won a good hand at poker two weeks back: then, I won the raffle at the Cancer Society relay, and my Tigers tickets been making me a fair amount on them interwebs."

"You don't use your tickets anymore?"

"Not with tickets sellin' like they have. I just as soon sit here and watch with Mom while they make me that much money."

Skeeter was one of those people who never worked, always had schemes, and never hurt for money. I was the opposite of Skeeter.

"I've had a string of bad luck lately, Skeeter. Any advice?"

"If it ain't workin', don't do it."

"I don't know if it's that simple."

We were up to the house, and he opened the door for me.

"Well, that motto works for me."

"Anything you could recommend that I should do?"

"Do what you want to do."

I didn't know what that was either. "The only thing that I knew I wanted to do was spin in the hills."

"Well, you done did that. Mission accomplished."

Skeeter grabbed my bag from the porch and followed me up the steps. I walked through the mudroom and up to the kitchen where Grandma was cooking.

"Mission accomplished!" I said to Grandma.

"Ehmm," she said as she shuffled past me. "Can you peel the potatoes?"

She passed me the peeler as she walked by. I started peeling over the trashcan, sitting by the window. Grandma's kitchen was remodeled to the top of the line, best appliances, and counter tops from the year 1957 and had never been changed a bit since that day. The wood cabinets had brass pulls and accessories, and the countertops were yellow and bordered with sturdy silver metal. The brown combination range and stovetop had reliably made a casserole a day for more than fifty years. While the kitchen wasn't much to look at, it had big windows that looked out over the farm, a beautiful view. And while the cabinets were small, the counters were tight, and the sink was drippy, it got the job done.

I sat on the stool by the window and looked out as I peeled potatoes and carrots and shucked corn. It wasn't long before Corey rolled up in his Ford Ranger.

"Corey's coming for dinner," Grandma called out as I saw him walking up the back steps.

"I have a Jell-O salad from my mom," Corey said. He took off his hat as he entered the kitchen, and Grandma walked over to him to collect the salad.

"Thank you," she cooed. And he bent down to give her a hug. She gave him a peck on the cheek and a one-armed pat on the back.

"So, we have a mission tonight," Corey said, looking at me. "Tammy's still missing. Her mom asked if we could go out and look for her."

"Tammy?" Grandma asked. "Your little friend with the red hair and the bad temper, that Tammy?"

"Well, she's not so little Gram, I think she's 5'7" and her hair is dark now, but yeah, she's been missing for a few days."

"Any idea where she went?" Grandma asked.

"She said she was going to Cedar Rapids."

"Iowa?" Grandma asked.

"I think she meant Cedar Rapids, Michigan."

"There is no Cedar Rapids, Michigan," Grandma said without looking up from her pot.

Corey chimed in, "Well there is, and there isn't. See we all went on this class trip in the third grade to this place called Cedar Rapids and this farm, but later it seems like nobody can remember exactly where it was."

"There's no Cedar Rapids. I'm sure of that. What was the farm called?"

"Pendelton's." I answered.

"Hmm, that I've heard of. Grab Skeeter for me."

"Skeet," Corey yelled, and Skeeter came up the back steps.

"Whatcha need?"

"Skeet, have you heard of Pendelton Farm?"

"Hmm, that sounds familiar."

"How about Cedar Rapids?" I asked.

"Iowa?"

Corey and I both shook our heads.

"Aint' never heard of another Cedar Rapids."

"That's what I said," Grandma added as she unwrapped an orange-colored Jell-O "salad" filled with mandarin oranges and pocked with mini-marshmallows and coconut flakes.

"Call down to the barn, Skeet. Let everybody know supper's ready."

Skeeter and Corey unfolded two more tables for the living room and rolled Grandpa to the head of the twelve-seat table in the dining room. They finished placing the last tablecloth just as a handful of my aunts, uncles, and cousins descended on us for dinner. Everybody had a dish in hand, but Grandma made the bulk of it, and the centerpiece was her big golden ham, adorned with pineapple and cherries, just like the Betty Crocker cover picture from 1972. Corey and I got a seat at the big table next to Grandma, an honor reserved for guests. Skeeter sat across from us and was eager to ask more about our missing town.

"What kinda livestock they had at Pendleton Farm?"

"They had cows, goats, and a lop-eared rabbit," I said.

Corey added, "Horses and ducks, I think. And a big barn with a yellow sign that had a hamburger on it."

"It was a steak," my cousin John called from the end of the table.

"It was a burger," Corey and I both said in unison.

With food in his mouth John mashed out the word, "It was a steak."

"Ignore John. Anyway, they had their own milk bottles, and they said Pendleton on them. I remember that."

"Hmm," Skeeter said. "That sounds mighty familiar."

"Cedar Rapids though, maybe you mean Cedar Springs or Grand Rapids. Could be one of those got all gummed up together in your mind. You all going out as far as Grand Rapids tonight?"

"No," Corey said setting down his corn on the cob. "Tammy worked at the bar out in Dairy; we're going to stop by and see if anybody knows where she might of went."

"Then Corey's going to take me out to the camper."

"You're not staying out here?" Skeeter asked loudly. The room got quiet.

"I want to stay out of the way. And get some time in the water. Just really clear my mind."

My aunt Sandy shook her head at me.

"Well shoot, you come all this way, and you ain't even visiting," Skeeter said.

"I'm visiting now, ain't I. I mean aren't I, Skeet?"

"I'd prefer you stay out here with us," Grandma added. "I have the room upstairs all made up."

"I'll be here for lunch and supper most nights. I'll be here to help. So, you'll get all the best parts of a house guest without having me get in your way. Plus, Grandma, you have one bathroom and a million people around here."

"I raised five kids with one bathroom. Seems plenty."

CHAPTER THREE

COREY AND I FINISHED OUR MOUNTAINS of food and a hearty slice of zucchini cake, which is a regular cake filled with shaved zucchini and topped with cream cheese icing. We took our final bites on our way out the door. My family had heaping desserts with every supper, and salads made with Jell-O, plus chocolate milk with breakfast, lunch, and dinner, and yet diabetes had somehow missed every generation. It was a medical mystery. Corey said he could only eat like us at Thanksgiving.

The sun was down as we headed out of town. We passed the plaza and the two trailer parks that touched each other, marking the separation line between two different towns. Our town was known for its annual leaf festival and low property taxes. The other town was Dairy, whose claim to fame was selling fried chicken gizzards at their annual festival. It was a part of the chicken that I was completely unsure of where it was and also unwilling to learn about.

"Want to get a gizzard?" Corey asked, knowing I wouldn't.

"Not in the least."

We took the old highway, the one that had been bypassed thirty years ago. It was marked 20 miles per hour slower than the main highway and was in a perpetual state of disrepair but had the fortune of being a slightly more direct route to downtown and had an adult store with mannequins dressed in over-the-top lingerie costumes like scantily dressed ears of corn or naughty Bob Ross standing in the window that greeted you just before you got to town. It was always a laugh to see what the teens who worked there chose for the window display.

"Oh," Corey said, "Barbeque Burlesque. You would have thought they would go with hot dog costumes. I guess that was too obvious."

I looked over to see that rather than dressing the mannequins in costume this time they dressed various barbeque items in scantily clad lingerie.

"It was too easy to make a hot dog sexy," I said. "I guess propane tanks with thongs were a little more creative."

We were just one turn away from town and that meant one turn away from everything Dairy had to offer. Dairy was the sort of town my dad would have said, "If you blink, you miss it."

I didn't need to ask where Tammy worked to know where we were going because she worked at the only bar in town. We parked downtown, and I followed Corey into the town bar, just next to the county animal shelter and across from the post office. Other than the park, that was the town. It didn't even have a grocery store anymore; that closed up when they built the new Walmart in Marsh.

Corey grabbed all of the attention as we walked in; he had that rugged, handsome quality of a man who had been slinging bales of hay all day—probably because he had been slinging bales of hay all day. Ladies swiveled in their stools and men looked over, huffed, and turned back around. The bar had dark, wood-paneled walls on three sides and a big mirror behind the bar. There were old neon signs advertising gas stations that had long since closed and beers that were no longer served. On the far side of the bar, which was very close to the near side of the bar, there was an air hockey table.

"Hey," Corey shouted.

"Corey," the bartender nodded at him. She was a small woman with a long-braided ponytail that reached down to her rear. "What can I get you?"

"Just a beer, whatever you got on tap."

She started to fill a mug.

"And your friend?" She looked at me, and I stepped up to the bar. "Uh, White Russian?"

She winked at me. Corey took a seat beside me.

"Hey, Julie. Any chance you've seen Tammy around?"

She paused. It was a brief pause, but she definitely stopped moving.

"No," she turned around with big a smile on her face. "Can't say I've seen her."

"Is she supposed to be working tonight?"

"No, she's not due till tomorrow. She's supposed to be in around 3:00."

I whispered to him, "I thought her mom said she missed her shift yesterday?"

"I'll talk to you about that in the car," he whispered back. "But she was here Thursday night?" he asked Julie.

She bristled again. I noticed it, but I wasn't sure if Corey had.

She looked back at Corey and nodded.

Corey seemed satisfied, but I wasn't.

"Were you here that night?" I asked.

"No, only Tammy was working Thursday," she said looking away from me. I bent down to meet her eyes as I was half a head taller than her. "I wasn't asking if you were working, I asked if you were here."

Corey kicked my shin.

She met my eye and said, "I popped in for one drink. Not that it's any of your business."

Corey looked at me, trying to tell me something with his eyes, but I missed the message.

"Did you hear her say anything about where she was going?"

She shook her head casually.

"Cedar Rapids maybe?"

She scrunched her face and looked at me like I had two heads. "Where's Cedar Rapids?"

"It's this place we went when we were kids. Well, we think we did."

Corey kicked me again.

"Is there anybody else who was here last time you saw her?" I asked.

She looked around the bar and lingered on a bald man with a barbed-wire wrist tattoo stooped over a pint at the end of the bar. She moved on quickly from him, trying to cover the look she gave him, and quickly scanned the rest of the room. She turned her head to me and shook it.

"So, that guy down there?" I said, stepping away from the bar and heading in his direction.

"Hey, don't," she whispered. When I kept my pace, she jutted her hand out to stop me. But I stepped out of her reach and barreled forward.

"Hi," I said as I approached him. He pulled his head up from his beer and gave me the same look I would expect from an agitated Pitbull.

He looked me up and down, and his expression remained unimpressed. I could usually elicit something of a glance in Mid-Michigan as I was just shy of six-feet tall. I was not so out of place in Chicago, but in my hometown, and enshrined in my yearbook, I was given the distinction of "Tallest Girl in School," placed often in photos next to David Blanch "Tallest Boy in School," a feature that helped propel him to football captain, prom king, and basketball star. He used to date Anna Shepherd, "Best Smile." And she was short—of course.

"What?" the Pitbull said it so angrily that Corey stood from his bar stool and took a step closer to me.

"Um," I managed to squeak out as he made me a little nervous. I shook off my nerves and took a tiny step closer and looked him in the eye, just to show him I wasn't afraid.

"Hi, I'm Michelle," I held out my hand to him and he ignored it. "I'm looking for a friend. She works here. I wondered if you might know where she went after her last shift a couple of nights ago. Maybe you heard something or saw her talking to somebody."

"Nope," he said, clenching his jaw.

I was going to have to use my grandmother's superpower of asking a question in a way that demanded an answer.

"That's odd. I didn't even say who my friend was. I didn't catch your name by the way?"

That was a shot across the bow. If ever there was a time to take a step away for my own safety, it was now. He had narrowed his eyes at me, trying to size me up, and I stared straight at him, refusing to give ground. Corey took another step in my direction which made the man move his head just enough to lose our staring contest and give me a chance to step away the winner. I shrugged and turned.

"What makes you think I was here?" he asked while my

back was to him.

Without turning around, I answered, "You were. I can tell by the way you answered."

"Hey," he shouted. He sounded a little closer to me than I expected. I turned and found him within arm's reach of me.

I hope you're on this, Dad, I thought, and caught a glimpse of Pabst Blue Ribbon beer on the counter, just to his right. That was my dad's drink and that was enough for me. *Message received, Dad.*

"Don't you dare…" He pointed his finger down into my face and without thinking I whacked it away from me. I could tell my strength surprised him. He puffed up at me, getting ready to say something. Just as he opened his mouth, a thin old hippie wearing a Grateful Dead T-shirt who had been sipping the Pabst jumped up between us.

"Hey man," the small man said, acting as a barrier. Though the real protection was the much larger Corey who had darted to my side.

There was a new staring contest brewing between the Pitbull man and Corey. After sizing up Corey he decided the fight could be lost. He turned and went back to his seat.

I looked back at Julie; she was shaking and trying to hide it while she popped the top on a Budweiser. She slid the drink across to a customer and said to him, "I'm going to go grab a smoke, Teddy. Keep an eye on the bar for me."

She glanced at me as she stepped outside; I assumed that was my cue to go with her.

Corey and I followed her out together and found her shaking as she tried to light a cigarette.

"Hey," Corey said gently. "Let me get that for you."

He reached forward and smoothly lit her cigarette, like a country James Bond. She took a puff and closed her eyes, sending the jitters away as she exhaled.

"What was that?" I asked.

"That was Randy."

"Why was he so mad?"

"I tried to warn you not to talk to him."

"I mean not really," I said.

"I said don't."

"I didn't know what you meant by don't." I had known exactly what she meant. "So, do you think Tammy went with him?"

"No." She looked up at the sky and stomped her foot. "Look, Tammy's been getting into like bad shit lately, like bad, bad shit, like drugs."

Corey added, "She's been having a lot of trouble lately keeping calm, and I knew she was starting to drink too much. I didn't know about the drugs. She said she was going to get some help."

"Well, when she tried to stop drinking, she started some worse stuff."

"So, is that guy a dealer or something?" Corey asked.

"He works for her dealer. He was there to make sure she paid up. He took all the tips she made, all of it, and he told her it wasn't enough."

"So, then what happened?" I asked.

"I don't know. I left after that. I didn't want to see whatever was going to happen."

I felt my cheeks flush, "So you just left her when she was in trouble?"

"Listen," she took a drag of her cigarette. She isn't my friend. She's my co-worker. Her business is her business, and I've got my own problems, and I've got my own kids, and she ain't neither of those."

"You could have told me," Corey said. "I could have helped."

"Yeah, well. She didn't want your help. She didn't want you to know."

"So after all of this, why did she call me and tell me she was heading to this fake city we used to talk about?"

She shook her head, and another patron walked out of the bar, waving at Julie as he stumbled past.

After another drag on her cigarette she said, "That Cedar Rapids place you talked about? I've never heard of it. She was probably high."

The man stumbling out of the bar turned around.

"Did you say Cedar Rapids?" he slurred.

We all turned to him.

"Yes," we said in unison.

"Well shoot. I haven't heard of that place in years, then all of a sudden, I hear about it twice in two days!"

"You've heard of Cedar Rapids?" I asked. The man was far too old to be one of the Marsh Elementary field trippers.

"Heard of it and been there once."

"Where is it?"

"Couldn't say. That was… hick… way back. I think they closed up shop."

"What did you hear about it recently?"

"Oh, that. She was.. hick.. talking about Cedar Rapids… hick…"

"Who was? Tammy?" Corey asked.

"No, Cherry Stein."

"Do you mean Charity Stein?" I asked.

"Stage name," Corey whispered to me.

"Don't know Charity. I only know Cherry," he slurred. "And Cherry told Tammy she found Cedar Rapids, and would she like to go visit with her? And Tammy goes, 'Sure I'll go.'"

"When did they leave?"

"I don't know, but Cherry stayed 'round all night. Even when Randy started pushing everybody around, yellin', making a fuss."

"Did they leave together?"

"Probably. Randy in there took her car keys, so if she didn't go with Cherry, I don't know who she'd go with."

Corey and I exchanged a look, and on my end my eyes were saying oh shit, and I couldn't tell what his eyes were saying because his eyes clearly spoke some other language.

"Anything else you can remember?" I asked.

"Nope," he turned to walk down the street and got a few steps away. He stumbled for a minute and looked around the sidewalk, before turning back to us. "Oh, he took her phone, too. He's not out here, is he?"

We shook our heads.

He whispered, "Son of a bitch," and stumbling down the

street he headed away again, mumbling an imperceptible song.

"That explains why she called me," I said to Corey. "I gave Charity my phone number a few weeks ago. She was on the decorating committee for the reunion, and I volunteered for it, so she had my number."

He nodded. "That's why she didn't call any of us. She didn't have her phone."

"But why did she call any of us at all?" I asked. "Like did she think we should know for some reason? She's a grown woman; she didn't need our permission."

He shook his head, "I don't know."

"But that doesn't answer the biggest question of the night," I said.

"What's that?" Corey asked.

"Um, why does Charity have a stage name? She's not the stripping type. I thought she was a dental hygienist."

"She is a hygienist, and she's not a stripper," Julie bristled. "She's a burlesque dancer."

"Isn't that, like, a fancy stripper?"

"No," they both said in unison.

Corey continued, "She's a real dancer. Like they promote her at big halls and stuff. She's a big deal around here."

"In Dairy?"

"All of mid-Michigan." Corey said.

"I'd say all of Michigan, and some of Ohio," Julie added.

She had stopped shaking and tossed her cigarette to the ground to stomp it out. "Well, I'm going back in."

"Sorry, I messed that up in there. I hope I didn't make your night worse."

She shook her head and waved me off.

"Here," Corey said, and he held out his hand with a $20 bill to her. "Take care of yourself out there. If you need anything, call me. And if you hear anything about Tammy, anything at all, let me know.

She took the money without looking at him and went inside.

When the door was closed Corey started walking down the street toward the car. Once we were out of earshot of people at the bar he said, "What were you thinking? That guy could have killed you."

"I'm fine."

"Oh, you are not fine; if that guy hadn't jumped between you, he would have torn your head off."

"I knew I was fine. The PBR guy was drinking my dad's beer, so I knew he'd be cool."

"That's not a thing!"

"Well, but it is, and it always has been. You know it. If I see my dad's beer, or Michigan State University stuff, or John Deere Green or corn, I know he's looking out for me."

He stopped and turned to look at me. "Corn, Michelle? This is Michigan. There's corn everywhere. It's not a thing, Michelle. Also, didn't you feel the many kicks to the leg I gave you to try to get you to lay off?"

"I got the kicks. I assumed you were encouraging me."

"Lies! Isn't your family Quaker? Aren't you supposed to tell the truth?"

"Correction, my grandmother is a Quaker, or was I guess, but I'm not."

"Well, I didn't like how any of that went down."

"We got the information we needed. She went with Charity to find Cedar Rapids."

"And where are they now?"

I shrugged.

"Let's find Charity. There's a show tonight in Lansing."

CHAPTER FOUR

COREY AND I TOOK OFF FOR LANSING, twenty minutes away but practically on another planet. Dairy was a quiet commuter hamlet with one stoplight and residents who all knew each other. Lansing was the bustling capital city with over a hundred thousand people. We were headed to an uptown theater which was nestled in a mid-century modern building that used to be the four-story Sears Shopping Center. It stuck out like a sore thumb in town with its yellow and blue enamel façade, rounded corners, and rounded glass prism windows. It was a symbol left from the era of the multi-level department store. Since then, it had been a state department building, a mixed-use commercial building, and more recently a nightclub and theater.

Corey parked two blocks away so we could observe the club before we went in.

"When did she start doing this?" I asked.

"Oh, you remember how she used to be in all the theater stuff in school, and she was always in dance? I think she's been into it for a while."

"Have you been to one of her shows?" I asked.

He hesitated. "I've been to some."

"Some," I prodded. "What do you get out of a burlesque show with dancing women?"

He blushed. "It's not just women, and I like art."

When we rounded the corner to the newly shined-up mid-century modern building, the entry was adorned with up lights and a red carpet. I looked at Corey and punched him on the arm.

"What?"

"We can't go in there like this, Corey."

"Like what?"

"You look like a lumber jack, and I look like I've been rolling around in a field."

"So?"

"So, that's fine for a Dairy bar, but there's people in

sequins walking in there."

He looked at the entrance to the club and down at himself, then at me and shook his head.

"Yeah, you look bad," he said.

"Do you have any ideas?" I asked.

"Missy lives around here; you think she has something we could borrow?"

I turned him around and we headed back to the car. Within ten minutes we had pulled up to Missy's apartment. "Oh, my God," she squealed after she buzzed us up. "I didn't know you were coming tonight."

"We weren't planning to but we're looking for Tammy, and we need to go to a nightclub and…"

"And," she looked at me quizzically.

"We need some clubbing clothes."

"Oh," she looked me up and down. "Yeah, you need something all right. Uh, let me see what I have."

Missy was, in the style of every woman, smaller than me. She bobbed into her closet and pulled out a black wrap dress with silver details. She held it up and pulled it in several directions. "This has a lot of give," she said.

I held it up to me.

"It's going to be short," Corey said.

I shrugged.

Missy went back into her closet and pulled out a tiny tight blue dress with sparkly fringe. "I can't wear that," I said.

"That's for me. We're going clubbing!"

"Well, we were actually looking for Tammy." I corrected.

"Yeah, and after we find her, we dance."

She started stripping and Corey turned around. I followed suit and turned around.

"So, you guys are going to this club to look for Tammy?" she asked.

"Well, we are looking for Charity Stein. She should be there, and we heard Tammy left with her the other night."

"Hmm, no, Charity works at my dentist's office," Missy corrected.

"She works there too," Corey said. "This is more of a

weekend thing."

She tapped me on the shoulder. I turned around and found her wrapped in her tiny blue dress motioning like she had just performed a magic trick. "Ta-da," she smiled.

"You look great," Corey said. She popped back into her closet and threw out a black shirt. It landed in a heap on her bed.

"Some guy left that here, Corey," she shouted from the inner recesses of her closet.

He held it up; it was a shiny black button-up, with printed on blue and silver flames. He shook his head as he looked at me. I held up the black dress and pointed out the plunging neckline.

"If I wear it, you wear it," I whispered.

He walked out of the room and across the hall to her bathroom.

I pulled off my t-shirt and jeans and wrestled myself into the little black dress. There was a lot more "little" in that little black dress than I was expecting. I managed to pull it just below my bum and not a centimeter lower.

"Ahh, perfect," Missy screamed running out of her closet. She handed me a pair of black flip-flops.

"I don't have any shoes that will fit you," she said.

I kicked off my sneakers and slid the flip-flops on. A full two inches of my foot hung off the back.

"These don't fit."

She shrugged and slid her own feet into spikey heels.

She maneuvered her way behind me with a brush and started to wrench my hair, pulling it back into a ponytail.

"I don't think I can go anywhere in this dress."

She smacked me with the back of her brush. "Shush, what are you talking about? You look gorgeous."

Corey walked out of the bathroom with his blue-flamed fiasco, far too tight around the biceps and open in the front.

"It's too tight," I said.

He looked at me, "Well, at least we match."

"You guys look great. We need to get a picture."

"No," we both shouted.

IT WAS A SHORT DRIVE BACK to the club. We pulled up in

front and sauntered past the red carpet. As ridiculous as our clothes looked, they seemed to fit the theme: sparkly, dark, and tight. At my height I looked like I was in heels, and nobody noticed I was practically walking on the floor. I felt the cold marble of the steps touch the bottom of my feet as we made our way into the night club. It was in a big sunken room that I imagine was once accessible by an escalator that lowered you down to housewares. It was now a gleaming black and white bar with workers dressed like they were out of the 1950's. The women wore short skirts and tiny hats, and hanging around their necks, they carried what looked like old-style 1950's cigarette boxes filled with drinks. The men wore arm garters and had neatly trimmed facial hair.

On the stage there was a jazzy lounge singer belting out a deep brassy number, accompanied by a piano and a bass.

"I've wanted to see this place for weeks; it just opened you know," Missy said, turning to me. She was a stunner. In a matter of minutes, she had managed to get her bright blond hair tamed in a bun, accentuated with sparkling butterfly clips and with just mascara and a swipe of lipstick she looked like a tiny Barbie brought to life.

"You literally live ten minutes away."

She looked at me and pouted. "I don't have anybody to go with. Everybody is like married, or pregnant, or getting married, or getting pregnant. I feel like I'm the only looo," she stopped herself.

Corey looked down. We both knew what she was going to say, loser. We knew by most measures that was true. Corey lived with his parents, and worked for his parents, and I was broke and living in a hovel.

She turned around and pretended nothing had transpired. "Anyway, we're here now."

We walked up to the bar.

"What do you want?" Corey asked.

"I'm sure I can't afford to drink here," I said.

"I got it," he said.

"That White Russian that I didn't get at the last place is calling my name."

"You got it."

He looked at Missy.

"Oh, a Cosmo, like on 'Sex in the City'." She smiled. "Oh, I'm such a Samantha," she said. "Corey is a Carrie. What are you, Squishy Mishy?" she said, looking at me.

"I don't know any of the words that just came out of your mouth," I said, puzzled.

"Hah," she laughed. "You are such a Miranda, but you look like a Charlotte, but with like the boldness and the height of a Samantha."

"If you say so."

She saw something in the distance and wandered away.

"What's a Carrie?" Corey asked. I shook my head.

We turned our attention back to the bar and a young man with garters on his arms and a handlebar mustache gave Corey a long look.

He ordered our drinks, then asked the bartender, "Do you know Cherry?"

The young man looked crestfallen.

With Corey oblivious to what had just transpired, I interjected. "We went to school with her. We just wanted to see if she knew what happened to another friend of ours."

"Oh," the young man said, brightening as he turned his attention back to Corey. "I know her. She dances at a lot of bars in town. She should be here tonight."

"When would she go on," I asked as he mixed our drinks.

"I don't know. You can go in the back and look for Heather. She runs the line-up." He beamed at Corey, looking for approval. Corey laid down some money on the bar and without looking at him said, "I'll be right back."

The bartender was just getting started on my drink, but I didn't want to wait for it and lose Corey. He made his way to the corner of the stage and boldly walked up it and behind the curtain. I didn't have his brave stride in flip-flops, but I tried and failed to match his cool demeanor.

As soon as I passed the curtain a person tried to stop me, but without turning around Corey said, "She's with me," and I was given a pass to follow as if Corey's say-so meant something.

We passed behind the main stage and made it to a hallway where he found a small man holding a clipboard.

"I'm looking for Heather."

He pointed down the hall, and Corey charged forward. A small, older woman with dark hair looked up as Corey approached.

"Can I help you?" she said, chewing seductively on a pencil.

"I'm looking for Cherry," he said.

Her face fell, and again, I had to intervene before Corey ruined our chances to use his good looks for information.

I jumped ahead of him. "She's a friend of ours from high school."

She rolled her eyes, "Yeah, lots of girls around here have, she made air quotes, 'friends, who are looking for them.'"

"Well, we are actual friends; we know her as Charity Stein, she's…"

"Shh," she cut me off. "We don't go around blabbing real names like that."

"Oh, sorry," I said. "We're looking for her. She left with another friend of ours the other night, and now we can't find her."

She shook her head and let out a long breath. "Well, I wish I could help you, but we have the same problem. I haven't been able to get ahold of her all day. She missed rehearsal earlier, and her phone goes straight to voice mail."

Corey had a delayed reaction to the news. "So you haven't seen Charity either?"

"Nope," she said, shaking her head.

"Does she have an emergency contact that we can reach out to?"

"No, but her roommate is sometimes around here."

She pointed to the stage. "Angel."

A small woman in a blonde wig was on stage in a bright red dress, swinging her hips like Marilyn Monroe. She had stuffed all she had into the little red dress, and it was a lot of stuff in a small amount of dress. Her face was plump and cheerful, and a huge smile crossed her face as she reached behind her and snapped something on the back of her tiny gown, unclasping it, and flinging it off. She spun around and, while I was sure I was about to see her in her birthday suit, I was surprised to find she was somewhat covered by a layer of thin sequins that wrapped around her ample assets in a way that did not, moments ago, seem possible. When she spun around again and whipped an impossibly high kick in the air, her eyes met Corey, and her playful smile turned coy as she bit her lip. She spun back for the audience, and somebody off stage threw a feather boa to her. She used it to cover herself as she spun again and released the string of beads that had been keeping her from the Full Monty. She worked and spun with the boa in hand and managed to cover herself in the important places with every flip and spin. Corey was right about burlesque. It was not stripping; it was twirling and teasing. And exhilarating. She swirled again, turned around, her back to the crowd, and tossed the boa over her shoulder. Just as she was about to spin around, the lights went down, and she stepped off stage.

She came right to me and Corey, and when the lights came back up, we could see she had been held in by flesh colored nylon. She was never actually close to nude, but on stage it sure looked like it.

"Hi, I'm Angel," she held her hand out to Corey. She had a million-watt smile. "Hi," he said.

I stepped forward. "That was so beautiful. Nice to meet you, Angel. I'm Michelle, and this is Corey."

She didn't take her eyes off Corey and said, "Thank you, hon."

"Um," Corey was somehow stunned into silence. Maybe he did appreciate art.

"What is it, Sugar?"

"Uh," he shook his head. "We're old friends of Cherry. We were hoping to see her tonight, and we heard she didn't show."

Angel made an exaggerated frown and then made a pouty face, and in a baby voice said, "Nope, no Cherry today."

"So, are you concerned?" I asked.

Still looking at Corey she said in her baby voice, "Are you concerned?"

"Yes," he said, and then he seemed to snap out of his trance. "We are very concerned. Do you know where she could be?"

She shrugged, "Nope."

I couldn't believe how casual she was.

"So, did she come home yesterday?"

"No."

Corey looked to me for advice on what to do. I rolled my eyes, trying to say to Corey, "Is she this big of a bimbo, or is she messing with us? Or is she a psychopath?" I was going to have to dig deep into the recesses of my brain to get this girl to talk. What did I know about her: she was a good dancer, so she couldn't be that stupid; she lives with Charity, so she's probably not a psychopath.

I was trying to think of just the right way to ask a question when Corey just blurted out, "Are you right in the head?"

"Yes, I'm right in the head," she dropped the baby voice. "I've had about enough of Cherry's stalkers."

"Charity," I said. "Charity. We went to high school with her. The reunion is next weekend, and we're trying to find her. She ran off with our friend Tammy the other night, and now they are both missing."

"Oh," her attitude changed entirely. "Let's talk someplace quiet. There's a lounge down at the end of the hall. I'll throw on a robe and meet you there."

We walked down the hall and found a dusty room fitted with velvet couches and chairs. There was a low coffee table in the middle of the room with a tray of lit candles on it. The light was low, and there was a couple making out in the corner.

Angel swept into the room with only her wig cap on and fluffy white robe.

"Privacy," she snapped her fingers, and the happy couple from the corner made way. She sat in the velvet chair across from us and started picking at the wig glue around her scalp.

"So, she got your friend wrapped up in her mess, huh?"

"What mess?" I learned forward.

"This new prick that she started dating. I told her to stay away from him. Bad news."

"Who?" Corey asked.

"Bryce something or other. He's terrible. She said he's like a college professor or something, but he's not right. Like there's a screw completely loose with that guy. She couldn't see it; she just saw the Mercedes."

"That doesn't sound like Charity," Corey said. "She's not about money like that."

"You haven't seen her recently, I bet. He's been hanging around for a few months, and he does these like mind games on her. It's so messed up. She can't even see it. He says things like, 'Imagine how good your show will be when you get fit' or 'You would think you'd have the best teeth working for a dentist'."

I made a disgusted face and said, "That's not like Charity at all to allow that sort of thing."

"I know," she said as she pulled at her wig cap, revealing locks nearly as dark as mine. "He didn't spring that on her right away. Like months in he starts with this negative compliment stuff. It's out of this play book to trick women into liking you by making them insecure. I've had men try it on me before, and my brother told me all about it, so I knew what to look for. Bryce follows every stupid trick in that book."

"How do you fight against that sort of thing?" I asked, genuinely curious.

She let out a maniacal laugh. "My go-to is to tell them I'm not like other girls; I really like small things, like small hands or dainty feet, whatever looks smallish on them. I let them know I love those tiny things. I throw their playbook right back in their tiny faces."

Corey made an ouch face. "That would work."

"So did you tell Charity this, so she knew what he was doing?"

"He's a next level manipulator, not like these dweebs at the club. I couldn't get her to see it."

"So, weren't you concerned when she didn't come home?"

"She's barely been home in months. She's always with him now. As soon as I tried to pull her away, he started to pull her in."

"Does she still pay her rent?"

"He pays it, mails a check right to the office. I never see it, but it's always paid."

"So, Thursday night, she met our friend in a bar out in Dairy. One of the guys at the bar said she was there all night and that she left with our other friend. They were looking for this place we went to when we were young; it's called Cedar Rapids. Ever heard of it?"

She smiled. "Yeah, from Charity. She said it was this place where she visited a farm when she was little. She said it was from a time in her life when things weren't complicated."

I remembered the farm. Holding a bottle out to feed a baby sheep. I feel like I could remember Charity there with me; we weren't close friends, but we were friendly and in the same class. We laughed and petted the sheep together. It was a hot day, and I remembered the sheep bleated at us, begging for their bottles. They let us pet their heads while we fed them, and we giggled. It was pure; it was uncomplicated. I knew exactly what Charity meant. My heart almost ached at the memory of it and the thought that it might not be real.

"Oh, darling," she said, and she reached into her bosom and pulled out a cloth handkerchief. "What's the matter?"

A tear must have escaped me.

"It's uh…"

Corey picked up what I couldn't say. "It's just that they say that we never really took that trip. Like a false memory. But we all have it."

"No," Angel shook her head. "That's not possible. All of you have this memory?"

I nodded. "I've heard of this before. It's like that movie The Matrix; they say there's like a glitch, you know, in time. If you all remember it, and you feel it, maybe it happened, and there's another like dimension or something where it happened, but you all ended up in this one for some reason."

I wiped my eye and chuckled. "I don't think I've left dimensions."

She looked lost in thought. Then she looked me straight in the eye. "She said there was a picture. Somebody had a picture of this farm. She was so excited. It was somebody who came in just the other day. He gave her the picture, and she was just beside herself. Gosh who did she say it was? Oh, I can't remember."

"What did he look like?"

She shook her head, "I didn't see him, but his name. Uhh, it will come to me. I just, it was like this distinct name, never heard it before."

I thought back to school, went through names in my head, "Blaine, Gibbon, Dario?" She shook her head. Corey searched his memory for names, and we couldn't get there.

"Sorry guys, it's not in there. But if I think of it…"

I wrote my cell number on a piece of paper. "Call me, after six preferably, I only have night and weekend minutes."

Corey rolled his eyes. "This could be life or death. I'll risk daytime minutes." He wrote his number down and slid it across.

"Well, if it's life or death then yes, anytime minutes. But let's keep it short, to the point."

CHAPTER FIVE

WE COLLECTED MISSY, RETURNED to her apartment, and changed back into our own clothes. When I peeled Missy's dress off me, I saw that I had stretched it beyond repair. I folded it up and put it on the top shelf of her closet. She'd had enough to drink so that she was half asleep as we walked up to her house. I helped her into sweatpants and a t-shirt and set a glass of water and two Tylenol on her bedside table. She mumbled to me while I tucked her in. I felt her head and listened to her chest, making sure she was just tired and not something worse. Corey and I sat in her living room for a minute listening to her mumble before it gave way to snoring, and we felt safe leaving her home.

It was a dark drive out to the campground, with no moon in sight. The only lights out that far shined on the signs for the campground. They featured a family of bears welcoming us to Trident Lake and campground, reminding us to slow down and watch out for cubs. I had expected the camping office to be long closed, and the couple that worked the desk fast asleep, but we were surprised to find the shack open and Ernie, a retired farmer who was a friend of my grandfather's, sitting in the booth in his oversized overalls, feet up on the desk, watching an old episode of *Will and Grace*, a show with a hearty number of storylines focused on gay characters. It was a surprising choice of show for an old farmer in a conservative town.

He was shaking with laughter as we pulled up. When he saw us, he quickly placed his feet on the floor and scooted his rolling chair up to the window.

"Boy howdy," he said. "That Karen gets me every time."

Corey and I looked at each other and suppressed a laugh.

"Hey, Ernie," I said.

"Well shoot, Michelle. Haven't seen you round here in an age. I just need you to fill out this here form for me." He passed over a clipboard with two lines to fill out, unit and name. I filled in the clipboard and handed it back to him.

"Y'all take care now, ya hear?"

We pulled away, and soon the light from his TV and the little shack was out of sight, and the night was once again dark. We drove slowly, ten miles per hour or less, per the rules, down the little lane that led to my family camper.

They had been renting a spot at that campground for more than forty years, and with each year they were given a better spot in the campground. They had started with their camper in Row five, Spot 525, near the porta-potties. Now the camper was all the way up to Lake View Row one, Lot number 001. We had the best view of the lake and the spot nearest to the boat launch. To the north was nothing but water, to the west other campers, and to the east the woods. It was the quietest and most desirable spot, and my grandparents had earned it through their skill of outliving every other original camper. They were celebrities at the campground and given status as the only space allowed to erect a permanent deck on their lot.

When my cousins and I were young, we would ride our bikes around the place, from the pond to the bingo barn, to the playground, to the lake, and if we were lucky, we ended our day at the ice cream shack. We would haul around our bug and amphibian catches in our bike baskets; we had containers for frogs, lightning bugs, water bugs, slugs, butterflies, fuzzy brown caterpillars, and just about anything else you would find in or around a pond. While my cousin John was built like a brute, he always took prodigious care of his little creatures and would chastise anybody who mishandled them. He would let us spend the day with our catches and examine them, but he had a rule that we had to have adequate air holes, and we had to put them back where we found them before the sun went down.

At the lake we would float in big black innertubes or climb the raft, covered with green astroturf, in the center of the lake, and play king of the mountain, pushing each other in until one cousin was the victor. With twenty-two first cousins, I never had that distinction as I didn't have enough fight in me. We would do this from sun-up to sundown, and if anybody ever put sunscreen on me, I never noticed. I burned my shoulders and knees constantly; my cousins, who had the gift of pigment, fared better and rarely had to sleep coated in a thick slime of aloe as I did. Luckily, a night bathed in Banana Boat often did the trick though my ability to sleep was less certain. I was often relegated to the floor, or if I was lucky I would get the bench seat cushion in the breakfast nook. Lying in those precarious places, covered in cold, green, smelly gel made for difficult sleeping conditions.

Corey pulled up to the camper; it was severely dark around it, with no lights on in the neighboring units and the camper closed tight. He walked me to the door, and we found it unlocked, as always. I hefted my suitcase inside and flicked on the porch light. When I stepped back out to say goodbye, I found Corey had moved to the edge of the deck and was looking over the water.

"You going to be okay going home this late?" I whispered.

"I'll be all right," he said.

It was darker than a typical night, but the darkness helped reflect the stars. There were gentle ripples in the water bobbing the stars around in their reflection. It was almost otherworldly, but peaceful.

He looked lost in thought. "Ten years," he said.

I didn't follow his train of thought.

"Ten years since we've been out of school," he said again, still looking out.

"Are you thinking about what Missy said?"

He nodded. "Everybody having babies, getting married, buying houses."

"We could do those things."

He shook his head.

"Oh, I forgot. You can't. Well, you could do one, maybe two out of three."

He nodded.

"I don't think it will be that way forever, Corey. It's 2009, like I just heard they made gay marriage legal in Iowa now. So, you could go to Iowa. I'm sure it's coming to Michigan soon too."

He looked sorrowful, and he was too quiet. I wanted to give him a big hug, tell him it would be all right. I couldn't imagine what he was going through. I felt a powerful need to cut the tension, and I fought my urge for nearly five minutes.

"I mean, it could be legal tomorrow, but you still have to find somebody who will put up with you, so that's another ten years at least."

He let out the smallest snort and said, "I know; you can't stand silence. So, I'll forgive you for trying to get me to laugh even when I'm feeling very serious, and I'm pouring my heart out to you."

"I'm sorry, Corey. I wish there was more we could do."

He looked back at me and held out his arms to hug me.

I hugged him back and rested my face on his shoulder. "So, is there anybody in the picture you would marry?"

"Oh my God, not you, too."

"Oh no, I'm becoming my grandmother."

"You are," he said. "Bye."

He walked quietly to the other side of the deck and waved. He took a step off the porch and got only a few steps down the lane when he stopped in his tracks.

Snap!

Corey turned around. The sound had emanated from the woods. I stepped off the porch and stood next to him; my gaze followed his. We both stared into the woods, looking for any sign of movement.

I felt a shiver run down my spine.

Corey held his hand up to his mouth and made a shush gesture toward me.

I quietly padded away from him up to the camper. I gently opened the door and reached inside, opening the closest drawer and pulling out my grandfather's Maglite.

I snuck back to Corey's side and handed it to him.

He snapped it on and shone it on the woods, sweeping in both directions. The woods were thick, and when he scanned the ground there was no sign of disturbed grass or twigs near us.

After a few moments he snapped off the light.

"I didn't like the sound of that," he said. "That was something heavy."

"Could be a deer or maybe something fell out of a tree."

He shook his head.

"No, I hunt a lot with my dad. I've heard a lot of animal sounds in the woods. That was something different."

"Maybe we should go inside."

"Why don't I just take you back to your grandparents' house? I know it's late, but I'd feel better about it, and I'm sure they won't mind."

"It's fine. Nothing has ever happened here, and my cousin Andy is like two campers over." I pointed down the row. "That's his Jeep right there."

"You have your phone, and it's charged?" he asked. I pulled out my pink Motorola Razr. "I'll plug it in now."

"If you're sure. Lock your door. And call me if you hear anything. I'll turn around and come right back."

I watched him get into his car, but he didn't move, just stared into the woods. I walked into the camper and made a big show of locking the door. I did as promised and plugged my phone in. Then popped back over to the window. He was still out there, and he had moved his car to position its lights to look out at the woods. I waved at him, and he seemed to settle and pulled away.

I looked around the camper, decked out with the best the 1980's had to offer: white wallpaper with a pattern of geese wearing blue bows between brown hearts. Hanging on the wall were various wooden heart accents, jigged out by my grandfather, like a wooden heart key hook and heart coat hanger, currently holding towels. There were also family photos set up between practical items like a coffee percolator and the toaster. I walked to the wall to look at them. Several were staged photos from Olan Mills, with all of us positioned in our Sunday best. But my favorites were the old family ones, with my grandmother and her parents in black and white, wearing the plain garb required from Quakers in those days, including bonnets and muted colors. She was just a toddler in the photos, and she and her brother were held by her parents who had smiles on their faces, a rare capture in old photos. There were also sepia-tone pictures of my grandfather standing along the Lake Michigan shoreline sand dunes fishing with his brother and dad.

I placed the photos back where my grandmother had them and set my sights on the bed. I was going to get the most coveted spot of all, the bed, the actual bed. I had never, in my nearly 30 years of camper visits, been allowed to sleep in the bed. I ran up the small steps to the queen-sized mattress waiting for me at the head of the fifth wheel and jumped in. I relished it for a moment before kicking off my jeans, shoes, and socks and grabbing my oversized *Friends* T-Shirt; in the friendly font that matched the show was written the words "Pivot, Pivot, Pivot."

I turned on the small black-and-white tv which only received antenna channels and surfed through the two channels still active; it was a Ken Burns documentary or a just beginning episode of *Golden Girls*. It was an easy call. I clicked off the lights, closed the plastic shade that separated the upstairs from the downstairs, and watched Rose, Blanch, Dorothy, and Sofia with their antics in Florida. I was a notoriously poor sleeper and would often stay up late into the night watching shows. By three episodes deep I wondered how Blanche, adorned in shoulder pads, sequins, and short cropped feathered hair managed to pull in just about any man she wanted in her mid-50's when I couldn't even get one in my late twenties. I was about to doze off to sleep to the comforting sound of the laugh track when I heard another crack. This time it was closer. I leaned up in my bed and turned down the tv. I looked out the window to the side of the camper facing the woods, but I couldn't see anything.

Creak!

The next sound was close, like it was on the deck.

I jumped to the window on the other side of the camper to look out, but the awning blocked my view of the deck from that side. I moved to the end of the bed and with shaky hands tugged at the corner of the plastic divider so I could see out the windows in the kitchen. I had managed to open it only a crack when I heard the handle on the door to the camper jiggle. I screamed and jumped back.

Jiggle. Jiggle. The pace was more frantic. Then suddenly a loud *Slam.* The person hit the door with force. I was sure it was hard enough to break it.

I grabbed a pillow from the bed and held it in front of me

as if it could protect me and jumped down the stairs, trying to get a look out the window. Then I heard a squirrelly, scratching noise to my side, and I realized there was another way to get into the camper, through the storage compartment. There was a crawl space between the storage area, which we used to house beach toys and marshmallow sticks and the cabinet that came up under the sofa. I jumped to the ground and put my ear against the cabinet. I heard frantic scratching; they were cleaning out the storage area. I moved to the floor, pushing my back against the breakfast nook, and planting my feet squarely on the center cabinet, pushing hard against it.

I scanned the room for something I could use to defend myself as I still only had a pillow in my hands. Then I heard heavy, quick steps across the deck and split my focus between the crawl space and the door. My feet jerked back toward me as the cabinet cracked open. I kicked against it, hitting something, and the cabinet catch clicked back into place. The cabinet shook under my feet frantically, and I kicked back with everything that I had, steeling myself like a wedge, still gripping my pillow tight.

"Go away," I screamed piercingly, kicking the cabinet door one last time.

It went quiet. I should have gotten up and checked the locks, but I was paralyzed with fear. I looked down at the pillow in my hands, it was embroidered with the words "Bless this Mess." I hugged it to me and lamented that I had left my cellphone on the kitchen counter just out of my reach. I heard more noise in the woods and closed my eyes, *"What do I do, Dad?"*

Just then the light on my phone went off, lighting up the whole kitchen. I steeled myself and jumped up to look at it; it was set to silent, but the screen showed it was Andy calling. I picked it up and heard a ragged voice on the other end.

"Hey, so uh are you at Grandma's camper? I just heard screaming?"

"Yes, oh my god, oh my god, come down here."

"Argh." He hung up.

Within minutes he was down at the camper in his boxers and a t-shirt, his hair crumpled on his head, and a baseball bat in his grip."

"What the hell, Michelle?"

"There was somebody here; they tried to open the door, and then they tried to crawl through the storage space. Corey heard them earlier out in the woods."

He woke up at that, "Are you serious?"

"Yes."

"And you had locked the door?"

"Yes!"

He stepped out onto the porch and looked at the door; it had a dent in it. Then he went to the back of the camper and saw the beach toys thrown hastily on the ground.

"They punched the door," I said.

"Okay, I'm going to go get my stuff. I'll sleep on the couch. We'll go look in the woods in the morning."

"Thank you, thank you, thank you."

CHAPTER SIX

POOR ANDY SPENT THE ENTIRE NIGHT bent like a pretzel to fit his 6'3" frame on a five-foot couch. His neck was up on the armrest, and his head was propped up on the wall. His legs hung over the other arm rest; no part of him was straight. I, on the other hand, slept like a log with a nice breeze from the bedside fan and the cushy trappings of a real bed on a bed frame.

I crept slowly down the stairs and into the bathroom at the bottom of the steps. I pulled my toiletry bag out of the closet, where Grandma had kept a small LL Bean toiletry bag for each of us with our names embroidered along the side; bags she bought for all of us grandkids for Christmas more than twenty years ago. I opened it to find a new travel-sized tube of toothpaste along with mini-versions of my favorite shampoo, conditioner, and soap. My heart leapt a little. I hadn't been able to afford the items in that bag for over a year. In my current financial state, I'd been reduced to using Suave 2 in 1 from the dollar store and no-name white bar soap that never produced suds and never got any smaller. Looking at my mini-travel bag stuffed with my favorite items, I got a little emotional. I knew Grandma could afford these little comforts, but I was too stubborn to ever ask her for them. I grabbed my bag and a towel from the rack in the kitchen, then stepped quietly out of the camper, easing the door closed behind me. I looked at the deck. The chairs were where I'd left them; the deck box was closed up tight. The awning was intact, but the door had a noticeable fist-sized dent in it. I reached up to feel it and put my hand in it; it was a big fist that hit that door, I thought. I pushed it out of my mind and turned to the steps and headed down the lane that ran parallel to the lake.

It was a beautiful and mild July morning. The sky was reflecting bright blue in the water, and it was calm. There were a few early-bird fishermen out, but they were floating serenely, no nibbles to excite them yet. It was a quiet morning, and I closed my eyes to soak in the gentle breeze as I made my way past the other camp sites. Most people were still sleeping, so I had the lane all to myself.

I stepped into the barn-shaped shower house. It had little individual stalls, each with small sitting benches and hooks for bags. There was a small cube for showering. I pulled off my dirty clothes and hung them in the bag on the hook and pulled out my toiletries and towels, setting them on the bench at the ready.

The showers were never my favorite; they had cinderblock outer walls, and cement floors that were cold, and well water that could only be described as smelling like a rotten egg. While none of that was comfortable, what really bothered me was what lurked overhead. The mostly senior inhabitants of the campground had collectively decided that spiders were to be left alone to keep the fly and mosquito population in check. As such, the rafters high above were always full of spiders dangling and crawling. They were far above, but I couldn't help thinking they might descend upon my naked body at any moment. On top of the unpleasant spider situation, the campground didn't trust us to turn off the water when our shower ended so the only way to turn on the water was by continuously holding a rope that opened the water tap to keep the shower flowing. The water was only one temperature, scorching hot, so I made quick work of it. I washed up and dried my dark hair just a little bit by dangling it in front of the hand dryer, giving it a scrunch with conditioner in my palm to bring out the natural waves.

I walked back to the camper, careful to take small steps in my flip flops so I didn't kick up dirt and mess up my just cleaned feet. As I approached the camper, I was surprised to find Corey's car parked along the road, and next to it, Grandma's burgundy Buick. As the fifth wheel came into view I found Grandma, Uncle Skeeter, Corey, and Andy sitting at the picnic table. Grandma's face was forlorn, tearful. She saw me and grabbed her heart. Corey followed her line of site and jumped up to run to me.

"We were worried sick," Corey said. "Why didn't you tell Andy where you went?"

"I just took a shower," I countered, holding up my toiletry bag and wet towels. "I just wanted to let him get some sleep. Why would he call you?" As the words escaped my mouth it occurred to me that I wasn't gone long enough for Corey and Grandma to get a call and get out to the lake. I stopped and looked at Corey and realized his expression held more than just annoyance; he was grieving. I stopped and stared up at him. "What's going on?"

He gulped. "Your grandma got a call this morning. The phone tree was activated at church: Mrs. Fowler, the police chief's wife, called Denise Rogers, the Reverand's wife, and sent out the call to bring meals to the Stein's. Thoughts and prayers are to go out to the family. Charity was found dead this morning."

I grabbed my heart and looked over to my grandmother; she was shaking almost inconsolably.

"Found dead?" I said, more of a rhetorical question as I looked out at the woods. "Found dead where? Like just died or murdered?"

"That's all we know right now," Corey said.

"What about Angel? Oh, my gosh, does she know? Should we call her?"

"That's all I know," Corey said. This all happened in the last hour. Your grandma called my mom, and we rushed out here to find you."

I walked to the patio with him and scooted in on the table next to Grandma. She let go of whatever she was holding in and started to sob uncontrollably. I reached over to hold her in my arms.

"It's just terrible news," Skeeter said.

Andy had gotten himself a little more clothing since I'd last seen him: gray sweatpants and a tank top. He ran his hands through his matted hair, but his lack of sleep showed all over him.

"I'm glad I stayed here last night. Who knows what could have happened?"

Corey turned to look at me. "What happened last night?" he asked, raising his voice. "I told you to call me if anything else happened."

"Well, for a long time nothing else did happen. I was practically asleep, then in the middle of the night somebody tried to get into the camper."

"What!" a collective shout came around the table.

Grandma wiped away her tears and turned from sadness to almost anger. "Somebody tried to get in last night, and you didn't call the police? Michelle Anne, what were you thinking!?"

Corey spoke almost in unison, "I told you to call me. How could you..." Within moments all of them were speaking over each other with various versions of, "What were you thinking?"

I held my hand up to shush them. "Andy heard me scream and ran right over," I said. "It was over as soon as it began. Whoever, or whatever it was, was gone by the time he came over, and it was so late it didn't make sense to do anything else. We locked the door, went to sleep, and that's that."

"There was somebody in those woods last night, and I knew it," Corey said. "We need to call the police."

He pulled out his phone and dialed, then immediately started pacing. Within a moment of making his call he was down by the lake wearing an oval in the sand.

Finally, he walked back up the hill. "They're going to send a deputy out. Told us to hang tight."

The energy had calmed, and we all sat in silence for a moment. Then Grandma neatened herself up and walked into the camper. I followed behind her. "Grab me the coffee off the top shelf," she said, pointing to her pantry cupboard. I nodded and went to work.

Grandma and I made coffee, fresh fruit, toast, and fried eggs. As we were wrapping up, Skeeter poked head in the door as if on cue. "Need anything?"

She sent him to work setting the picnic table and bringing out food. Within moments we had coffee brewed and a small spread at the table.

I sat next to Grandma, who couldn't seem to find anymore words that morning.

"I found my toiletry bag, Grandma," I said. "Thank you for keeping it stocked up for me."

She bristled for a minute, then looked at me and softened. "I make sure it's ready for you every year. You are always welcome back home, and I want to make sure you know that."

I didn't want to tell her how luxurious it felt to me to take a campground shower because I had such good soap. It would pain her to know how I lived. I simply smiled at her.

"So, what did Denise say?" I asked.

"Oh, such sad business," Grandma said. "She said she was found dead this morning. And she didn't give any details, and you know Grandma doesn't pry, but she said the circumstances were tragic; she said it's very likely she was murdered. I signed up to visit the family tonight as part of our church grief train; we'll bring over food to her family and offer comfort and fellowship. You will come with me, right?" she asked.

"Of course," I said. "Did she say anything about Tammy?"

"Tammy?" she sat her spoon down and stared at me. "Why would she say anything about Tammy?"

I looked to Corey.

"They don't know," he said, looking back at me.

"The last place anybody saw Tammy was with Charity a few nights ago," I said. Grandma held her hand to her heart and Skeeter said, "Shoot."

"Did you tell the police?" I asked Corey.

"I did on that call just now."

No sooner had Corey said it than a cruiser slowly pulled up the lane and parked in the grass between the road and the boat launch. An officer, short in stature but with a stocky build, stepped out of the car and tucked his hat under his arm. We all stood to greet him."

"Hey Corey," he said, holding his hand out; the two shook.

Corey made introductions, "This is Michelle, her cousin Andy, Uncle Skeet, uh I mean Steven, and..."

"This lady needs no introduction," he said, holding his hand out to my grandmother. "Mary Anne Fry, a living legend. My family owes you so much."

Skeeter and I exchanged a look, neither of us knowing what Grandma had done.

"I only do my duty to spread the light," she said.

He kissed her hand. "Thank you again."

Grandma gestured back to me. "This is Officer Fowler,

son of Captain Fowler."

Corey turned away from him to grab a chair from the other end of the patio. He pulled it up to the table and walked over to the storage box on the patio. "Do you need a cushion?" he asked.

Fowler shook his head.

"Can I get you a cup of coffee?" Grandma asked.

"No thank you, Mrs. Fry. I wouldn't want to trouble you."

"Nonsense," she said. "Skeeter, would you please?"

Skeeter jumped up and ran into the camper to fetch a cup of coffee. When we were situated, Fowler pulled out a pad of paper and wrote my name at the top and the date.

I spent the next half hour walking him through the evening, starting with our trip to Dairy and ending with Corey dropping me off at the camper.

"So, you heard something out in those woods." He gestured to the trees, looking both at me and Corey. We nodded.

Then, I told him what happened and how Andy came running to the camper to check on me. He scribbled more in his book. "Can I see your phone?" he asked.

I stepped inside and pulled my phone off the charger. I handed it over to him and he looked through the messages.

"It was 3:46 a.m." he said. He scribbled it in his book. Then he turned the page and wrote my name and date again.

"What about the message Tammy left you?" he asked. "Can you play her message for me?"

I pulled my phone back and dialed my house. "She left that message on my home machine." I said as I dialed in my remote access code and handed the phone over to him. He wrote down what she'd said verbatim and took a note of the time. He looked up and looked to me, "Is Chicago in a different time zone?" he asked.

"It is but my machine is set to Michigan time, because the only people who leave me messages are my family."

"Huh," he said.

"What?" I asked.

"The witching hour."

I have him a quizzical look.

"The witching hour, both your incident and the incident with your friend happened at the Witching Hour, between 3:00 and 4:00."

"Does that mean something?" I asked.

"It's just interesting. Your friend worked in a bar, so she probably got off at 2:00 or shortly after. So why did she call you at 3:15 and not 2:15? What happened in that hour?"

I shook my head. "I have no idea."

"So, where is Cedar Rapids?" he asked. "I've never heard of it."

Corey tried his best to explain it, but Officer Fowler looked perplexed.

"So, everybody from your class believes in this place Cedar Rapids, but none of you know where it is?" I nodded my head in agreement. He grabbed his walkie talkie, "Gladys, can you get me a location on Cedar Rapids, Michigan?"

"Back in ten," she said.

He stood and placed his hat on the picnic table.

"I'm going to go take a look in those woods."

He walked past the storage compartment on the camper and into the woods, moving slowly and deliberately, looking around as he went. Corey walked to the edge of the woods and watched him. After a moment I made my way to Corey's side. Fowler pulled out a blue glove and a plastic bag and slid something into it. After a few steps he grabbed something else and slid it into the bag.

He took a call on his radio and walked back to us.

"What did you find?" I asked.

"Somebody's definitely been in these woods," he said. "Cigarettes, a glove, a rose keychain, but some of it looks kind of beat up. Could have been out here for a while. The cigarettes are fresh."

"Any idea who it could be?" Grandma asked.

"Could be a vagrant, just looking for an open camper. Could be kids. Looks like chance that they got your camper, with you being closest to the woods."

"You don't think it has anything to do with Tammy and Charity?" I asked. He shook his head. "No, if it was a murderer,

I don't think they'd give up so easily. I don't think they were expecting you to be here and just got scared off. I'd recommend you keep it locked, though."

"How did they know about the crawl space, though?" I asked.

"Lots of fifth wheels have that. If they know camping, they probably know about that too. Just lock up the storage compartment next time."

Corey asked, "Did you find out anything about Tammy or Charity? Where they could have gone?"

"Gladys said there is no Cedar Rapids in Michigan. She thinks it must have been Grand Rapids. Maybe it's a township or something."

"There was a sign that said Welcome to Cedar Rapids," I said. "I remember it was in big blue writing. It had the Rotary Club symbol on it and a Free Masons symbol. They must have records of a chapter there."

"So, you say everybody from the class of 1999 who went to Marsh knows about this?" he asked.

I nodded. He pulled out a cellphone and dialed. "Hey Tara, this is Micky, ever heard of Cedar Rapids? The chatter from the other end of the line confirmed he was getting an earful." He nodded, then turned around and walked down toward the lake. After a few moments he came back up. "My sister said it's a thing; her husband was in your class too…said he's never heard of it. But my sister, who forgets nothing, said almost the same thing as you Michelle, so I think there must be something to it."

"I know your sister," I said. "She used to be a goth kid, all black, black lipstick, white face paint. That was her, right?"

"Never mention that, especially not around my father," he warned.

"Oh, I almost forgot to ask, have you talked to Charity's roommate, Angel?"

He nodded.

Grandma stepped out from behind me and stood between me and Corey and Officer Fowler, "Is my granddaughter in any danger now?" she asked.

"I don't think so," he said. Then he lowered his voice

almost to a whisper. "Charity had a second job that, well, it wasn't the most Christian activity that she was involved in, so I think she put herself into the line of trouble really."

He thought he would find a comrade in chastising un-Christian-like behavior with my grandmother, but he miscalculated. Grandma never judged another person's beliefs or their commitment to Christianity. She never let people say a cross word about Corey for being gay and derided Christians who judged others. While she had adopted a Methodist orthodoxy after meeting my grandfather, she held her Quaker beliefs close to her heart, and discernment, the ability to let anybody discern the will of God and their belief in their own way, was of fundamental importance to her. If Charity wanted to run naked in the streets, Grandma would have said that was no business of hers.

"A woman wanting to dance is not incompatible with Christianity or the teachings of Christ. In Exodus, Miriam, the sister of Moses, dances with other Israelite women to praise her Lord," she said crisply. "There is nothing that Charity, beloved daughter and.."

I interjected, "dental hygienist."

"Beloved daughter and dental hygienist could do to lose the light of God by dancing."

Officer Fowler, having been appropriately chastised, walked over to the picnic table and grabbed his hat. He held it in his hands and kept his head down as he addressed Grandma.

"You are right Mrs. Fry. It's not my place to pass judgement."

"Nor is it mine." She softened. "This is a terrible business, and I just want to make sure this young woman is on all of our hearts today."

CHAPTER SEVEN

OFFICER FOWLER LEFT AND PROMISED they were all hands on deck at the police station. But I felt a pit in my stomach. It didn't seem like they were that concerned with finding Tammy. If they had a poor opinion of a dental hygienist like Charity, I feared they would think even less of a missing barmaid with a suspected drug problem.

After breakfast Grandma insisted I was coming back to the house with her, but I wasn't convinced that I would be leaving the lake. While the night before was frightening, the morning had been glorious. I felt like my proximity to nature was trying to show me something—something I was missing. Even after a frightful night, even under the shower in the spider barn, I felt at peace that morning. Like there was a message there for me. I felt it right up until the moment of the tragic news.

I worried that Grandma was going to take me back home with her, and with Corey in her corner they would refuse to bring me back to the lake. I insisted on leaving my luggage in the camper, but when Corey turned around at the gate to the campground, I assumed he was going back to take my bag, a conspiratorial effort by him, Grandma, and Skeeter. When I asked Grandma what he was doing she shrugged, to her if she didn't say anything, technically she wasn't lying.

We got back to the farm, and no sooner had we walked in the door than the phone rang. Grandma hurried down the hall to catch the call, and I found my cousin John was in the kitchen waiting for us.

"You hear they are having a get-together for the class of 1999 at The Alpine tonight?" he asked.

"No," I said. "But I'm in. You and the wife willing to give me a ride?"

"She's not coming out. She doesn't want to be around all that smoke in her last trimester. You can ride with me and Blanch."

"Blanch?" I said, "Who's Blanch?"

"You know Blanch. David Blanch, he was the tall guy. I think you danced with him at the winter formal once."

"Uh, I was made to stand next to him at the winter formal so we wouldn't block other people in pictures, but I never danced with him. And I never heard anybody call him Blanch."

He chuckled. "Yeah, he hates it. So, you know that makes me do it extra."

"That's mean, John."

"Shoot, that's how you know I like a person. That's why I used to call you Xena Warrior Princess; that's how you know you were my favorite cousin."

I hated being called Xena in high school. It's not that I minded that everybody thought I looked like Lucy Lawless, but the Xena yelp calls, and the lesbian jokes got old fast.

He saw the annoyance on my face. "Don't worry; I won't call you that anymore."

"Well then don't call David, Blanch."

He rolled his eyes, "You don't understand men, Xena; he will appreciate it."

I slugged him on the shoulder and barked at him to move out of the way of the fridge. It was fully stocked, and the middle shelf was taken up completely with chocolate milk.

"Grandma's getting her supply ready for milk-barn work, I see."

"Yup," he said. "You and Corey are on shift tomorrow morning."

Grandma entered the kitchen from the hall, and her face was anguished again.

"What's wrong?" I asked.

She shook her head. "It's dreadful, dreadful. Mrs. Fowler called; she said Charity was murdered. She was..." Grandma took a deep breath. "They said it looked like she'd been in a car accident at first, but then they said it just looked like too many bruises for the accident she was in, and well, they could tell when she got to the coroner that she was dead before the accident."

"How could they tell?" I asked.

"Grandma doesn't pry," she said.

"Grandma, this is a time to pry. Did they say if they saw any sign of Tammy in the car?"

"Oh, shoot. I forgot to ask about that."

"Can you call her back?" I asked.

"No, we will see her tonight at the Stein's, and we have work to do; go out to the porch and grab my apron."

Grandma and I spent the next four hours mixing, rolling, slicing, and spicing to make two apple pies, two cherry pies, and two dishes of raspberry crumble. We left three pies at home and gathered the rest to deliver to the Stein home.

WE HAD TO PARK A BLOCK away as the ladies of the Methodist church meal delivery brigade had already descended upon the Stein home, filling their driveway and their street. With pie and crumble in hand, we walked two blocks to the beautiful two-story craftsman at the center of the street. We walked up the steps to the wide front porch and found the door to the house open with just the screen door for a buffer. We could see church ladies moving to and fro in the house and stepped inside the foyer, which was abuzz with activity. An elegantly-dressed, tall woman noticed us, wiped her eyes, and greeted my grandmother.

"Oh, thank you for coming, Ladies. You can put those in the kitchen, Mary." She steered us to the back of the house. In the kitchen we saw at least six different types of casserole, fifty mini-sandwiches, and trays of cookies that looked like enough to serve an army. Various cheeses, pickles, and salads were tucked into different places around the room.

"The fridge is full," the tall woman said as she straightened the table to make space for our desserts."

I wondered what exactly the Stein's, two adults and a dog, would do with this mountain of food. But food wasn't really the point of the food train, as Grandma had told me when I was young. The point was to show people going through a tough time that you cared. Watching a gaggle of church ladies fuss over an overabundance of food made me think of my place in Chicago. If I died, who would come to mourn me? My boss? Probably not, he wouldn't even take the time off to go to my funeral. What about my neighbors? I didn't know a single one of them by name.

The only person to mourn me in the city where I lived was maybe the sports reporter, but only if he could get a half-day off.

"If I die, bring my body back to Michigan," I whispered to my grandmother.

"Oh, what brought that on?" She stopped nudging plates and looked up at me.

I shook my head. "Nothing, I'm just having morbid thoughts, I guess. Oh, don't forget we need to find out about…" No sooner than she had scooted her pie into place, somebody popped their head around the corner asking for her help. She dutifully ran off, leaving me standing awkwardly alone in the kitchen.

After several moments of pretending to straighten up the table, I looked around and found nothing else to do. I decided to look around the room, finding a wall of family photos. They mostly featured Charity and her dog. Her big blue eyes followed me in the photos as she stared straight into the lens. I found myself walking through the kitchen out into the hallway and following the line of school photos that took her from kindergarten up to graduation. There were also rows of framed playbills on the wall; some were shows she went to, but many were shows she starred in at our school. I stopped to look at her final school picture. It was her in a cap and gown; it was hard to believe it was ten years ago. She had the bright make-up popular in the late 90's, eyes frosted with silver eyeshadow, thin eyebrows, and her lips a deep burgundy shade, no blush in sight. In another photo she wore a spaghetti-strap slip dress that every girl of the time was wearing.

After only a moment looking at the picture, I overheard a conversation in the living room that made me take notice. I stepped just to the side so I could see who was speaking out of the corner of my eye while I kept my gaze on the photo in front of me.

"Strangled," I heard. It was Mrs. Fowler, the wife of the police chief, whispering.

"Oh, my," the smaller woman in a flowered hat replied.

"Windpipe completely crushed, bruises all over her face and arms. The State Police think the crash was supposed to make all of those injuries look like an accident."

"Oh my."

"And who do you think did it? Nobody knows, so I'll tell you what I think. She was last seen with that Tammy girl. You know the one with the silly black hair?" Then she leaned in and whispered, "The one who lived at Eagle Bay."

They both raised their eyebrows and nodded as if that meant something, confirming my suspicion that nobody would care about Tammy. If the police didn't think much of Charity Stein, daughter of respected town dentist Randy Stein, I didn't hold much hope that they would care at all about Tammy. She lived with her mom in what was referred to as the "bad" trailer park. Not the pretty one with the fountains and the new double-wides. She lived in the one with the old single-wides that was close to the city waste-water treatment plant and the Dollar Store. It straddled the township line, half of its residents resided in Marsh, and the other half resided in Dairy. It had long been a bone of contention among the Marsh area school board that they couldn't nudge the township boundary just a little to get all the Eagle Bay students and their test scores out of their city.

The two women started to whisper softly, and I struggled to hear anything more. "Bruising… wrists were rubbed raw…" I took a cautious step toward the living room, craning to learn more when I heard a noise close behind me. I turned and let out a startled, "Oh!"

There was a man standing far too close to me. We were practically nose-to-nose when I turned to face him. He was about my age, with hair slick with oil and a dark suit. He looked like he was trying his best to channel Charlie Sheen from *Wall Street*, but he wasn't quite good-looking enough to pull it off. His expressionless gray eyes sent a shiver down my spine. They were hidden behind dark rimmed-glasses. I knew instantly this was the creepy boyfriend Angel told us about.

"Who are you?" he asked. His voice and demeanor were cold.

"I knew Charity in high school. I'm Michelle, and you?"

He looked annoyed at me, "Bryce, her fiancé."

I held out my hand to shake his; he looked at it and looked

back up without making any effort to shake my hand.

"I've never heard Charity mention any Michelle."

"Like I said, I knew her in high school. I hadn't talked to her in years until a few weeks ago."

That made him snap to attention. He narrowed his eyes at me. "Why did you talk to her a few weeks ago?"

"Reunion," I said.

He continued to stare, and I continued to offer no additional information.

"What did she say?" he asked.

"Reunion stuff," I said nonchalantly. "Hey, do you know Angel? She's a friend of Charity's. I just met her recently. She said Charity had a real prick ruining her life; any idea who she was talking about?"

He clenched his jaw, and we ended up glaring at each other. He looked like he could outlast me in an uncomfortable silence contest, but I was willing to give him a run for his money. Luckily, my grandmother rounded the corner with Doctor Stein by way of the living room and broke the tension, allowing me the chance to declare yet another staring contest win. When Bryce noticed them, he immediately took a step back and abandoned his intimidating posture.

"Is everything okay?" Doctor Stein asked. He must have noticed the look.

"Of course, Doctor Stein, just meeting an old school chum of Charity's."

Chum? I wondered at that wording. I certainly never said chum. I would have said acquaintance.

"How are you, Michelle?" he asked.

I'm sure he remembered me more for my dental work than as a friend of Charity's.

"I should be asking about you. How are you and Mrs. Stein holding up?"

He smiled weakly and shook his head. I supposed not so well.

Mrs. Stein's tiny frame stepped into view for only a moment, and she squeaked out a thank you, before immediately burying her head in a handkerchief and disappearing to another room. Doctor Stein followed her, and I was left with Grandma and Bryce.

"We should go," Grandma said. "They have had quite enough visitors for today."

"I can walk you out," she said to Bryce. Grandma must have been tasked with getting him out, or she would not have been so forward. He looked incredulous but only for a moment. Her straightforward demeanor and obvious position of respect made him acquiesce to her request. I'd never seen anybody try to stare-down my grandmother. He considered it for only a moment, then thought better of it. One day I hoped to have that level of gravitas.

"It's time for me to go anyway," he said. "I didn't catch your name?"

She held out her hand to shake his and said, "Mary Anne Fry."

He nodded without introducing himself and stormed out the door.

After he was out of earshot Grandma leaned into me and said, "he's been making everybody uncomfortable all day."

"I didn't care for him at all, gave off bad vibes," I said.

She shook her head. "Didn't seem like there is much to like. Let's round up the troops; the family needs private time."

Grandma walked around the house and gathered all the Methodist church ladies and told them it was time to go. If Grandma willed it, thy will be done.

WE WALKED SLOWLY BACK to the car, and I waited at least a block before I asked if Grandma had gotten any more info.

She said, "Nobody seems to know what happened to Tammy. Mrs. Fowler knew that they were last seen together. She seems to think Tammy is more of a suspect than a victim."

"I know Tammy didn't have the best reputation, but she wouldn't murder somebody. No way. They were going on an adventure together; it just doesn't make sense that they were going to go have an adventure, call me to tell me about it, and then Tammy was just going to murder Charity. I overheard Mrs. Fowler say she was strangled and beaten. It doesn't make any sense, Grandma; that doesn't sound like Tammy at all."

She stopped and looked up at me. "I remember Tammy from when you were young. Sweet girl. Very troubled. We don't know who Tammy is anymore, but I never saw that kind of evil in her heart. I don't believe it's in there."

"She's a victim, Grandma, and I'm going to find her."

She nodded. "And I will support your efforts."

We drove back to Grandma's house, and I found my bag waiting for me on her back porch. "That Judas," I said, cursing Corey for taking my luggage as I had suspected.

"Oh, good, you can stay the night," Grandma said.

"Et tu, Brute?" I said to my grandmother.

"Brutus and Judas? Really, that's overly dramatic," Grandma said as she ascended the stairs up to her mud room. "And John said you are going to see some of your old friends tonight. You may want some of your nicer things to wear."

I looked down at my t-shirt and jeans. I was not in possession of nicer things except the dress I had packed for the reunion. I supposed I could put on some mascara and lipstick and put a little gel in my hair.

I lugged up the suitcase and rolled it down to the bathroom. I had my iron heating up and was dabbing on eye makeup when my grandma came in and said, "You look lovely."

She smiled up at me, then set another newspaper clipping on the counter for me. It was an advice column.

This is for you, dear. She kissed me on the cheek and said, "Skeeter is here to take me and Grandpa to Wendy's. We'll be back late."

"Wendy's as in the fast-food restaurant Wendy's?"

"Mmm hmm."

"I'm sure there's a story there."

"Don't wait up," she said, and she shuffled down the hall. "Me, don't wait up for them?" I shook my head.

When she was out of sight I read the question from the advice article, "How do I open myself up to love after years without a meaningful relationship?"

I groaned as I scanned the highlights: be myself, don't be closed off, don't be bothered by what ifs."

"Riveting advice," I said sarcastically to myself, scrunching my waves. After a few swipes of mascara and a hint of lipstick I was ready. I unplugged my curling iron and picked up the article, crumpling it, ready to toss the generic advice where I thought it belonged. I noticed there was ink on my hand and opened the article again, turning it over. In the margins of a JC Penny ad there was a hand-written note, "You will have to be vulnerable to find love, and I'm afraid I made that hard for you. I'm sorry that I wasn't stronger when your parents died. I let you be the strong one, instead of me. I can't go back in time, but I can try now."

I felt a lump in my throat. How could my grandmother put something so emotional in the margins of an ad for discount slacks? I unfolded the article and slid it into my pocket. Just as I did, I heard a knock at the back door.

"You ready, Warrior Princess?" John shouted.

CHAPTER EIGHT

I BOUNDED DOWN THE STEPS and went out the back door to find John sitting in his old Mustang convertible with the top down.

"You still have this thing?" I asked.

He grinned. The little white car was well past its prime, peeling paint, rust over the wheel wells, but in high school he was a legend for driving the Stang. He'd gotten it for a steal after it literally fell off the back of a stock truck. John, ever the entrepreneur, ran up to the dealership after watching the car roll off the back and bartered the price down enough to get a brand-new Mustang on a Little Caesars delivery-boy salary. It took him a whole summer to get it up and running, but when he did, everybody was in awe. In our poor little farm town, he became a God.

Now, however, the seats weren't in any better shape than the paint, rips and stains abounded. "How many miles are on this?" I asked as I slid into the passenger seat.

"Over two-hundred thousand."

He slammed on the gas the minute his tires hit the dirt road. He drove like a mad man, kicking up a cloud of dirt that billowed out behind us.

"Real mature, John."

"Yeehaw," he shouted as he sped down Old Fry Road, so named for our great-grandparents. "We gotta pick up David."

The wind whipped through our hair with the convertible top down, making the gel I had applied earlier an exercise in futility. After a few turns and a return to paved roads, we turned down Hampton Street and then down a long-paved driveway that went up the center of a perfectly neat and symmetrical apple orchard. We passed the trees, adorned with green apples still waiting to ripen. After a lengthy drive we reached the last of the orchard and were in view of a vast green yard and a big white farmhouse surrounded by perfectly manicured bushes. It was like my grandparents' house on steroids: a bigger porch, a bigger garage, bigger windows, bigger doors, and everything was symmetrical. My grandparents' house looked like it had been added onto a piece at a time, and the rooflines could be referred to as cattywampus. This fancy farmhouse even had a picturesque white barn with a black roof. It was an overly scenic version of a farm. I didn't see any cows, pigs, chickens, or cash crops, so I was very unclear as to what was supporting this farm. It likely wasn't the rows of neatly trimmed apple trees; there wasn't enough money growing on those trees to support this grand place.

David was already sitting on his porch waiting for us. John shouted, "Yee-haw," to David, who nodded in reply. He took the steps two by two, and the closer he got to the car I realized how tall he really was. I knew it in high school, but in my memories he seemed smaller.

"Can you scoot the seat up?" he asked. And I realized I had been staring at him.

"Oh, sorry," I said, snapping out of my trance. "I'll sit in the back."

"You don't have to," he said. "I've had to sit back there before, and I managed."

I stood from my seat at the same time he was bending down to pull the latch on the seat. I bumped him and stumbled back into my seat.

"Oh, are you okay?" He leaned down and held his hand out to help me up, but I forgot to take it. Instead, I stared into his face. I knew I'd seen his face before, but it was never like this. Were his eyes always that blue? I felt as if he was different. Or maybe it was me who was different. I only remembered his face in black and white, through yearbook photos. I hadn't remembered him in full color. I stared up at him and forgot to speak. With my mouth failing to find words, he reached down and gently pulled me back up.

"I'll just…" I jumped up and moved to the back.

"Thanks, Shell. I would have tried to fit back there, really."

"No problem," I said. *Shell*, I thought. *Did he know me well enough to call me Shell?*

He looked at me for a moment longer than he had to and said, "John used to stuff me back there all the time when he had a girl in the front."

"Yuck!" I found my voice. "I can only imagine who sat in that seat back then."

"Sherry…" David started before John reached over and punched him on the shoulder.

"No, not Sherry Dilts!"

"Don't say a word," John said in warning, and David gestured that he would zip his lips.

As we pulled away from the farm, I noticed all the lights inside were out. I wondered if David lived there alone, or if he was like Corey, still living with his parents. Maybe he lived in the basement of this beautiful farm or in some corner of the big garage, and his parents were at Wendy's having hamburgers with my grandparents, doing God knows what.

The roads to town from David's house were all paved, and we couldn't help but yell, "Woohoo," as John sped down the hills. We listened to a "That's what I call the 90's" C.D. that had been stuck in the player for more than ten years. David and I threw our arms up in the air like we were on roller coasters as we whizzed up and down old roads. We couldn't' talk much while we were travelling fast down the old highway, but once we got to town, bumping down to 25 mph, it was quiet enough to speak. I wished I had thought of something smart to say on the drive, but when it was suddenly quiet, I couldn't find the words. The only thing on my mind was wondering why David and I had never gotten together in high school.

I was about to open my mouth to ask about his parents when John said, "So why didn't you guys ever get together back in high school?" There was a lump in my stomach, and David's neck turned red.

I wanted to know what he would say to that, but he stayed tight lipped.

I offered my reason. "Because people always thought we should."

He chuckled. "Exactly. The minute somebody suggested we would make a good couple, I knew it would never work."

"Y'all are stupid then," John said. "You would have made a good couple."

We pulled into the parking lot behind the bar. It was already packed with cars, and the sun hadn't even gone down yet.

After we parked, David and I walked back to the trunk, planning to help with the convertible top.

"Shouldn't we put the roof up?" David offered.

"Oh, that don't work at all."

"What if it rains?" I said, looking up at a not entirely cloudless sky.

"We'll worry about that when it happens."

I shrugged, and we walked toward the bar. My head didn't even reach up to David's shoulder. It was odd to be standing next to somebody so much taller than me. I figured that's what other girls must feel like all the time, small next to men. I found my gaze drifting over to him, and he looked away quickly every time I looked his way.

A din of chatter and the smell of fried garlic pizza dough greeted us as we walked in the back door to The Alpine. It was our neighborhood bar. It had long ago been renamed Pete's, but we still called it The Alpine, the name it held for the twenty years before it was Pete's. It had high ceilings crisscrossed by dark wood beams and dark wooden walls. The lighting came from dim wall sconces and the tables were dark with red vinyl seats, unchanged since the time it was The Alpine. The long bar had red neon signs behind it and Budweiser advertising on every surface. On the far edge of the bar there was a poker machine. The place was packed. John pushed through the crowd and made room for us at the football players' table. He introduced me to the wives of some of his old friends, but I wasn't listening because all I could think about was David. He introduced me to a Deborah, and when I said nice to meet you, I called her Dave-ora. The slip was not lost on David, which was mortifying.

It didn't take long for John to abandon us, much to my delight. I wanted nothing more than to talk to David, but when I got the chance, I couldn't figure out what to say.

After a few moments the silence was killing me; I brought up the only conversation in my brain, "So, really, why didn't we ever date in high school?"

"What's your real reason for not dating me?" he asked.

"Well, remember back when we had to take pictures in gym class, or when we were both in debate? They always moved us to the back row, and when I was a teenager, I wanted to do the opposite of what people expected, so I never considered you an option. Well, it was half that and half that you were always dating somebody, and I don't break people up or date cheaters. So, now what's your real reason?"

"Well, don't take this the wrong way, but you were so different from everybody else. It was something I didn't really appreciate at the time."

I'm sure the insult showed on my face.

"Really, you didn't know you were known as, well, different?"

I shook my head.

"Like in middle school you wore one sparkly glove and a red leather jacket with zippers all over it and sang *Billie Jean is not my lover*, constantly."

"Oh, I can explain that. See, my Uncle Skeet gave me a Betamax "Making of the Thriller Album," and it changed my life. I went through a pretty hardcore Michael Jackson phase. I don't think there's anything weird about that."

"I mean, my mom and I drove by once, and we saw you trying to moonwalk through your chicken coop. And you fell over in gym class on multiple occasions because you were trying to defy gravity by doing this lean thing."

"That lean was from the *Bad* video. And I don't think any of that is weird."

"I don't think I said weird; that's your word. I said different. And when I was young, I didn't know how awesome different was. When I was older, I thought, damn, Michelle knew who she was when she was eleven better than I knew at twenty."

"I want to know more about that, but I need to put a pin in the conversation of your self-discovery because you just said you thought about me after high school. Expand on that."

He turned red again, "Yeah, I did. When I went to college. I lived my life doing whatever people expected me to do, and I hated it. My dad wanted me to go into engineering like he did, and I just didn't like it. And I thought about you and how you just did whatever you wanted. Either you didn't care about the opinions of others, or they didn't bother you. I don't know how a person gets that kind of confidence. I was probably twenty-two when I was finally as brave as you were in middle school."

"You wouldn't believe how brave I am now," I joked.

"Seriously though, how did you get like that?"

"Honestly?" I asked, and he nodded. "My parents died when I was really young and..."

"I'm sorry," he said.

"No, it's not like that; you don't have to be sorry. It happened a long time ago. I don't get sad about it or anything anymore. So, anyway. My parents died when I was young. They were in a car accident; it was just this fluke thing, patch of ice, we hit a bridge, and off we went."

"We? You were in the car?" he asked.

"Yes, I don't really remember it though. I get flashes, like a strobe light where I just see us going over. Then all the stuff around me starts falling in front of me, and then we face this river. Then I see flashes, like my toys were floating in the air in front of me, then my mom's purse floats up, then my mom is looking back at me, panicked. It's all just flashing now, and I don't feel sad when I see it like I used to."

He looked stunned.

"Anyway, the confidence. Well, the worst thing that I could have imagined ever happening to me happened—and I survived. So, I figure I can survive anything, and if I don't, well the world went on without my parents. Also, my grandparents weren't ready to take on kids when my parents died; they were definitely in grandparent mode and not parent mode, so they pretty much let me call the shots."

"Like they didn't parent you?"

"They never really acted like parents. They were more like friends. But I really didn't get into any trouble, so I made their lives easy. I had to ground myself a few times because I thought they went too easy on me."

"I know you're trying to be funny. But that sounds like a

lot for a kid."

I shrugged.

"It's weird that you don't remember the crash, isn't it?"

"No, I went to a lot of therapy when I was younger. We talked about it constantly, and now I don't even think I really remember it. Just the stories of it."

He stared at me, like he wanted to say something. Just as he was about to open his mouth, I shouted, "Oh my gosh, Tammy!"

He turned and looked behind him.

"No, Tammy is missing. I'm supposed to be looking into that. Do you know about it? I'm sure you heard about Charity, right?"

"I did; my mom is on the phone tree for the church."

"Tammy was with Charity the night before she died. Remember Tammy? She was a red-head when we were young, but she dyed her hair black in high school. I used to hang out with her."

"I remember her. I didn't know Tammy was with Charity."

"I know; the cops don't seem to care about that part. So, Corey and I have been trying to figure out what happened to her."

I told him all about my phone call, my meeting at her bar, and then meeting Angel at the burlesque club.

"How can I help?" he asked.

"Well, we need to find Cedar Rapids so we can find out where Tammy and Charity went. Do you remember anything about it?"

"I remember the barn with the steak on it, the animals," he shook his head. "Not really, but we're here with like forty of our old classmates; somebody has to remember something."

"Oh, and Angel told us somebody has a picture of it. A man with a weird name she hadn't heard before."

"Let's divide and conquer. I'll ask everybody I know about it; you ask everybody you know. Somebody must remember more."

I went table to table, asking about the farm and getting blank stares half of the time and vague conspiracy theories the other half. David came back around to me and asked me what I found out.

"Most of our classmates remembered even less than I did," I reported. "Sarah Berman thinks that it was on a Prime meridian, or that it must have been a place where two bodies of water met and created an energy vortex that swallowed it. Derrick Peters thinks we were all hypnotized and never went there in the first place, and weird Bill thinks it's a government conspiracy and has something to do with chemtrails. Did you do any better?"

"Not really, but somebody said the state library in Lansing has a historic maps room and we should try there and see if there's ever been a Cedar Rapids in Michigan because they said it might be a township and not a city."

"Are townships not on maps?"

"Apparently not on all maps."

"We need to go there."

"Want to check it out with me tomorrow?" he asked.

My inner teenager wanted to squeal. He was asking me on a date, well kind of, but I couldn't go.

"It's okay if you don't want to," he said.

"No, I do want to, but I have to work at the milk barn for my family tomorrow. I made a promise, and I roped Corey into it and everything." I was torn. "But Tammy is missing, and that's probably more important. What time do they open? Maybe we can get there and back early."

"We can try."

"Hey, thanks for asking around for me and not thinking it's crazy."

"It's not. I remember this trip. I can't believe so many people don't quite recall it. You know how earlier you said you don't know if you have real memories of your parents anymore, just stories of them? I think that happens around tragedies. Especially for kids. So, it makes me wonder if we have real memories of this place, or did something bad happen there? And now we all remember something different. Is our mind blocking something?"

It was getting louder in the bar and harder to talk. I learned into him. "My memories of it are wonderful though, nothing bad at all."

"What?" he shouted.

I hung my head. He held up his finger, gesturing for me to wait one minute and backed away from me. I tried to see where he went, but he disappeared into a sea of people. I sat at the table with the other football players and their wives, locked into their own conversations and ignoring me. I looked around searching for any familiar faces.

I had given up when a hand tightly clutched my shoulder, and I looked up to find a very drunk Jay Able, "Best Free Throw Shooter," trying to get me to stand up.

"What?" I shouted.

"You Michelle?" he shouted.

I nodded.

He pointed to his drink and then to me. I shook my head. And he nodded and pointed again.

"No thanks."

He shrugged and moved down the bar. I was thankful to see David coming back with two drinks in hand; one was a White Russian.

I smiled at him as he moved to sit by me.

"John told me," he shouted.

I held the drink to my lips, excited after missing two previous White Russians destined for me, when suddenly I heard soft synthesizer music on the juke box, followed by the whispers of Michael Jackson. I almost tossed my drink with excitement. I looked at David, and a broad grin shone on his face.

"PYT, Michael Jackson?" I shouted. He nodded back.

I jumped up and pulled him with me to the dance floor. It was already packed, which was perfect because I was certain I was not a good dancer though what I lacked in skill I made up for in enthusiasm. David had neither, but he was smiling at me as I made wildly robotic moves during the interludes and all, and he seemed not the least bit embarrassed by my intentionally over-the-top moves.

After the song I made my way back to the table, and I found my White Russian had grown legs. I hung my head in disappointment and looked around for David. Instead, I found

John stumbling in my direction. He sat across from me and slid his keys across the table. "We better go; they say it's starting to sprinkle."

I nodded and thought it was better that I hadn't had a drink so I could be our driver.

We got up and pushed through the crowd. I held tight to the back of John's shirt so I wouldn't lose him in the crowd as he ambled around shouting, "David."

He was near the bar, holding Jay Able by the back of his hoodie. He looked mad.

"What's wrong?" I asked.

"Nothing," David said, and he pushed him away.

"It looks like rain," I said. "And we need to get John home."

When we got to the car, John slid over the back door and landed in the back seat with a thud. David came around to the side of the car and pulled John further into the seat; I pushed his legs over the other side and onto the floor. He was lying across it, so I stepped onto his back, wrapped a seat belt around him, and buckled it under his stomach.

"Good enough," I said.

I drove the Stang with far more caution than John had. It wasn't a smooth ride anymore; it shifted hard, and the suspension was shot. We felt every bump and stone. I didn't speed even though I thought the clock was ticking on beating the rain.

"Do you mind if I take John home first?" I asked. "He's already going to be in huge trouble with his wife."

"Of course. I think I'm going to have to carry him in."

We rolled slowly down the dirt road, and the sprinkles picked up. David only had to guide John into the house, not carry him entirely, but that wasn't going to keep John out of trouble. His wife, with a baby on her hip, was not in good spirits as we practically rolled John through the door.

We pulled away and started back down the dirt road when the rain started to come in big droplets. A flash of lightning moved across the sky, and David took off his flannel shirt and tried his best to hold it over my head.

"I don't think we're going to make it to your place in this.

Do you mind if we park this in the barn until the rain lets up, or I can borrow my grandma's Buick to get you home?"

"I don't mind at all," he said. We drove a few houses down to the family farm and into the equipment barn. We pulled in between the combine and the hay bailer. Just as we pulled inside the rain let loose to a full downpour. We got out of the car and walked to the door of the barn. We could see the house down the lane, but the lights were still out, and the Buick was nowhere in sight.

"What time is it?" I asked.

"About midnight," he said, checking his watch.

"My grandparents are still at Wendy's. I can't believe I beat them back."

"Should we make a run for it?" he asked, just before a clash of thunder rang out around the farm. I took a quick jump back away from the door as the rain fell even harder.

"Maybe not."

"We could go up in the hay loft and make out," I said, half joking, but not really joking. He laughed.

"We can go up in the hayloft," he said. "Wait out the storm."

We took the ladder up to the second story of the barn and found a soft spot of hay to sit on. We could see the storm raging outside through the wide-open barn door.

He scooted in next to me, and we watched the storm for a few minutes.

"What have you been up to since school?" he asked.

"I live in Chicago now. I'm a journalist."

"Oh, wow. That's a really good job for you. I feel like you always asked a lot of questions."

I nodded. "What about you? What do you do now?"

He hung his head. "Uh, well, I guess the biggest thing going on with me is I just finished my divorce."

"Oh, did you marry Anna after high school?"

"No, nobody you would know. We have a son together. She has primary custody, but I see him on weekends and a few weeks in the summer."

"I'm sorry."

"You know how when I said I was sorry your parents died, and you said it's not sad like that?"

"Yeah."

"Same for me. It's not sad. It was okay. It was okay with both of us. It was just for the best, and I think we'll come out better for it."

I wondered what happened. Did somebody cheat? Did he cheat? I wanted to ask all of it and decided it was none of my business.

He clearly didn't want to say any more about it and changed the subject, "So, what's it like to be a journalist in the big city?"

"Well, I wish it was like the movies. It's not. I'm really busy all the time covering city council meetings, school board meetings, and zoning meetings. I never work on anything exciting, and the pay is terrible, but other than that."

"Really, I figured you probably had all these fancy events to attend, probably knew some pretty important people."

"Nobody in newspapers has any money for fancy events, and important people try their best to avoid us. If I'm completely honest, it's lonely in Chicago. All those people around me and nobody knows me. I thought living in a city would be like *Friends*. I thought when I grew up, I would meet my friend-family, and we would have all these great adventures. I had a friend-family for a little while in college, but it turns out that friend-families turn back to their real families when they get married and have kids, and if you don't turn back to yours, you end up spending a lot of time alone."

"Are you going to go back?"

"I don't know. Everything that happened to Charity made me think about how lonely it is there. If I died, nobody would notice for weeks."

"Don't go back," he said, looking in my eyes. He held my hand in his. "Life's too short to be lonely, Michelle."

I looked in his eyes and was about to lean into him when lights flashed in front of us. I looked forward; it was my grandparents pulling up the driveway.

"They're back."

CHAPTER NINE

THE RAIN LET UP AND DAVID took John's car back to his place, with a reminder that he would pick me up in the morning. I stayed in my old room at my grandparents' house and woke up to the familiar sounds of my giant family eating breakfast downstairs. I threw my hair up in a top knot and went downstairs in my sweatpants and tank top. Most of my family had already dressed for the day, but I was on vacation.

There was a buffet set up along the outer edge of the dining room wall. It had eggs, bacon, biscuits, gravy, and some sort of egg casserole. There was also coffee and chocolate milk. I piled on eggs and a biscuit and poured a big glass of chocolate milk. John's wife was staring daggers at me, so I moved past the adult table to the kids' table on the porch. I sat in the tiny chair with my legs scrunched up around me with my nieces and nephews, well that's what we called them, the children of my cousins, and tried my best to eat in silence, though there was a rather heated argument going around about what happened to Steve from *Blue's Clues*.

I was wondering what time David planned to get there. I checked the clock, and it was just after eight. My grandmother came out to the porch, somehow fresh as a daisy, showered and coiffed after having made breakfast for fifteen people. She must have been up for hours, which was a shocker to me after she'd closed the Wendy's the night before.

"Don't forget you're working the milk barn today," she said, bending over to kiss my head.

"I know, Grandma; I'm supposed to be there at eleven, right?"

"No, by ten."

"Corey will be there at ten; he's very punctual."

"So will you."

"I may be a smidge late."

I looked out the window of the porch looking for any sign

that a car was coming, but the dirt road had no cars in either direction; the dust was usually a clue that somebody was on the way, but it was completely clear in all directions.

"Or maybe not."

John looked out from the kitchen and leaned back in his chair and teased, "You thinking 'bout David?"

My grandmother beamed at me. "Oh, is that who you were with up in the hay loft last night."

"Ohhhh," the kids all said in unison. Followed by a chant, "Michelle and David sitting in a tree, K-I-S-S-I-N-G."

I waved my hand in the air, "It's nothing; there was no K-I-S-S-I-N-G in a tree or in the hayloft," and the kids all went "Aaww," then were quiet.

Grandma took a step back toward the dining room, then turned around and finished the saying, "First comes love, then comes marriage," and the kids all rolled around with laughter.

I just wanted to get to the K-I-S-S-I-N-G part. I stabbed my eggs and took a big swig of milk when I saw dust billow up from the corner of Fry and State, the direction of David's house.

I perked up, but when the car passed quickly, my face fell. I collected my plate and dishes and grabbed the other dishes from the table and carted them off to the kitchen.

Grandma was already by the sink, washing. I grabbed a towel and moved in beside her, drying and putting things on the top shelf for her. We worked in silence, and it was another half hour, and almost all the dishes were put in their place, when I finally gave up and assumed David forgot about asking me to go to the library with him. I ran off to get ready for the milk barn. I had to wait for the bathroom, with the line three deep. I held my towel and my red polo shirt with my name and Fry Farms logo, "Eat Beef, Drink Milk, Wear Wool, Fry Farms," emblazoned on the back.

I showered in about two minutes, as the line was already forming outside the bathroom again. I was ready in record time. I ran upstairs and grabbed my old work boots. I braided my hair and put on a swipe of mascara, then grabbed another flannel to change into so I could go to the library after the milk barn.

Skeet drove me to the fair. It was early, and they hadn't

opened the rides. When we got to the gate at the back, they saw me in my work shirt and waved us through.

"I heard you're dating David Blanch?"

"What?" I said shocked. "I'm not dating David Blanch; did John say that?"

"No, Jackie from The Alpine said that."

"Who is Jackie from The Alpine?"

"She's the bartender. We're on friendly terms."

"Pretty darn friendly if you saw her between last night and this morning."

"Well, yeah. Anyway, she said David got into this fight with this other guy at the bar over you."

"Really, I saw him get mad at this one guy, but I didn't know what it was about."

"She said it was all about you. And she said he seemed pretty sweet on you."

"Well, that's interesting because he was supposed to pick me up this morning, and he completely forgot."

"I don't know what that's about," he said.

He dropped me off near the horse barn, and I walked past it and the pig barn to the little red milk barn parked near the Farmers Insurance food tent. Corey was already pulling out the awning on the front of the barn. I stepped up and opened the windows.

"I heard you're dating David Blanche," he said.

"Are you sleeping with Jackie from The Alpine too?" I asked.

"I don't know who that is. I heard my news from Skeeter. He didn't act like it was a secret."

"When did you see Skeet?"

"At breakfast."

"You were at breakfast?"

Yeah, I was there early; a sheep got out, and I helped Skeeter get it back in."

"That gossip. I'm not dating anybody. I hung out with him last night, and he was supposed to come see me this morning and never showed up."

"I'm not surprised. He probably has to work."

"What does he do?"

"You don't even know?"

"No, we talked about other stuff. He said he's divorced."

"Yeah, I heard about that."

"Do you know what happened?"

"No, I'm sure John does."

"Well anyway, he was supposed to pick me up this morning to take me to the library to look at maps. We were going to look for Cedar Rapids and try to figure out where Tammy went, but he never called or showed up or anything."

"So, you two did hit it off last night?"

"Well, we ended up in the hay loft."

"You trollop," he joked.

"Yeah, nothing happened. We just talked about his divorce and my horrible job."

"That sounds, well, terrible actually."

We stepped into the barn and looked through the fridge to locate the different milks. I opened the deep freezer and found we were low on chocolate ice cream bars and sent Corey to grab more. He was back before the fair opened, and we had a slow trickle of visitors through the morning. I couldn't help but scan the crowd for David, but he wasn't there.

"So, I had a reason for asking you about David, actually. My cousin Corey Two is coming to town, and he wanted to see you. I told him you would be here today, and he wanted to stop by."

"Oh, Corey Two. I haven't seen him since, what, high school?"

"Well, I told him you were single and ready to mingle. He seemed pretty excited about that. So, I wanted to make sure I wasn't lying about your singleness."

"Still single," I assured him.

We waited on a customer who wanted a gallon of chocolate milk. We had only trickles of customers until lunchtime, and then the rush was on. We flew through ice cream sandwiches, chocolate bars, strawberry popsicles, and cheese sticks quickly. At one point the line reached almost over to the pig barn, but by two o'clock it had died down, and we were just killing time again.

"So, can you take me out to the library this afternoon?"

"Yeah, I can drive us over there."

"Has anybody heard from Tammy?" I asked.

"Not a thing."

I had started to sweep the barn while it was quiet when Skeet came up and opened the side door.

"Hey guys, I found a clue," Skeet said. "Come here."

Corey flipped the sign on the barn that read, "Be Right Back," and we followed Skeet to the calf barn.

"Look at that," he said pointing to a baby calf. I searched the stall, but I couldn't tell what he was talking about. We both shook our heads. He walked into the stall and pointed to the bottle sitting beside the calf. "Look," he pointed to it. It said Pendleton Farms; it was just like the bottles I remembered. I felt a rush of adrenaline go through me.

"Where is this cow from?" I asked, frantically looking around the stall for more information. He walked over to the next stall and pointed to another bottle.

"It's not those cows that are from Pendleton Farms; it's the bottles. I knew it sounded familiar. Pendleton Farms makes milk bottles."

"Oh," I said, and the rush was gone.

"This is important. It means you really did see a Pendleton Farms bottle. We never used these on our farm; nobody did in the 1980's. They were this little company back then; I saw their display at a trade show in Illinois. They were too expensive for any of the farms around here. So, you did go to a farm, it must have been a big one, it just wasn't called Pendleton."

Corey and I marinated on the new information about the bottle most of the afternoon. I told him about the reactions from our classmates at the bar. He was surprised that people had forgotten about the trip. When I told him about the theory that David had, that some people might have blocked it out, he thought that was plausible. We were going over our memories again when I saw Corey look past me, and a cheeky smile crossed his face.

"What?" I swung around and saw Corey Two standing behind me. He had gotten better looking with time, too. He looked a lot like Corey One, painfully handsome, with a killer smile and a body that showed off years of hard labor.

"Hey Corey," I said.

"Can I come around and give you a hug?" he asked.

"Sure," I walked over to the side door and met him on the steps.

"I haven't seen you since," he searched his mind. "Before you went away to college, right?"

I nodded. "Yeah, that sounds about right."

I held out my arms, and he embraced me in a big hug. His arms were hard, and he smelled like cedar.

"How did college go?" he asked.

"I finished. So, I guess it went okay. How about you?"

"Yeah, I went into Civil Engineering. I do land surveying now."

"That sounds exciting. Do you like it?"

"I love it. It takes me all over the state. I'm surveying a property for the city this week, so I'm staying with my aunt and uncle. I love that I get to do that."

I fell into a long conversation with him about his family, how he lived up north in the winter and spent time at a family lake house on Lake Michigan in the summer. He was so easy and friendly to talk to. Familiar and new at the same time.

"Hey, so I have to meet with my co-workers tonight. but do you want to get dinner with me tomorrow?"

"Yes, for sure," I said.

"So, I better go. I actually snuck in here to see you guys and went right past the gate. So, I'm technically a criminal right now. I'll pick you up tomorrow at your grandparent's house if that's okay?"

I nodded.

"Can other Corey give me your number?"

"You call him other Corey?" I laughed.

"Yeah, well at home we call him Corey Two."

"That's what we call you," we laughed.

"Okay, I've gotta go," he said, and he leaned in for

another hug. I returned it, more enthusiastically this time.

Just as we pulled away, I saw a large form bobbing through the crowd over his shoulder. It was David. He saw me hugging Corey, and his face fell.

He walked up just as Corey Two walked away.

"I'm sorry I couldn't make it this morning," he said. "I called John to tell him, but he wasn't home."

"You could have called my grandma's house."

"My mom wouldn't give me the number. She said the phone tree was sacred, and she wasn't allowed to give out numbers."

"Sure," I was unconvinced.

"I'm sorry. I got here as quickly as I could, and I wanted to see if we could go tonight after your shift at the barn. I'll take you to dinner afterwards and everything."

"I already told Corey I would go with him."

"Oh," he said. "I'm sorry. I had an emergency at work, and I couldn't get off."

I was still unconvinced. "What was the big emergency."

"Appendectomy," he said.

"Oh," I was surprised. "You're a doctor?"

"I'm an anesthesiologist; well, I'm in a residency," he said. "I was supposed to be off today, but the hospital got a little overwhelmed and asked me to come in."

I suddenly felt like a complete jerk.

"I didn't know you were a doctor," I said. "Sorry, I thought you were just making an excuse. Hold on."

I popped back into the milk barn, "Corey do you mind if I go to the library with David tonight?"

He made a face at me. I was pretty sure the face was meant to convey you just agreed to a date with my cousin.

I poked my head back out. "He said it's fine."

David promised he would be back in an hour to pick me up. Corey and I needed to refill the freezer before the next shift and put up our away sign to make the trek across the grounds to the big freezers.

When we got to the barn, we filled milk crates with ice cream, and I told him what had happened with David.

"So, are you dating David?" he asked.

"I'm going on a date with David," I said.

"But you're going out with my cousin tomorrow."

"Yeah, funny thing, because I haven't dated anybody in a year and now two dates in twenty-four hours."

"Well, you're like a Minnesota,-Michigan ten, but a Chicago seven."

I laughed, "Don't I know it. What's your excuse? You're an internationally rated ten, and you won't say if you're dating anybody."

"I was dating somebody, but it didn't work out. There's not that many people to choose from around here if you know what I'm saying. I'd probably have better luck in Chicago. There are enough people to actually have real gay bars."

"Well, maybe we should trade locations," I said.

"Chicago sounds terrible, honestly. I don't think I could live where there's no greenspace. That's just not me. I need to fish and hike."

"You could visit."

"I could do that."

"So, what's wrong with Corey Two? He's amazing. Why doesn't he have a girlfriend?"

"He has had girlfriends. Not in a while though. I don't think there's anything wrong with him. Just see how it goes."

"Will he be weird about me seeing David tonight?"

"No, he wouldn't be weird about that. He's not like that. I don't know about David though; he strikes me as a little more sensitive."

We had filled the milk crates and trudged them back through the fair. When we were back at the barn, we found John waiting for us; he looked like he hadn't gotten completely over his hangover.

He had a jug of chocolate milk in his hand, which he passed over to Corey.

"Grandma said to give you this."

"My pay," he said.

"I assume my pay is back at the house," I said.

"Yup, oh, and when I got home, David had left like five

messages telling you he wasn't going to make it this morning. Can you give your suitors your phone number, so they don't fill up my machine?"

"My suitors? It is one suitor," I said.

"Well technically," Corey coughed.

John woke up at that, "Are you dating somebody else already?"

"No, I haven't been on a first date with even one person. Possibly, tomorrow night I will be dating two people, but today I have been on a date with no one."

"Where are you going tonight?" John asked.

"David's taking me to the library."

He shook his head. "We have a very different idea of what to do on dates."

CHAPTER TEN

DAVID PICKED ME UP ON TIME and in far better comfort than we had been in the previous evening. He drove a black luxury sedan with a beige leather interior. I patted the seat when I got in; it was so soft and comfortable, I could sleep on that seat easier than on my bed.

Seeing his car brought me to the realization that the glorious hobby farm we had visited the day before was his. I suddenly felt a major sense of inferiority. My net worth hovered around $300 plus some secondhand furniture and a plastic cart on wheels that I bought at IKEA. I didn't own a car, couldn't see that owning a house was in my near or distant future, and David was driving in a vehicle with a value that doubled what I made in a whole year. Who knew what else he had in that garage and in his barns? I'd felt a lot more comfortable the day before when I thought he lived in his parent's fancy basement.

I was quiet for most of the ride to Lansing. He pulled up to the library building and paid an attendant $10 so we could park close to the building. I suddenly became very aware of how much he was spending. I would have parked blocks away and walked to avoid the fee.

He stepped out of the car and walked around to open the door. I stepped out, and he was smiling down at me. I didn't return the look.

"Are you okay?" he asked, and I nodded.

We went into the building; it had a beautiful round foyer with a glass wall that wrapped around a three-story pine tree. We walked around the loop and to the floating staircase at the back of the building. We followed the signs for the map room and found it with a very formidable librarian standing at the desk and a younger looking man stocking shelves behind her. She eyed us as we walked in and while I tried to look like I knew where I was going, she stopped me anyway.

"What are you looking for?" she asked, looking down her

nose past her glasses. She didn't say, "Can I help you," but instead it was a sharp, "What do you want?"

"We are looking for old maps," I said. "We're trying to find a town that might have existed in the past, but it doesn't anymore."

"Oh," she said. "There's a lot of that in Michigan."

"Really," we were surprised.

"Oh, yes. You will find these in many areas that have an abundance of water, and especially at a place where waters meet. The water will move the earth and bend cities to a new location, and it will take the earth with it. Sometimes water can move a whole city."

I laughed. "A drunken friend told me that at a bar, that where waters meet cities disappear or something about prime meridian lines."

She did not return my laugh. "Just because something seems implausible doesn't mean it does not happen. Cities do go missing along prime meridians. Sometimes they go missing because something happened to the landscape, or sometimes, something so very bad can happen in one location that everybody decides it is best to pretend the place never existed at all. But a well-drawn map will always reveal the truth."

"Do you know some of these towns? Is there a way to look them up?"

"There is no single repository for missing towns; they usually go missing for a reason. But you might want to start with the town of Singapore; it went missing back in the 1800's. It was on the west side of the state, just north of a town called Saugatuck. I recommend you look at maps from 1838 to 1870; you can see what happens when a place is literally wiped off the map."

"What happened to it?"

"Like I said, some places face a physical challenge to their location, and some face a tragedy. Singapore is unique among cities that have disappeared; it was a victim of its own success, and unlike many cities that are gone, Singapore is still physically right where it has always been, though for all intents and purposes it is also not there."

"We are looking for a specific city; one that isn't that old. We were there back in the 1980's with a bunch of our classmates, but none of us can find it again. It was called Cedar Rapids."

She tapped the side of her glasses, "I've seen every map in this collection. I've studied them for years, and I've never seen a place in Michigan named Cedar Rapids."

"Not even a township or anything?"

"No, but tell me what you know about it."

"It's to the west of here, at least an hour but not more than two. It had a city sign that had symbols on it for the Mason's Lodge and Rotary Club, and I think it said Welcome to Cedar Rapids or something like that.

She tapped her glasses again. She slid a piece of paper over to me and told me to draw what I remembered on the sign. I doodled the little symbols and the shape of the sign and the bubble-style font that I could recall and slid it back over to her.

She looked it over. "What you are describing is a city gateway; they often have signs for the local clubs. But the rest of what you describe and the lettering here, that's not what I've seen on a city sign."

She took out a second sheet of paper and doodled something and passed it to me.

"What I think has happened is you have two bits of information in your mind, and they have melded together to form one memory. I think what you are looking for is a city with the words Cedar or Rapids in it, and there are many on that side of the state, and I think you are looking for a sign that welcomed you to a location, like an amusement park, which may also have the name Cedar or Rapids. You have conflated two signs. To find a sign from this time period, I will direct you to the section for 1985 to 1990." She gestured for us to follow her and pointed down a hallway.

"Concentrate on the west side of the state. Look for any cities with the name Cedar or Rapids and write those down. I think you will find you have a mislaid memory. Why a whole classroom full of students have this mislaid memory is beyond me. That is a bigger question."

We walked down the hallway where she had gestured and

pulled out a map from a glass case. David held it for me, and I ran my finger along the cities on the west-side. "Grand Rapids is obvious, and it's a huge town; we would have remembered that. Look north; here is a place called Cedar Springs. There's a town called Cedar, but it's too far north; there's the Red Cedar River."

"What about Cedar Point, Ohio?" he asked. "Maybe we saw a sign for Cedar Point, and we mixed it in. I mean, a lot of us went to Cedar Point that year too, and it had that bubbly type of font."

"Yeah, but it's in the wrong direction. Cedar Point is South and East, not West."

I directed him to put that year's map back, and we pulled out maps from further back. We looked back to 1985 and then flipped to 1990. I couldn't see any big changes.

"Let's go look at Singapore."

We stepped a few rows over to the 1800's. David pulled the rack and found a map labeled "County Map of Michigan and Wisconsin." Tucked along the Kalamazoo River, north of South Haven and South of Grand Haven, was a little marking for Singapore at the edge of Allegan County.

We tucked the county map back in and looked for a map from the 1890's. The town was gone; in the place of Singapore the map now said Saugatuck, Douglas County. No city markings or landmarks existed over the land that used to say Singapore.

We tucked the historic map back into the shelf.

"So, towns do disappear, from maps at least. But she thinks our town is still there, and we got it wrong."

"Yeah," he said. "And it really bothers me that she said that we all have a mislaid memory. She said it like it was bad, like a conspiracy or something."

"I noticed. It bothered me too."

We walked back to the counter, and the librarian we had talked to was gone. Only the assistant remained. I had a small list of cities and rivers all on the west side of the state to check, and I was going to thank her for her help.

"What happened to the other librarian?" I asked.

"She's gone home for the day," he said. "We're about to close."

David checked his watch, "It's almost six."

"Could you thank her for helping us? Oh, and do you by any chance know what happened to the city of Singapore?"

He shook his head, "I haven't worked here that long, and I haven't read up on the historical maps."

We thanked him and headed on our way out of the library. It was nearly empty, and by the time we made it out to our car we were nearly the last vehicle in the paid lot.

My mind was racing; I wanted so desperately to know more about Singapore and to see if any of the Cedar towns or Rapid rivers held clues to where we could find Tammy.

I slid into the car, and David asked, "Are you hungry?" My mind skipped a beat, and he said, "I know a little Italian place nearby; want to try it?"

"Oh, yes, I'm starving. I've only had cheese sticks since this morning."

It was a short drive down Michigan Avenue, and he pulled up in front of a little mom and pop Italian eatery. I was relieved that he didn't bring me somewhere fancier. I didn't want to feel any more out of place with him.

The wait staff greeted us warmly, and they seemed to know David well. Within moments of sitting down we were served a warm basket of bread and tucked into a quiet corner of the little restaurant.

"They seem to know you here," I said.

"I might come here a little too much. I can't really cook, and it's close to the hospital so…"

"Why doesn't anybody call you doctor?"

"Well, at work they do. And sometimes when I teach classes, they do, but who in Marsh is going to call me doctor? Not John. He still calls me 'Blanch' half the time. Not my parents. Some of our old teachers still call me Davie."

"So, you don't make a thing out of it."

He laughed. "No, not at all. I know who I am."

"I remember you said that. It's like we changed places. I knew who I was at age 11, a budding pop star, and in college I knew I was a writer, and now I'm not sure about any of it."

"Your pop career never took off?" he said with a grin.

"It never got off the ground, sadly. So, how did you figure out who you were?"

"I was in college; I had a fight with my dad about school. I had a bad first year, and he said he wasn't going to pay for it anymore. So, I started paying for it myself, and took out a bunch of loans, and then strangely started attending classes on a regular basis and getting better grades, and I also changed majors to biology and away from engineering, and I finally started to do well."

"So, you paid for college by yourself? I did that too."

"Well, not quite," he said. "My dad came back around and took care of it again, but only after I did a year on my own. We are on better terms now."

"But he doesn't call you doctor?"

"He does to his friends, annoyingly, always putting the emphasis on the word doctor and not even on my name, like this is my son *Doctor* Blanch."

"Eek," I said.

We had a perfectly lovely dinner, and I tried my best to relax as I had the night before, but the David I was learning about today didn't seem like the sort of David that would ride around in a beat-up convertible with me or the sort of person I would ask to make out with me in a hay loft. Oh God, I forgot about asking him to make out with me in the hayloft. I was so embarrassed. I hadn't even had one drink.

We skipped dessert and decided to go for a walk. He showed me where he went after work and on breaks to get a rest, The Riverwalk. It was a paved walkway that ran north-south through the city and bordered the narrow parts of the Grand River, which split into two as it went south, one branch becoming the Grand River and the other becoming the Red Cedar and running through the zoo and nearby college campus.

We walked along the path and chatted about his family and mine. He told me all about his work. I wasn't one hundred percent sure how anesthesiologists spent their time at work. I learned that he could be in an operating room, a recovery room, emergency room, or even a labor and delivery ward. He took time between each patient to learn about them and make a case plan, and he was usually the first person in an operating room, testing all equipment and making sure all of his supplies were on hand in case of an emergency.

"I find order important, so that's good for me," he said.

"I'm not the most ordered person," I admitted. "I like to go off the path and try new things. I think it's good that a person like you is saving lives, and a person like me is writing about them."

I could see he was smiling, and the backs of our hands kept bumping as we walked, and after a few moments I made a move to hold his hand. He smiled at me and pulled my hand up and kissed the back of it.

I felt a flutter in my stomach and looked back at him.

"So," he said. "I have a real day off tomorrow. Do you want to go out to Saugatuck and see if we can figure out what happened to Singapore?"

"Yes," I said excitedly; then, I remembered I had just agreed to a date with Corey Two. "Uh."

"What is it?"

"I, uh, have a date tomorrow night with Corey's cousin, so I have to be back by dinner."

"Oh," his hold on my hand loosened. The rest of the walk was quiet, and I wondered what he was thinking. When we were almost back to the car, I blurted out, "I agreed to dinner before I knew anything would be happening with you."

"Well, I would hope so," he said. "I only invited you ten minutes ago, so, if you had accepted a date between now and then I'd be really worried."

"I thought you blew me off, and when he asked, I didn't know you were literally minutes away from coming to see me, or I wouldn't have accepted."

"Really?"

"Really, I feel bad about it. But like I told you, I wouldn't date a cheater, so I'm laying it all out there. Any chance you have a date tomorrow night and want to clear the air?"

He walked around the car and opened my door. "No dates, no hints of dates, no lunch breaks with an old friend, no sidelong glances at a co-worker, nothing. I won't even pretend to be playing hard to get. I've been lonely for the past five years, and this is the first date I've been on since my wife left. I don't feel comfortable flirting at work, and the hospital is where I spend all of my time, so I just don't meet anybody."

"I'm sorry. I haven't dated anybody in at least a year, and I just happened to get two dates in one day, and I have no idea why."

I stepped into the car, and he gently closed the door.

I patted my jeans pocket and said, "Well, maybe I do know why," and pulled out my grandmother's newspaper clipping and looked at it. He leaned over to look at it and asked, "What's that?"

I showed him the article and he read the headline. "My grandma gave me this yesterday. I guess it did the trick."

He couldn't suppress his amusement. We laughed together, and he reached over and grabbed my hand again.

CHAPTER ELEVEN

I BOUNDED DOWN THE STAIRS BRIGHT and early the next morning and helped Grandma make breakfast. I hopped the bathroom line to get in the shower and took all my make-up and hair styling equipment upstairs to let the rest of the house have the bathroom because I was going to be a while.

It was the first time I was going to go all out with the primping since I'd gotten to Michigan. I dried my hair, straightening out all of the natural curls, then adding big soft curls, teased the back and brushed it into big soft waves. I dabbed on foundation, mascara, eyeliner, lipstick, and wore a real blouse, a white wrap top with a light blue skirt, and even strappy sandals, borrowed from one of my more fashion-forward cousins. I would be able to wear the healed wedges with David and not make things awkward for him. I'd probably move back to flats for Corey Two. He was at least 6'3' and would still be taller than me in wedges, but he didn't tower like David; I threw flip flops in my bag for date number two.

I grabbed the white sweater that was hanging over my bed and bounded downstairs searching the house for a big straw hat; I knew Grandma had many for gardening.

"Where are you off to this morning?" she asked.

"I'm heading to Saugatuck with David. We are looking for a missing city."

"Oh, Singapore."

"You know about it?"

"I do; your grandad's grandmother lived there for a while when she was a baby."

"I've never heard you mention it."

"Well, there's not much to tell; much of our family history from that time was buried with the city."

"Buried? What happened?"

A knock came at the back door; it was David. He was dressed up too, in chino shorts and blue button-up polo shirt. He was holding a bouquet of colorful summer flowers.

I walked down the stairs to greet him, and he enveloped me in a big hug.

"You look stunning," he said as he handed over the flowers.

Grandma called to us from the top of the stairs, "Good morning, Doctor Blanch."

"You can call me David, Mrs. Fry," he called back.

She slowly moved down the stairs with a hat in her hand; she handed it over to me and said, "I'll put those in water for you, dear. You two have a nice day. I'll see if I can find Grandpa's mementos about Singapore for you for when you get back."

Just then Skeeter walked by the kitchen and shouted down to the mudroom, "You all trying to find Singapore?"

"Yup," I called back.

"Take a ride on the sand dunes; you'll find it."

"Will do," I called back.

We walked out to David's car, and he opened the door for me. Before I got in, he asked, "Does this count as a third date?"

"Sure, why?"

"Do you mind if I get some third-date, end-of-the-date business out of the way at the beginning of the third date?"

"I don't follow you."

He ran his finger along the edge of my jaw, and I looked up at him. We were on the same page. I went up on my tippy toes, and he bent down, and we met in the middle. It was a sweet and very welcome kiss. That flutter again, from my belly to my toes.

We rode to Saugatuck listening to songs from our teenage years: Smashing Pumpkins, Nirvana, TLC. We decided that neither of us liked Ace of Base, both of us liked The Beastie Boys, and we both secretly liked boy bands. We liked scary movies that were a little scary but not gross, and we liked comedies. He was a bigger fan of action movies than I was, but I said I was willing to watch them, and he said I was a bigger fan of chick flicks, but he, too, would sit through those.

By the time we had made it to Saugatuck we had made plans to watch more movies than we had time for with my remaining days in town, and we talked about plans to go see bands that weren't coming for months. We planned like I would be in town though nothing on that point was settled.

A big colorful sign greeted us not far from the interstate and announced Saugatuck. It was situated around a lake that was part of an inlet canal that opened to Lake Michigan. Unlike the flatter part of the state where I lived, this area was hilly and lush with greenery. To my surprise, in addition to the colorful landscape, the town was draped in rainbow finery.

"I didn't know it was a gay friendly town," I said. "I need to tell Corey."

"Oh, is he gay?"

"You didn't know? Sorry, I thought that was common knowledge by now. I've known for almost fifteen years, and he hasn't been in the closet since we graduated."

"I always thought he was a good dude."

"You thought correctly. He's a little quiet these days, but still good. Terrible gossip though."

"Really, he gossips a lot?"

"No, like he's a terrible gossip. He won't do it. Sad really."

"I'm not so good myself."

I pretended to be annoyed. He parked along the main thoroughfare, which was surrounded by art shops and little cafes. He ran to the other side of the car to open my door, but I had already done it. I jumped back in so he could do it again.

We walked along the paved shore path that was abutted by docks with schooners and small yachts. At the center of town, we came to a chain ferry boat. It was a hand-cranked boat that was navigated by two burly teenagers cranking a gear that moved us along the canal by a permanently-installed chain. On the other side of the canal, we walked up the path to a lookout tower, and we were able to see the channel and lakes for miles from our perch. It was a tough climb in espadrilles, but David was patient with my many stops. By the time we had descended the stairs, I remembered I had flip flops in my bag, and my aching calves were mad at me for my lapse in memory.

We walked through town and were stopped in our tracks when we saw a historical marker that said Singapore, Michigan, in front of an old church. It read, "Beneath the sands of the mouth of the Kalamazoo River lies the site of Singapore, one of Michigan's most famous ghost towns."

According to the information on the sign, the town was built in 1830 by speculators who wanted to give it an exotic name to attract visitors. It had its own bank and currency system and was home to what was once a busy inlet to the Kalamazoo River. By 1870 the town had disappeared, and its inhabitants moved south to Saugatuck.

"So, this is where everybody went. But what happened to Singapore?"

"Let's take a dune ride; Skeet said we'd find it."

We asked around town, and they told us just to travel north up the main road and we would find Mac's. It was a quick trip and just a few minutes outside of town where we found the very place: a little shack with big red and blue topless jeeps. The sign advertised fun for all and offered two types of dune rides: easy rider or thrill. We were in agreement; we wanted the thrill ride.

We paid, or rather I should say David paid our $20, and we were seated on the next available buggy. The first twenty minutes of our ride rivaled any roller coaster; the buggy whizzed up and down dunes, and we held our hands in the air screaming as we plunged down each hill. The driver handled the truck with expert care, and even though we were speeding across sand, the ride felt secure. David reached over like he had to keep me safe a couple of times, but we both knew I was fine.

It was when we finally stopped, at the apex of the largest hill to look out at the dunes that we had just traversed, that we had a chance to really look for the town. David asked the driver about Singapore.

"Of course, we know all about it," he said. "You can still see some parts of it over there. We are standing on the remnants of it right now, and if you dug right here, you would find the ruins of an old farmhouse right beneath us."

"So, what happened?" I asked. "Was it a flood or a fire?"

"Nope, nothing of the sort," the driver countered. "Singapore is buried beneath us, a victim of the success of its residents and their generosity. The town, up until it went under, had been saved from flood, famine, blizzard, and fire before it finally gave up the ghost. What took Singapore down was not its own fire, but the great Chicago fire of 1871. The people of Chicago needed help to rebuild their city, and with three sawmills and a booming logging industry, Singapore was where the citizens of Chicago looked to help them rebuild. They took the trees from this land bit by bit, ferried them across the lake, and rebuilt the city on the other side, using Singapore timber. They didn't realize that the trees were what literally rooted this place. With each tree that was taken, the landscape suffered massive erosion, and within just four years of the Chicago fire, the logging company called it quits and left the town burying itself in the sand."

"They couldn't do anything to stop it?"

"Nope, there were people who tried to stay. One man stayed too long. They say he stayed after the banks were closed, the school was gone, the lumber mills moved, and he still refused to go. They say he would work in the city by day and climb the dunes at night to get back to his home, buried except for the third-floor attic. He would crawl through the window, with no kitchen or bathroom, praying that the sand might wash away and give him back his home. His prayers went unanswered, and soon his house was buried just like everything else. The only part of it that remains is the tip of a chimney that you can see over on that ridge."

"What happened to the man?"

"Nobody knows for sure, but the people who left Singapore had a string of uncommon good luck if you ask me. A cursed town gave way to create charmed people."

"Why do you say that?" another woman from the tour asked; everybody on the buggy was now in raptures at the story.

"The people of Singapore moved North to Holland or South to Saugatuck and experienced a boom of unusual success. No matter which direction they went, their next move seemed to be the right one. Growing tulips and fruit to the north and making art and baskets to the south all turned out to be very lucrative. No matter which way they went they were okay. Seems like the only person who suffered might have been the man that refused to follow the winds of change."

"Maybe they were charmed by their generosity and not the sacrifice of the town," I said.

"That would be poetic if true," he said.

I thought about that. With my newfound knowledge that my great-great-grandmother might have been a resident of Singapore, I wondered if I could be considered amongst its lucky descendants. I was poor, very poor, and I'd lost both of my parents when I was young. That didn't feel very lucky, but I had more than twenty first cousins and grandparents that remained in uncommonly good health and were there when I needed them. I wondered if that could be considered luck.

"Look, it's a place where two waters meet," I said to David, pointing at the great lake and the inlet.

"It is," he said.

The second half of the dune ride was only slightly tamer than the first half.

I was thankful that Skeeter told us about the ride, or we might not have learned more about the city. We walked back to the car, and I was lost in thought. I knew what happened to this town, but I wasn't any closer to figuring out what happened to our town.

"What's on your mind?" David asked when we were back in the car.

"We just aren't any closer to finding Tammy. I feel bad that I'm wasting time, and she might really need us."

"I don't know if you want to hear this, but my mom said Tammy was known to have a drug problem, and she's not sure that Tammy missing has anything to do with what happened to Charity."

"But she called me on Charity's phone before Charity showed up dead, and she said she was going to Cedar Rapids."

"Did they find Charity's phone? Did she have it with her when she died?"

"I…I didn't think to ask that."

"What if they had parted ways after they found the town, and something happened to Charity after, and something different happened to Tammy?"

I slapped my hand against my head, "Oh my gosh, what if Tammy's been calling me this whole time? She has Charity's phone, and she doesn't know anybody else in her phone book."

I rifled my phone out of my purse, then looked at the clock; it wasn't a night or weekend.

"Do you have a cellphone?"

David pulled a phone out of his center console and handed it to me. I dialed my number back in Chicago and let it ring until the answering machine picked up. At the end of the greeting, it beeped; I had a message. I dialed my code and then a message started, Sunday 2 p.m. It was quiet at first, then a whisper, "Michelle, we found it. We need help, hurry. Charity is..."

The message was cut off. I grabbed David's arm.

The machine beeped again. I pressed seven to hear the next message. Monday, 1:45 a.m. "Michelle. Help me. It might already be too late; tell my mom I love her. I'm so sorry I got us into this. I can't call her..." the message cut off.

There were no more messages.

"She called me. She's been calling me. We need to tell the police." I handed him back the phone.

He dialed the police station and put Detective Fowler on the speaker phone.

I blurted out, "Tammy called me. She left me messages, and she used Charity's phone. She needs help."

"It's not possible; we have Charity's phone."

"How's she calling me?"

"Oh shoot, hold on." The sound of shuffling went on for a few moments, and he came back. "Did Tammy also by chance use a pink flip phone?"

I pulled my phone out of my purse and showed it to David. "We all have pink flip phones. They were on special when the new Walmart opened."

"Shit, we have Tammy's phone."

"You can't," I said. "Somebody took Tammy's phone, too. I don't know whose phone you have."

I gave the detective my log-in code for my phone so he

could get the new messages.

"Why do you think she's calling you?" Fowler asked.

I opened my phone and examined it, thinking about why she was only calling me.

"I don't know."

"Okay, sit tight, and I'll let you know what I find out."

"She said she found Cedar Rapids though. I've at least got to look for it."

"No, wherever she went you don't need to go there. We are looking into it. I'll call you as soon as we know more."

"Can I call her mom? She asked me to tell her she loved her."

"No, not yet, but I'll make sure she gets the message."

I closed my eyes for a minute to think. And it was as if David knew I needed that moment. He patted his hand on my back while I curled up. I sat up, rifled in my purse, and pulled out the tiny bits of paper that I had written on at the library.

"These towns, we are close to some of these towns. Let's go find them."

He reached across me and to the glove box and pulled out a map.

"Tell me where to go."

CHAPTER TWELVE

I CALLED COREY ON THE DRIVE TO TELL HIM what had happened and cancelled my date with Corey Two. I gave Corey my list of cities and townships, and he said he was going to search as well. We drove around the edges of Grand Rapids first. We drove through the small hamlet of Grandville and up through Wyoming, then to center-city Grand Rapids and did one loop before deciding we never went through a city that big when we were on our field trip. We moved through to the township area on the East side of the city.

That area was still not rural enough for what David and I remembered. We made our way north to Rockford, and the landscape was getting a little more rural, but there was a large body of water in the center of town that was very memorable and certainly not something we had seen before. We stepped out to look at the dam at Rockford. We found Corey and our friends assembled over the bridge at the base of the dam. There was Missy, Corey Two, and Jen, looking at a map of their own.

"Jen!" I exclaimed when she turned around, and I got a look at her pregnant belly for the first time. It was so out of place on her tiny body it almost looked like she'd stuffed a basketball under her dress. I carefully embraced her and said, "Should you be out here looking for a kidnapper?"

"That's what I said," Corey chimed in, looking up from his map.

"She's been missing too long, and I'm worried."

I felt the same way.

David was trailing behind me, being quiet, and I realized he didn't know the people in this group. "Oh, everybody this is David. David this is Missy, Jen, Corey, and his cousin, also Corey. We call him Corey Two."

The two shook hands, and David stared at him with more intensity than I expected. I realized he was inspecting my other date.

Noticing the tension Corey one joked, "You can just call him Corey."

"I always thought it was weird you were both named Corey," Jen said. "Why did your parents do that?"

Corey said, "We are both named Cornelious, for our great-grandfather. He meant a lot to our moms, so they both wanted to honor him."

"Oh," she said. "I guess I didn't know you were named Cornelious, either."

"Well, Corey Two, if you are going to be around us a lot, we need to call you something other than Corey Two, how about Neil?"

"Sure, if that's easier," he said.

I interrupted. "Back to the maps."

We ran our fingers along the map lines. "So Grand Rapids isn't right at all," I said. "There's not enough rural land. What we are looking for is flat; I remember corn fields."

"It's got to be north," Jen ran her finger over the map. "I think we should go North, then East."

"That seems right to me too," I said. "Let's go to Cedar Springs first, then start heading toward Kent City and Muskegon."

We agreed. I jumped in the car with David. We followed Corey north up 131. Corey pulled off and into Cedar Springs. We were trekking along well until suddenly Corey's truck started swaying and then went across the center line. He had to jerk the vehicle back over to correct. We were taken aback by the erratic driving. Suddenly, he slammed on the brakes and pulled over onto the shoulder.

David followed him and pulled off, and I ran up to the truck to see what was happening.

"Jen pulled the damn steering wheel," Corey said. "Gave me a damn heart attack."

Jen looked like she was about to jump out of her seat.

"Did you see the sign?" she shouted. "We have to turn around."

I waved to David to follow us, and I crawled into the back seat. We turned around and got back to the edge of town. Once there, Jen directed Corey to turn down a side street. How she had managed to see that sign, which was so far from the main road, was beyond me. It took a moment for it to come into full view. When it did, I knew why she was excited. My heart did a flip flop, "Cedar Springs," I said.

She jumped out of the truck, and I followed her. We ran our fingers along the letters, and it's like something clicked in my brain. We had been here before. This was the shape of the sign I'd drawn for the librarian. I pulled it out, but the words were different, and the logos for the town associations weren't on the sign at all: they were behind it.

"This is it," I said. "But it's not exactly like I remember. Where did the Rapids come from?"

Missy looked at the sign, "I've seen this sign, but this isn't the one that I remember."

Corey pulled out the map again and said, "If we were heading to a school field trip, we would have taken 96 up 131 or 57 to here. If we were heading East, which we all think is right, why wouldn't we take the more direct road, 37 or stay on 96?"

"Maybe there was a traffic jam." I offered.

"I don't know," he said.

"We need to go further." Jen said, "We're getting closer. I can feel it."

I ran back to check on David behind us. "Do you mind if I ride with them for a minute? We're going East to Muskegon, and we are kind of vibing on the stuff we see."

"Is there room for me to ride in there with you?"

"Oh, sure," I said, and realized he felt left out.

We found a shopping center where we could safely park his car and crammed, three to bench seat, in the extended cab Ford. Jen and Missy sat up front, with Missy taking the center, straddling the stick shift.

That left me in the back between Neil—formerly Corey Two—and David. I debated putting them next to each other, but David looked like he was going to eat Neil if I left him unprotected.

Corey drove carefully down the straight road that took us from Cedar Springs to Muskegon. We passed a skating rink, parks, golf club, and it was all starting to feel eerily familiar.

"This is like high school," Missy squealed from the front, "all of us on a road trip with the Coreys. Remember that horrible fake Pizza Hut we went looking for?"

"Oh God," Jen said. "It was a Pizza Shack, remember; they built it in an old Pizza Hut."

"Remember the waiter?"

We all laughed, except David. He wasn't in on the joke.

"Sorry, David," Missy said. "You were too cool to hang out with us back then."

"I was not," he countered.

"Oh yeah you were. You and John and all the football players only hung out with the other football players, and we were just band and drama nerds."

"I would have hung out with you if you had asked. Playing football wasn't even my idea; the coach and my dad pushed me into it," he said. "And besides, Corey played football and you hung out with him."

"Yeah, but Corey was both a football player and a drama kid," Missy argued. "And in football he was a kicker, so you knew he wasn't like a real football player. You guys never hung out with him."

I thought for a moment; they probably hadn't hung out with Corey for other reasons, but I didn't want to make the drive more tense. I wondered if Corey was bothered by the topic of being left out in high school; it was once a touchy subject, so I moved the conversation along.

"So, I don't know where you got the idea my cousin John was popular; he certainly was not," I said in response to Missy's earlier comment.

"Oh, my gawd, yes he was," Missy said. "I had the biggest crush on him."

"Turn here," Jen jumped out of her seat and smacked the window.

Corey took an abrupt turn onto a highway. We drove just a few miles when suddenly we were all quiet.

"This is it," Corey said.

"This is it," I repeated with Jen and Missy.

It was as if he suddenly knew the way. Just a few miles down the highway and he took an exit, following a sign for a state park. I felt a tingle on the back of my neck, and I reached out to David, who held my hand. Corey proceeded slowly and turned onto a side road, slowing more until he came to it. Right in front of us was a faded blue sign and written in chipped white paint were the words: "Cedar Rapids."

We all stared in silence. I barely registered the words below it, the words that I could not see in my memory, "Whitewater Adventure Park."

My mind flashed back to the bus ride in 1989. The sign was bright back then, the paint fresh, and the sun was shining. A student called from the back of the bus, "Coach Perry, what's whitewater?" He answered, "It's another way to say fast-moving water."

The flash ended, and the letters of the sign appeared before me, peeled away, revealing the decay of twenty years. We got out of the truck and walked up to the sign; I felt it and imprinted the true sign in my memory.

"It was a water park," I said, but nobody was by me any longer.

The others had walked past the sign and started up the hill behind it.

Corey had bounded up and was nearly to the top. When he got there, he turned and shouted, "Hey, guys come up here."

I took off, running up the hill, only just beating Jen to the summit. It was a steep climb, and I had to catch my breath. As I did, I looked out, able to see for long stretches in all directions. On the other side of the hill was an abandoned water park, every inch of it faded.

What was once the main attraction of the park, three intertwined waterslides which let out at a giant lake of green mossy water, were cracked and pale. The gates that surrounded the park were covered in ivy. Cartoonish bear signs, meant to verify height at attraction entrances, had their paint chipped away, especially around the eyes and mouths, leaving gaping dark holes in place of what were once cheery features. The food court buildings had all the glass broken out of them, and where there were once counters, there were now wooden panels vandalized with graffiti. The grass had grown tall all around, and the yellow umbrellas over the picnic tables had torn away and were hanging in shambles from their metal supports.

"Cedar Rapids was never the town," I said.

"No," Corey said, shaking his head.

We all stood in silence for a moment, trying to connect the dots of the past we remembered and this place. I had been to this water park when it was open. With each feature I saw, my mind filled in the blanks of what the park used to be. I remembered the water of the lake used to be a crystal-clear blue, and it housed swan boats that we could pedal with our feet. Now the water was murky, and the boats were gone.

Corey looked like something had just occurred to him. "So, the farm…"

He never finished his thought. Instead, he turned away and bounded down the hill and over to his truck. The other guys took off after him while Jen, Missy, and I strolled down, making sure we paid special attention to Jen, who was still catching her breath from the trek up the hill.

When we made it to the base, they were all putting their heads together over a map laid out on the tailgate. We pushed our way in to look at the map.

"What is it?" I asked.

He pointed to the map, and we followed the path of his finger to a big green space not far away, "The farm has to be in here."

There was a lot of green space east of us.

"I think we should follow this road," I said, pointing away from the city.

He agreed. He folded up the map and tucked it into his back pocket. We were all still in a bit of shock at the revelation that Cedar Rapids really wasn't a town. We quietly turned back to the cab of the truck, and just as we opened the door several things happened all at once.

A dark car with tinted windows drove slowly down the abandoned road and came to a stop when it was opposite us. The driver's side window rolled down, and I saw the Pitbull man from the bar. I only just registered his face when he pulled a handgun out and aimed at Corey's truck. He hit the passenger's side door, not aiming at anybody. We all ducked, then moved to the ground, except David. He stayed standing; as soon as the shots stopped, he kicked off fast, rounding the front of the car, then taking off at a sprint to the car. He was only a few paces away when the man pulled the gun back in and sped away, squealing his tires and kicking up dust behind him.

My heart was racing out of my chest. I was shaking as I went to push off from the ground; my palms shook as I pushed up and tried to steady my breathing. Just as I was able to get control of myself, I noticed Jen had rolled on to her back next to me, and her breathing was not steady at all, 'Hee...hee…hoo… hee...hee…hoo."

"Shit," Missy said. "Get her in the truck; we have to get her to a hospital."

"We need a blanket," David ordered.

Corey jumped into the back of his truck and pulled a plaid blanket out of his storage box; he laid it on the back seat, then jumped from the back of the truck to the front, firing up the engine. Missy and I gently guided Jen into the center position in the rear and snuggled her in between us.

Corey started to pull away, and David said, "Wait, my car and we need to call the police."

Jen was breathing hard again.

"I don't think we have time for that," Neil said.

Jen closed her eyes and between gasps she said, "Could be a Braxton Hicks Contraction."

But within a few minutes she was breathing heavily again.

"We need to find a hospital now," David said.

"No," Jen said jumping forward, grabbing the collar of his shirt. "You get me back to Lansing. I have a doula. I have a birth plan."

"I don't know if we have time to," Corey started.

"I will make time," she seethed.

Corey went speeding down the highway, making a quick trek back to 96.

"I'll figure out how to get my car later," David conceded when he realized the quickest way back to Lansing wouldn't take us anywhere near his car.

After we all had a moment to collect our breath Neil asked, "What just happened?"

"That was the guy that said Tammy owed him money."

"How do you know him?" David asked.

"I confronted him at the bar after she went missing."

He shook his head, "You're going to give me a heart attack."

CHAPTER THIRTEEN

AFTER A HARD NIGHT OF LABOR, AND one birth plan thrown completely out the window, Jen gave birth to a happy healthy baby boy, born two weeks early. Her husband developed an eye twitch when he heard what had brought on the early labor.

The police met us outside of her birthing room; this time Detective Fowler had backup from Captain Fowler and Sargent Sarita. He was not pleased that we had taken up sleuthing on our own, gotten shot at, and sent a woman into early labor, but we gave him a solid lead on a possible suspect for Charity's murder and Tammy's disappearance.

"I'm sure we were close to finding her," I said. "What did you find out about the phone?"

"We had some burner phone; it didn't have a plan on it. Tammy had missed some payments, so we thought it might be hers. We weren't thinking to track Charity's phone."

"The key is the farm, and it's going to be up where we were. I'm sure of it," I said.

"So, you solved the mystery of your missing town?" he asked.

"I think we did," I said.

"I'll tell my sister. It's been bothering her all week."

"We didn't find the farm though."

"I'm going to find it," Fowler said. "We're going to go up there today. We have some help coming in from the locals."

"Do you think it's too late for Tammy? She stopped calling."

"I don't know. The phone probably died after this many days without a charge. I wouldn't count her out just yet."

Jen had her baby at the hospital where David worked, and we were there so long he slunk off to take a nap wherever residents sleep in a hospital. We saw him walk by later in the morning in his white coat and green scrubs. He looked like he'd had a shower, but he certainly didn't look well-rested.

He nodded to Corey and Missy when he walked by and stopped to say good morning to me.

"Good morning, Doctor David," Neil interrupted, and David managed a pained smile at him.

It wasn't long before it was just Missy and me at the hospital in day-old clothes, as the Coreys both had work to do. My grandmother was enroute to pick us up.

After the police left and the baby had arrived, we both crashed, the surge of adrenaline wearing off. We sat low in the boxy hospital chairs. If we'd had even a bit of comfort, we would have been fast asleep.

"Do you think that guy has Tammy?" Missy asked.

I hadn't thought about it. My mind had been totally occupied with survival mode.

"Huh, I don't think so. She wasn't in that car."

"Why would he shoot at us?" she asked.

"Well, that's the weird part; he didn't even shoot at us, did he? It was more of a warning. Like he shot near us."

"What was he trying to warn us about?"

"Stay away from Tammy, I guess."

"But you don't think he had her?"

"I wonder…"

"What?" she asked.

"I wonder if he was looking for her, too and didn't want us to find her first."

"And holy shit, what about David, just rushing right in? I kinda wondered what you liked about him; he's like tall and all, but he's got a total dad bod."

"He doesn't have a dad bod."

"Too close to a dad bod for me. In high school he was like this chiseled tall Adonis."

"Hey, he's still good looking."

"Don't get me wrong; the way he ran in there was like, hot." She fanned her face. "But not like Corey's cousin. My god, he's hot like twenty-four-seven."

I was about to defend David more when Grandma rounded the corner. She had her hands full of lilies, a tiny bear, and a card.

She passed the card to us to sign.

"She'll know we didn't get this, Grandma; we've been at the hospital all night."

"It's about the thought; the card says we wish you blessings of joy, and I'm sure you do."

"We do." I signed.

Grandma got to be a normal visitor and dote on Jen and the baby, shaking hands with the riled-up father and hugging her parents. Missy and I were clearly not welcome parties, but Jen insisted that they bring us in. She gestured for one final hug before we left. As I was pulling away, she grabbed me by the shoulder and pulled me back down and whispered in my ear, "Find Tammy and get that fucker."

I looked at her sweetly and smiled, "Anything for you, new momma."

CHAPTER FOURTEEN

AS MUCH AS I WANTED TO SET OUT on the sleuthing trail again, my eyes betrayed me, and I fell asleep on the drive back from the hospital. I fell asleep in the Buick and woke in my bed when it was dark. I assumed Skeeter or John must have relocated me.

My mouth was full of ick, and I realized I'd completely trashed my borrowed white blouse when I'd dived into the dirt.

I ambled down the stairs with a toothbrush and pajamas in hand and made my way to the bathroom. After I was presentable again, I walked out to the kitchen to find dinner was finished, but Grandma had left out a plate of turkey, gravy, and potatoes for me with a little note, "Gone to church, hope you get this before it's cold. Your milk is in the fridge."

I felt the plate; it was cold. I walked into the kitchen, pulled the cling wrap off my dinner, and popped it into the microwave. Then I opened the fridge and found a gallon of chocolate milk with a Post-it note with my name on it that said, "Thank you for working the barn."

I ate in the kitchen on the stool by Grandma's phone. I started to come out of my fog and looked up at the clock; it was after eight. I had to search my mind for what day it was, Wednesday, maybe Thursday. I looked at the calendar. I worked at the milk barn on Monday. Sleuthed on Tuesday. Delivered baby on Wednesday. I hung my head. I was supposed to be working with the design committee for the reunion. The committee that Charity was in charge of, and I'd slept right through it.

I wracked my brain for who was in charge now and called Missy. She woke as groggy as I'd been just moments ago. "Hey, Missy, who's in charge of decorations now?"

"Oh, probably Abby or Anna," she said. "I don't have a number for either of them, but I know a lot of people are heading to The Alpine again tonight. Might be able to figure it out there."

"Are you coming out?" I asked.

"Not a chance, I need to sleep for another twelve hours at least. Are you going to go?"

"If I can get a ride to town."

We said goodbye, and I walked around the house. It was another too-dark night. I looked out the big front window that faced the sheep pasture and big red barn and saw stars gleaming in the night sky. I could enjoy the view for hours—a view completely obscured in Chicago. We had nearly the same sky, but I could never see it with the city lights blocking out the night.

I sat in my grandfather's rocking chair, thinking it would be a good idea to rest for a night, but something was nagging at me, telling me to go to town.

"Okay brain, what's the issue?" I said out loud to myself. I went over the events of the previous days and wondered what I might be missing. Charity was on the decorating committee. She died. Was it her creepy boyfriend, or Tammy's drug dealer enforcer, or somebody else entirely? They crashed her car, a car that she and Tammy took to an old water park.

It was something earlier that I was missing. That night at the bar the old man said he'd heard of Cedar Rapids: why would an old man be under the same delusion as the rest of my class about a city that wasn't a city at all? He said he hadn't been to Cedar Rapids in years; why would he have thought it was real? Was he on the trip with us?

Then something else came to mind. Charity's roommate said there was a picture of it. Some guy with a strange name gave it to her. Then it struck me. Charity was on the decorating committee; she was collecting photos; the Cedar Rapids picture might be with the committee.

I ran back up the stairs and changed into my last clean outfit. I gathered all of my clothes scattered around the room and ran downstairs, throwing a load in the washer before stepping outside and realizing my plan ended there. I had no way to get to town.

I looked around the farm for lights. Skeeter's apartment over the shed was dark. Aunt Pattie's lights were out. I scanned all of the houses and found that nobody was home. Then I remembered Wednesday Night church. I realized everybody, except Skeeter, would be at the Methodist evening service. I looked around the property. Lots of tractors and a combine, but nothing I could get on the road. I remembered Skeeter said he won a side-by-side at a breast cancer raffle. I didn't see it in the equipment barn, so I figured it had to be in my cousin's barn. I headed down to her property, walking along the dark dirt road, and snuck into her outbuilding. I saw something covered by a tarp and pulled it off to see a little two-seater vehicle that looked something like a bat mobile. It was dark and solid and to my horror had a big pink decal across the windshield that said, "Booby Bouncer."

I shook my head and walked to my cousin's house, correctly assuming the door would be unlocked. I poked my head in the kitchen door, announcing myself in case anybody was home. Complete silence greeted me. I saw a key hanging under a chalk board with a little pink brassiere hanging from it. I grabbed it off the hook and scribbled on the chalk board, "Borrowed the Booby Bouncer, love Shell."

I ran back to the barn and fired up the side-by-side. It had a full tank of gas and ran as loud as any tractor. It growled when I stepped on the gas, and I floored it out of the farm; it topped out under thirty, and I wasn't sure it was street legal, but I didn't think either of the Officers Fowler would issue me a ticket after our history together.

I saw why it was called the 'Booby Bouncer' on the dirt road. It had almost no suspension, and I felt every bump and rumble. I guessed that might be half the point with these, to feel the earth as you drove, but it was a little flashy and loud for a ride through my quiet town. It wasn't until I turned onto the paved road at Packard that the ride smoothed out.

I made it to The Alpine and found the lot full again. Reunion weeks must be a boon for this little place. My bouncer didn't fit neatly into any space, so I made sure to park away from the action, especially since I hadn't exactly secured permission to take her out.

I followed the noise into the bar and found it hopping yet again. There were vaguely familiar faces. I scanned the crowd looking for Abby, "Most Organized," hoping she could point me to the new head of the decorating committee.

I found her sitting at a long table that I'd sat at two days before with the football players.

She was smiling and laughing until she saw my face; then, she very abruptly looked angry and pointed. I looked to my left and right, then pointed to myself and she motioned for me to come over.

"Where have you been?" she seethed. "I've been calling."

"You have my house number in Chicago, so I haven't been getting those calls."

"Why would you give us that number? Don't you have a cell?"

"I can only do night and weekend minutes on that," I said. "And I'm sorry I didn't make it today. Jen had her baby last night, and I was up at the hospital with her."

"Oh," she squealed, and it seemed all was forgiven. "What did she have?"

"Bouncing baby boy," I said.

"I knew it. She was carrying low."

"But I do need a favor. Charity had some pictures from different classmates, and I think she had one from our third-grade trip to that farm. Do you know where she might have put those?"

"I have no idea," she said, rubbing her temples. "I'm starting over at square one because I don't know where any of that went. In fact, I was going to ask you to ask around and see if you can get any old class pictures because I have literally nothing."

My heart fell.

"Hey," a man came up behind Abby. "Are you looking for pictures from that third-grade farm trip?"

"Yes!" I shouted, much louder than I planned.

"I have those," he said; he held out his hand and introduced himself, "Long Fei."

"Michelle," I said, holding out my hand. "I'm sorry, I don't exactly remember, did you go to school with us?"

"Up until third grade. My dad is military; we moved right after that trip."

"Did you give your farm pictures to Charity?"

"I did, but I got doubles."

"Oh, my gosh, where?"

"Out in my car."

I jumped out of my seat and practically pushed him out of the bar. We stepped out into the quiet of the night, with Abby in our wake. As we were stepping away from the back door David and John were walking in, and we nearly bumped into each other.

"I thought I would find you here," David said, steadying me after I nearly barreled into him.

Without even thinking to greet him I said, "He has the pictures of the farm."

"Who?" David asked.

I introduced him, "David, this is Long Fei. Long Fei, this is David." The two shook hands, and Long Fei said, "I know you, David, and you can call me Long."

He pointed to his car. It was a white rental sedan with a Nationwide sticker on the back bumper. To our surprise the rear window was smashed.

"Oh, shit," he said. "Somebody broke into my car."

We looked in the backseat. It was empty.

"The pictures were sitting back there," he said.

Abby and I walked around the parking lot looking into the other cars, but we couldn't find any evidence of the pictures.

Long Fei opened his trunk and found his luggage intact.

"That's crazy; they took my pictures."

"Why would they do that? What was in the pictures?" I asked.

"Really normal stuff. Just us petting like goats and sheep and stuff. It wasn't anything special. I'm sure you guys all have the same pictures."

I shook my head, "We don't, and nobody really remembers this trip. We've all been mixed up about it for years."

"Are you serious?" he said. "You guys don't remember this trip. It was crazy, and you really don't remember?"

"No," Abby and I both said.

He went completely pale and said, "I'll never forget it."

CHAPTER FIFTEEN

WE WALKED INTO THE BAR AND ORDERED Long a stiff drink. He was visibly shaken. He went to the head of the big table where Abby had been sitting earlier, and everybody gathered around him, eager to hear what he had to say.

"It was a great trip, at least the first half of it. We were feeding baby animals, and we got to put our hands in this feeder corn, it was like normal corn, but hard you know, and they were showing us how you feed animals. I remember learning a lot about farming there. I think I was with you for a while in the bunny barn, Michelle. Remember we had that bunny with the big ears; do you remember it?"

I had a flashback.

I was standing in a big barn next to Long. Beside us was an elaborate rabbit hutch. It was more like a rabbit mansion. It had two floors of hand-crafted wooden bunny housing. They had little walkways and arched bunny sized doorways. I remembered his big smile as he held the giant velveteen rabbit with droopy ears. I pictured the way he held the bunny; his grip was a little precarious as he was hugging the top of the rabbit tightly, but its ample bottom hung out of the hold. The rabbit was not secure, but he seemed not to mind. I remember the other kids were excited to see Long holding the gentle giant and ran up to him to pet it. I don't recall how Long came to be holding him. We were all smiles, Jen and Corey included, petting the docile bunny. Then a woman, the farmer's wife I think, came running over and screamed at Long, startling him. He dropped the massive creature. "Don't you touch him," she screamed. Her reaction was out of proportion to what had happened, and Long welled up with tears and ran out of the barn.

My mind snapped back to the present, just as Long said, "After the bunny incident we separated. Some of you went to the other side of the barn, and some of us walked out back to the field, and that's when things went really bad."

I flashed back again.

I went to the barn. I filled bottles and helped feed the baby goats with the small glass Pendleton bottles.

Long continued his story, bringing me back to the present.

"I ran to the back of the property, by the fence that was next to this big field. I was upset because the farmer's wife yelled at me for the way I held the bunny. I stood with some of the other adults after they helped calm me down. We watched the farmer bailing hay, and he was standing by this big green bailer with yellow stripes on it. He stopped his tractor, and he got off and waved at us.

He was a little far off out in the field; we could see him, but he was too far away to hear him. He shouted something, but we couldn't make it out. There was a bunch of kids there, like David you were there, and Anna Shepherd, John was there, and some of the other chaperones. Everybody was all happy. I remember watching the farmer make these big round bales of hay; it was kind of mesmerizing you know, baling and then balling, and it was just a beautiful day, perfect weather with a nice breeze. So, things were like calm and friendly, and then the farmer steps back to the bailer and reaches his hand under the machine to pull on something. It was like this big yellow stick; it didn't belong out in a field, and then suddenly he just gets sucked in."

A collective gasp went around the table. Long took a swig of his drink and steadied himself. His hands were shaking.

"He just like went right in the machine, and I felt like time stopped. All the adults started screaming around me and running in all directions. Us kids, we just stood there; we couldn't process what we'd seen. I remember just staring at the machine and wondering when he was going to come back out; then all this red just started oozing out, and I realized he was dead."

He looked around the table at the shocked faces. "You guys seriously don't remember this?" We remained stunned.

"Why don't you remember this? I think about it all the time. Like I had to go to therapy; my parents were so worried about it."

I was the first person to find words. "Nobody remembers

it. We can't even find pictures from it, pictures we remember taking. We don't have one mention of it in the school year books or newsletters."

"Do you remember it, David?" Long asked.

He gulped and shook his head.

He looked down the table, "John?"

He shook his head.

Long finished his drink, "That's messed up. That's so messed up."

CHAPTER SIXTEEN

THE MOOD IN THE BAR TURNED. I think some people did remember the farm accident after he said it and didn't want to admit it. I wasn't one of the witnesses, but I didn't recall anybody ever talking about it. I had had nothing but pleasant memories of that day up to that point, but I forgot about the woman yelling at Long and him dropping the bunny. How could half the kids in my class witness something like that and none of us remember it? I thought back to the bus ride and the sign for the water park. That memory must have been before the accident because I could see smiling faces all around the bus, people playing patty cake and cards. The mood was one of excitement. I couldn't picture the return ride. What had happened on that return trip?

I didn't feel like drinking, and David kindly ordered me a Shirley Temple, and I sat in the bar poking at the cherries.

"What are you thinking?" he asked.

"I don't remember any of that. Like with my parents I understand; I was young, and that we suppress some trauma. But how could so many of us just forget? Even the people that didn't see it."

"I heard about this before; it's selective amnesia. It's kind of what happens in anesthesia. Your body takes you out of something while it's going through trauma to save you the pain. But it happens even with average things; the mind is tricky.

"I can't imagine a whole class full of us would forget a town though."

"It happens on a global scale, like Monopoly. My little brother used to swear that the guy from the box wore a monocle, but he doesn't."

Thinking back to the Monopoly box I was sure I'd seen the guy on the box with a monocle, bag of money, and a top hat. I could picture it clearly. "He did have a monocle," I countered.

"That's what my brother thought too, but I never saw that. Here's another example; remember the Publisher's

Clearinghouse? It was that contest in the eighties, and remember Ed McMahon used to deliver checks to people? He'd run up with balloons and surprise winners, and he would say, 'This is Ed McMahon with the Publisher's Clearinghouse Sweepstakes.'"

"I do remember that."

He shook his head. "It never happened."

I tilted my head. "Of course it did."

"Nope, just like we forgot about the signs; they were us thinking of two different things and putting them together, conflating those two things. Ed McMahon did a commercial for this other company called American Family, and it sort of had the look of Publisher's Clearinghouse, and we've just put them together. Everybody has."

"He delivered checks with balloons. I can see those big checks."

"He didn't."

"Okay, maybe you say he didn't; after that sign thing yesterday I'm a little shook, but why would so many of us have such a fake and messed up memory of something that actually happened to us? Somebody had to mess with our memories, and that can't be good."

I pulled out my phone, thinking about calling Missy, telling her what I'd just learned. I opened my phone and closed it again and looked at David.

"The phones," I said, having a thought. "Will you drive me to Kmart?"

"Yeah, what are we doing?"

Before I could answer him, I was heading for the door.

He followed me to the car and started for Kmart.

"So," I said, talking to myself as much as to him as we drove. "Missy, Tammy, Charity—we all had this same pink phone. There was an introductory deal when they opened the new Walmart across the street from the old Kmart. You could get this phone, in pink or blue, for free with a new plan. So, we all have this phone. Our parents all bought the same toaster that week; it was like $10 toaster day. It was a whole thing."

"Okay," he said, turning into the nearly empty parking lot of the Kmart.

I jumped out of the car and continued sharing my train of thought. "So, we all have the same phone because we went to the same store."

"Yes."

"Well before Walmart the only place in town to get anything, like photos, was at the Kmart. We all would have taken our film there to be developed."

I stared at him, but he still didn't quite get it. "Okay, so you know how you're saying that we might all be confused about the signs, and maybe Ed McMahon didn't deliver checks, which I'm not sure I believe just yet. But Long was not confused, and he had pictures, and none of us do. So that means somebody went to a lot of trouble to make sure there were no photos developed from that day—or that the photos never got back to us. All the adults that were around us for years pretended that day never happened. Why would they do that?"

"Stop, Michelle," he put his hand out in front of me to slow me down. "I think it's really obvious why they did it."

I tapped my foot.

"They were trying to protect us. They didn't want us to have this horrible memory," David said.

"That doesn't make any sense to me."

"It makes perfect sense to me. We were a group of young kids who had never seen anything like that. They probably didn't want us to have horrible memories, mess us up for life. So, they just, pretended it didn't happen."

"Like Long said, 'That's messed up,'"

"I don't disagree, but I think what we should be looking into is some therapy to remember it and get past it, not chasing down a conspiracy theory."

"It's not a conspiracy theory if it really happened; it's a real conspiracy."

"Well," he conceded. "I suppose. But I can't be mad at them for it. I'm glad I don't have that memory. Did you see how upset Long was about it?"

There was a long pause between us when he finally, quietly said, "I don't want that memory."

"I understand that," I conceded. "But there has to be

something else in those photos. He said it was just normal pictures of kids and animals. Why would photos like that be worth stealing now?"

"I…" He thought for a moment. "Actually, I don't know."

"Precisely," I said, pulling him with me to the photo counter at the back of the store. It was an unmanned space. The counter was worn away where people must have passed things over it for many years, but the shelves for holding photos behind the stand were empty, and the little signs around the kiosk were chipped. Even the signs over the counter that were supposed to announce prices didn't have information on them anymore.

We searched for several minutes before finding a skinny teenager in a blue-light special vest to probe.

I bent the truth in my questioning of him, saying that I was with a reunion committee looking for pictures from an old school trip.

"We don't do photos much anymore," the kid replied. "People mostly do digital and put them on memory cards."

"Is there any way to look back at pictures that were processed a long time ago?" I asked. "Any old records."

He stepped behind the counter and looked absentmindedly through the drawers.

"Our records only go back five years, ma'am."

"Ma'am." It was like a knife to the heart as I was certainly still a Miss. I ignored the barb. "Do you have any records from farther back than that, like people who worked here or what the procedure would have been for photos?"

He bent down under the counter and pulled out a three-ring binder.

He opened it to the first page which said, "process notes." He flipped through the binder to a tab marked "Time clock procedure."

I bent down to look at it. "What is this?" I asked.

"Well, this binder was made like years ago, and the old-time clock procedure is in it. I noticed somebody copied the old timecards with the procedure, so you can see some names. I saw an Aaron guy in here; he works at the grocery store in town now. He's in here, and Mrs. Perry, she's the football coach's wife, she worked here for a while and…"

I slammed my hand on the page and pointed to it, "Coach Perry's wife worked here!" I shouted to David. "He was on that bus with us."

David gave me a knowing nod, and the young worker looked shocked at my out-of-proportion reaction to an old timecard.

I collected myself, "I know her is all. Thank you so much. That's all we need."

With that, we rushed away from the counter.

We walked back to David's car, and my mind was racing.

"We need to go find Mrs. Perry, and then we need to go back to Cedar Rapids—I mean Muskegon."

"Michelle, it's too late to do any of that. It's almost ten. People will be sleeping by now. I'm sorry to do this to you, but I didn't get any sleep today, and I worked a full shift. I need to get home and get some sleep."

I looked at him, and he did seem to have newly formed dark circles under his eyes. "I just wanted to make sure you were okay after yesterday and…"

A pang of guilt hit me. Missy and I had slept for a whole day to recover, and David went straight to work, and he pushed through what must have been sheer exhaustion to go to The Alpine to check on me.

"Let's get you home," I said. "Can you drop me off at The Alpine? I need to get Skeeter back his… uh… vehicle."

"Uh…vehicle…?" He wanted to ask more but thought better of it.

When we got back to the Booby Bouncer, I could tell it exceeded his expectations.

From behind the vehicle, I could see that not only did the front say, "Booby Bouncer" the back had a bumper sticker that said, "Save the ta ta's."

I started to open my door, and David told me to wait and jumped out of the car to walk around and hold the door open for me. His face looked fallen, and I wondered if he remembered the accident more than he let on.

"Are you okay?" I asked, and he hesitated. I reached out

and hugged him, and he squeezed me tighter than I expected, taking my breath away.

"Want to sleepover?" he asked. I did, but not with an exhausted David.

"You need your sleep, David."

"I'll get some."

"Some? There are lives at stake, David." I joked. "You need a good night of sleep."

He held tight to me and seemed to not want to let go. I was sure he was upset. Then I thought he probably saw people die all the time now; maybe it wouldn't affect him as much as it had back then.

I got up on tippy toes, pushing his arms up, and planted a kiss on him, a real one. He released his grip of a hug and let his hands wander to the small of my back.

He unlocked his lips from mine and whispered in my ear, "Sleep over."

I reached up to his neck and pulled him down, then whispered in his ear, "Booby Bouncer."

And he shook with laughter.

CHAPTER SEVENTEEN

I HAD A GAME PLAN FOR THE NEXT DAY: find Mrs. Perry, ask her if she ruined the film from our field trip, and find out why. Then go back to Muskegon to find the farm. I was also going to have to fill the two Coreys in on my plan as I needed a ride.

Corey One rolled in after breakfast. He looked like he'd had a bad night.

"Did you hear the news?" I asked. "About the farm."

"Yeah," he said. "Organized Abby called everybody; even Jen got a call in the hospital. I can't believe we all forgot about it. Hearing it kind of brings back memories, and they weren't all so great."

"I know. But I still want to know more. We need to go find Mrs. Perry."

I told him what had happened the night before and all about the pictures that went missing from Long's car. The missing photos were news to him.

We ran into some luck because we learned that morning that Grandma knew just where we would find Mrs. Perry. She was now the secretary at the school aquatic center.

COREY AND I WALKED INTO the aquatic center, and the smell of chlorine hit as we strolled through the lobby. Pre-school-aged kids were bouncing around the area wrapped in towels, likely waiting for the start of swim lessons.

We pushed through them to the reception area and knocked on the glass of the greeting window. Above it was a sign proclaiming $3 for a swim. A small woman with a bowl hair cut opened the window and greeted us, "What can I do ya for?" she asked.

"Are you Mrs. Perry by any chance?"

"Oh, don't ya know, I'm the very one."

"Hi, nice to meet you, I'm Michelle, and this is Corey." He nodded his head. "We know your husband. Corey used to be on the football team back in high school when he was the coach."

She beamed proudly at Corey. "My husband turns out such fine young men, doesn't he? Just the best."

"The best," I agreed. "We're here though to ask about a field trip we took with your husband back when we were younger."

"Well, I'll help you if I can, but if you want any specifics you might want to ask him. He did so many field trips I can't hardly keep them straight anymore."

"Of course, so the thing is with this trip I think you might know a little about it. It was back in 1989; we did this field trip to a farm; it was out near Muskegon."

The smile faded from her face, "Don't know nothing about that."

"Well, I haven't told you what I'm asking. My problem is we all took this trip, and now we can't find any photos of it, and we learned just last night that you used to work at the Kmart, and you might know how the pictures were processed back then. You might be able to help us figure out what happened to them."

"I don't know what it is you want from me."

"Do you remember any of those photos?"

"Nope," she said, and she closed the glass on us and ran to the back of the office, gathering her purse.

I shouted through the glass, "We don't care about the photos, or if you took some Kmart oath to protect picture privacy, or something. We just want to know what happened to the photos. Why they might be gone."

She shook her head and disappeared to the back with her bag in hand.

Corey looked at me, puzzled.

"She just took off."

"She just took off," I repeated.

"What the hell was that?"

"I have no idea."

We went downtown for lunch, and Corey took pity on my horrid financial situation and bought me a sandwich at the deli. I had contented myself with a tiny container of pickles from the condiment station, but he chided me, claiming taking pickles from the condiments station was stealing even though he had purchased food. Because of my rampant pickle theft, he insisted on buying me a sandwich to avoid potential prosecution or maybe just dirty looks.

We weren't there long before Neil walked in the door with the rest of his crew, all wearing their bright orange vests. He grabbed his sandwich and sat with us next to his cousin and across from me. The rest of the men from his crew were sitting at the table behind them. We told him all we had learned the previous day, and he was properly shocked.

"I'm going to go look for this place with you guys," he said. "We have to find Tammy."

"Don't you have to work?" I asked.

"Nah, these guys got this," he pointed behind him.

He took off his orange vest and handed it to one of the men behind him.

"So, what do you guys think happened?"

Corey offered his theory first, "I think the farmer died on our trip, and all of the adults got together and decided to pretend the trip never happened so we would forget about it."

He pointed to me. "Go for your theory, Michelle."

"I think it was more than that. I think the farmer died, maybe he was murdered or something, and there is evidence on the photos that we don't have. Because I don't know why Charity is dead, and why Tammy is missing, and why somebody stole the photos of something that really wouldn't get anybody in trouble today. I don't think a bunch of fifty-year-olds care anymore about a bunch of almost-thirty-year-olds remembering a guy who died in a farm accident twenty years ago."

"Maybe what happened to Tammy and Charity had nothing at all to do with your missing city, and it was all this other guy who literally shot at us."

"Nah," Corey and I both said in unison.

"You should have seen the Coach's wife, Cousin," Corey added. "She was shaken up."

CHAPTER EIGHTEEN

WE MADE IT TO MUSKEGON by mid-afternoon. As we crossed the highway to the old water park, my phone rang. It was David. I calculated how many minutes I could talk to him for free; it wasn't many. I flipped open the phone. "Hey."

"Hey, where are you? Want to get dinner?"

"I'm actually in Muskegon."

"What? The police told you to stay away."

"It's fine. I'm here with the Coreys."

"You are going back to that place where the guy shot at us? The guy who still hasn't been caught?"

"Correction, he shot near us."

"Go to a restaurant, I'm coming. I'm off work, and I'm heading out to you."

"David, it's fine. I'm out of minutes; I gotta go."

"Go to the pancake house off 131 and…"

I clicked off the phone. Under one minute, I congratulated myself.

Corey drove past the abandoned water park and out into the country. Paved roads turned to dirt. We were chasing familiar feelings; we went down one road, and it would look familiar but then change, and we would turn around. We zigzagged the back roads of little townships, and when we came to a little covered bridge, we knew we'd gone too far.

"We should go back and meet David," I said. "He seemed upset. Maybe something will look familiar to him."

We turned around and headed back to 131 and found a pancake house. We must have passed it two days before, but I hadn't noticed. David was clearly more observant than I. The Coreys walked inside, and I stayed back for a moment staring at the sign, "Paradise Pancakes."

Something about it was setting off my senses. I turned it over in my mind. Corey poked his head out the door, "Come on, what do you want to drink?"

"Water is fine," I said. He closed the door and walked back inside. "Paradise Pancakes," I said again, and it's the last thing I remembered before the world went black.

I came to in the back seat of a car with leather seats. My eyes hadn't yet focused, and I couldn't feel the seat as my hands were tied. I wondered if I was in the back of David's car. I struggled to sit up, but as I did, I saw a bald head over the seat in front of me. When my vision was clear, I could see the cracks and dirt in the once-luxurious Cadillac. This car was nowhere near as nice as David's.

"Where is she?" he screamed; it was the Pitbull man, Randy.

"I don't know," I blinked. My eyes were still cloudy.

"Of course you do; this is the last place anybody saw her, and now you show up, twice. Where's she hiding?"

"We don't know. We're looking for her, too. She's been missing for almost a week."

"She's missing all right. She owes us a lot of money, and if she doesn't pay up…well for your sake let's hope we find her."

"I don't have any money if that's what you're getting at unless she owes you $300 or less, which I'm happy to give you. Otherwise, I'm going to be pretty useless to you. My investment portfolio is heavy on chocolate milk at the moment."

"You have friends. A friend with a nice truck, too. I bet they'd pay to see you alive again."

"I don't think any of my friends have access to the kind of cash you're looking for." Except maybe David, I thought.

"Then we better find her."

"I'm telling you we don't know where she is."

"Why do you think she's here?"

"She left a message saying she was going to this farm we went to when we were kids, and it was over here somewhere, but we don't know where."

"I've been driving around here for days; what's the farm look like?"

"It's a big farm; it had a big barn with a sign on the side with a picture of a burger on it."

"I've seen a barn with a steak on it."

I jumped up in my seat, "Where?"

He pulled off into a parking lot and turned around.

We headed back down 31, past the state park signs and past the old water park. He drove further than we had before on the paved road and turned onto a dirt road we hadn't been down before.

"The last time you saw Tammy was she with another girl?" I asked.

"Nope," he said, offering no additional information.

I knew I should be more scared in my current situation, but I felt like things were happening as they should. I closed my eyes and thought, *"Dad you got this?"*

When I opened my eyes and looked around, I didn't see any signs. My heart sank. I might really be in trouble this time. The sun had begun to set as he turned down a pitted dirt street, the edges overgrown with tall grass on either side. He pulled slowly down the road, and when he rounded the driveway at the edge of the lane, it all came into view. I had a flash of the farm from when I was young: the glorious barn, the big brick house, the picturesque field, all bathed in the yellow light of morning sunshine. I could see kids running and playing, chickens in the circular driveway, the barn with the big sign. When I snapped back to reality, I saw the sign was now rusted and hanging upside down, held to the barn with one lone bolt. It proclaimed, "A Century of Excellence Hannah Farms."

The grounds were completely overgrown, the circle drive now covered in weeds; the once beautiful house was boarded up, and the wrap porch had caved in on itself.

"Is this the place?" he asked.

"It is," I said reluctantly. Then I saw a rusted green tractor in the distance. Its yellow stripes had faded, and the tires were flat, but there was no mistaking it; that was a John Deere, my dad's favorite tractor. I knew it was my salvation.

I breathed a sigh of relief, looked up and whispered, *"Got it, Dad."*

"Where is she?" he bellowed.

"I don't know."

He pulled off to the side of the driveway and jumped out

of the car. "Get out," he prompted, as he opened the door. He had a gun fixed on me, but I felt awash with calm after seeing the tractor. I knew my dad was somehow with me. We walked over to the barn, and there were more flashes. I remembered the mooing of the cows, the bleating of the sheep. I remembered the bunny again. I pictured his little hutch. I remembered Long and how he gently lifted the rabbit off the ground. He didn't take him out of his hutch. I wondered why the farmer's wife was so mad at him. He didn't drop the bunny until she scared him. I closed my eyes and tried to picture the moment; then, I remembered her apron; it was covered in blood. I wondered why she was covered in blood. The farmer died after the incident with the bunny, not before.

I searched my mind again, trying to remember what else I'd seen that day. The farmer's daughter showed us new baby kittens, and we fed the goats. I quickened my pace to the barn and looked around the pens, which were now bare. They were once filled with hay but were now gray, cracked, concrete floors, and the pens that were used to make the enclosures had completely rusted.

I walked along the edge of the barn, aware that Randy still had his gun trained on me. I walked into the calf pens and saw a glass bottle on the ground; I kicked it and read the logo on the bottom. "Pendleton Farms" just like I thought though now I knew it was the bottle company name, not the farm.

I stared at the bottle for a moment before Randy walked in front of me and kicked it across the barn. It shattered on the broken concrete on the other side of the building.

"She's not in here," he growled. He grabbed my wrist and pulled me with him out of the barn. We walked up the driveway to the boarded-up house, and I noticed a surveillance camera at the end of one of the poles. I stared up at it and mouthed, "Help." It had a light on; I didn't know if it was recording or transmitting.

We found a window had been pried open at the back of the house, the opposite side to the dilapidated porch. He pushed me in it first. I stepped in to find the house had been completely overrun by garbage, vermin, and vines. I moved to the center of the room, trying not to brush against the mounds of filth in the home. There was a putrid smell in the house that I couldn't place, and I longed to plug my nose.

"What happened here?" he asked.

"The farmer died on our field trip," I said. "It looks like that was the end of this farm."

"There's footprints." He pointed to the ground, and I followed his gaze. He was right, two sets of prints, made by feet smaller than mine. I was sure they had been from Tammy and Charity. They had stepped into the thick blanket of dust, leaving a clear path we could follow. There were no other steps; it was clear that at least when they were in the house, they were alone. We walked from the living room back to the kitchen. There were handprints on the drawers. Randy whipped the drawers out, looking through the paperwork, but didn't find anything. We moved around the house and found the steps stopped again in front of a book that said Ledger. He flipped open the book and scrolled through events.

"Check Spring, 1989," I suggested. He flipped to the back of the book and found that all the entries from 1989 had been ripped out. All that remained were curls of paper in the spiral spine of the notebook.

"Hmm," I said.

"There's nothing here. Go check upstairs," he pointed at a darkened hallway with narrow steps. I saw active spiders on either side of the doorway and begged, "How about you go first, and I'll be your back up? You be Diana Ross; I'll be the Supremes."

"Move it," he shouted.

"I need my hands so I can look around."

He reached behind me and cut the tie. "I have more rope where that came from," he warned.

"Got it." I tucked into myself as much as I could and held my breath to dart up the stairs past the spiders.

I made it by the tangle of webs untouched…I hoped. I searched the landing for signs of activity. It didn't look like either of them had made it up the stairs at all. There were no tracks in the dust. I didn't like the look of any of the structures keeping the second floor up and nervously shouted down, "They weren't up here."

"Check the rooms!" he shouted back.

I took a step into the master bedroom and found a possum slinking across the floor; it saw me and fell over on its side. I turned and ran out of that room as fast as I could. "Not in the master," I shouted.

I stepped into a nursery, which had been completely emptied out; then, I went into what looked like a girl's room. It had faded, peeling pink walls and a canopy bed with a tattered sagging canopy. Even in its state I felt like that room was the safest one. I walked over to the ledge and looked out at the farm; from this vantage point I could see the sun setting golden over the field all the way back to the forest. Whoever lived here had a beautiful view once.

Something shined near my finger, and I looked down at it and back up. The sunlight was nearly gone, and I traced the line of the light and couldn't figure out what was shining on me. I looked out the window and saw a prism hanging on the window on the other side of the house; it was spinning in the breeze.

"Is that you, Dad?" I asked. I turned over my hand and the shine focused on the ledge of the window. I knocked on it; it was hollow. I checked the sides of the ledge and found it pulled away, revealing an opening at the base of the window. Tucked into the little enclosure was a small diary with a flimsy lock on it. I pulled it out, put my finger under the lock, and pried it open with ease.

"What's going on?" he shouted.

"I'm looking."

"Get back down here," he said.

I tucked the diary into the back of my pants and ran down the stairs, faster this time as I now trusted that I wouldn't be touched by the timid hallway spiders.

"She's not here," he said, pointing the gun at me.

"I told you I didn't know where she went. This is where she said she was going. It doesn't look like she stayed here long."

"You better come up with another idea," he said.

"I'm going to go check out that tractor in the field."

"She's not staying in a tractor."

"I think we should leave no stone unturned." I walked swiftly back to the cracked window before he could bind my hands again.

"Stay where I can see you," he said as I crawled through the window. In my haste to get out I caught my arm on a nail. Normally, I would have backed up so as not to rip my skin, but I was in a hurry and propelled on through. I heard a tear in my bicep and felt a faint bit of wetness on my elbow, but I pushed it out of my mind and jumped through the window. As soon as I was out, I watched him try to suck in and turn sideways, getting ready to shimmy back through the window. I took my chance to sprint to the tractor. The smarter move would have been to run back to the car and hope he'd left the keys in it, but I had a message; I was supposed to go to the tractor.

Without looking back, I heard him shout after me, "Get back here."

A shot rang out across the farm, and the crows from the trees ahead of me took to their wings, shaking the leaves as they quickly created a black plume that rose from the forest ahead.

I reached the tractor and bounded up the step to the seat. It had the same gear set up as my dad's tractor and a steering ball on the wheel, just like my dad. It was a great sign. I looked around for any indication that it was the salvation I thought it would be, but another clue did not materialize.

"Dad, what am I supposed to do?"

I searched the tractor, pulling the gears, looking under the seat, not a key, not a crowbar, not anything that I could use to defend myself. I saw Randy running at me, mouth foaming. He was running furiously with his gun trained right on me. I held out as long as I could, but when he put his foot up on the step of the tractor, I abandoned my plan and jumped off the other side of the machine. He leapt up to grab me, but I was just out of reach. I landed on the ground in a soft pile of dirt. He had just missed me as he leaped from the step up to the tractor and grasped nothing but air. He was too far into his plan to grab me before he realized there was nothing he could do to stop his trajectory. He went headlong into the flattened tire of the tractor, knocking himself out.

I ran to the other side of the tractor, jumped up the step again, and checked that he was unconscious. I pried the gun from his hands, unloaded the bullets and dumped them on the ground, then threw it as far away as I could, not quite getting it into the woods. Then I darted from the tractor back through the field to the car parked in the driveway. I pulled at the door of the car and found it locked; I peered into the window and saw the keys in the ignition and a key panel on the side door. He had a code.

I searched the farm for something to throw through the window. At the base of the old silo, I found a large brick. I chucked it into the window and it spiderwebbed out but didn't break. *It must be bulletproof glass*, I thought.

I felt around my body for my phone, but it looked like he had taken that after he knocked me unconscious. All that I had on me was my clothes and a book.

The sun had finally winked away, and I was at the end of a long lonesome road. I suddenly wished I'd kept the gun; it might come in handy. I decided I'd better get back to the main road before full dark settled in.

After I'd started my trek, I finally had the courage to look at my arm and found the wound was deeper than I had expected. There was a wide river of blood flowing from my arm onto the ground. I didn't think it was a great idea to bleed out, but I also didn't want to go back in the house to look for something clean to stop it. I decided to take off a sock and rip it to make a tourniquet. The fabric was helpful at first, but it soon loosened, and I found it soaked.

Without another option to fix it, I put my arm up over my head and dropped my hand behind my back, like we did in high school gym when we were stretching.

I walked down the dirt road for what must have been miles and didn't hear another sign of life, not a cricket chirp or the buzz of a fly. That was unusual on a country road. When my arm grew tired, I alternated between holding my hand up in the air and trying to put pressure on it to get the wound to stop bleeding. It was finally slowing down, but I wasn't sure I hadn't already lost too much blood; I was feeling woozy. The shadowy sky gave way to gray and then pitch black. It was a dark night, and the shadowed crescent moon didn't give off enough light for me to see the path before me.

After nearly two hours without a car in sight, I heard a rumbling in the distance behind me. The only thing in that direction was the farm. I jumped into the grass and crouched low, putting my elbows into the dirt as I dropped my head, covering my face with my hair. The car was moving slowly, and I poked my head over the grass for just a moment to see what was taking so long. He had a flashlight, and he was shining it on either side of the road before moving forward. I scooted back, farther away from the road, and looked for something to shield myself from the light. There was nothing. I tucked myself farther into the grass. The light stopped in front of me, and I held my breath. It stayed and stayed, and I mentally prepared myself that I might have to go another round with him; then, the light passed over me, and he moved on. I stayed on the ground, waiting for the car to move completely out of view.

When it was past the hill, I finally got up on my palms and pressed them into the dirt as I lifted off the ground. My punctured arm waivered a bit but held up enough for me to come back to a stand. I debated walking on the road or staying in the grass, but in the dark, I couldn't see the terrain well enough to traverse off the road. I continued my trek over the hill where the car had passed and on to another dirt road. I couldn't recall how far we had gone down the different dirt roads, but I knew it had been several minutes, which was likely several miles. I turned onto the better road I remembered traversing earlier.

The gravel was better packed here, but the grass was also short and maintained, taking away my hiding places. I knew I was getting closer to the paved road where I might be able to flag down a car. I saw headlights come up over the hill again in my direction. The car was moving faster this time, and I moved to the side of the road searching for a place to hide. I was a few hundred yards from what appeared to be a thicket of bushes. I took off for the brush at a sprint. I pushed into the branches without hesitating, scratching my arms again as I jumped in. I bent low and hoped I'd managed to get into the bushes before he saw me.

As the vehicle passed, I could see the dark paint and the cracked side window. I crouched low and waited for him to move out of sight again. I stood up quickly, and I swayed a bit. I put my hand up to my arm and felt the wetness flowing again from my puncture. I had to do something and ripped off the arm of my t-shirt and shredded it until it was a long piece of fabric. I tied it as tight as I could with one arm and my mouth. I tried to ignore the pain as I continued on. I also ignored that the fabric was wet again, almost instantly.

You're fine, I said to myself.

The clock was running on how long I would be able to walk in my condition. I started to trot, hoping I would find the main road quickly and manage to get a ride to safety. Just as I could see the pavement coming into view the car came again, faster. I trotted to the nearest tree and leaned up against the back side of it, away from the road. I knew I couldn't bend down again; I was afraid I would lose consciousness. I nestled myself up against the tree, trying my best to turn as he passed, to stay just out of his view. I managed it one more time, and he turned onto the main road again.

I closed my eyes, to steel myself. *"What do I do, Dad?"*

Nothing, no light in either direction, not a sound. It was going to be my decision to make and mine alone. I turned toward the water park, deciding it was best to go the way I had been before.

I pulled myself by sheer will away from the tree; I longed to stay there and drift off to sleep. I moved out to the paved road. It was very late and still uncomfortably dark; while the road was paved, it was completely unlit. I walked at least another mile before I saw another car. It was coming from behind me; it had different lights. I knew it wasn't him. I turned to it and waved my hands in the air. The car came straight toward me and slowed down. I ran to it, just before it swerved away from me and took off. I could only hope they'd called the police and said they saw a blood-soaked woman out alone on this country road.

I let that hope propel me as I moved further and further along the road. Before I knew it, I saw the sign, Cedar Rapids White Water Adventure Park.

I stumbled to the sign. In the distance I saw a car again, moving slowly, flashing a light in the grass. I knew I had to get off the road. I thought about my options: keep walking to the highway at least another five miles to the main road, or find a place to rest and a better tourniquet for my wound. I didn't think I would last if I tried to walk much longer. There was also a chance that Corey or David would think to look for me at the water park. With the car still several hundred yards away from me I ambled up the hill and was pleasantly surprised to see a few of the lights still worked in the park. I walked down the embankment to the waterpark and made a beeline for the old concession stand.

The doors on the side were rusting around the edges, but still they were made of solid metal. They would be impenetrable. However, the windows had been broken and covered loosely with graffiti-painted plywood. I pulled up a corner and squeezed my way in. There were only shards of light around the plywood, but it was enough for me to see around the room. It was a cinderblock building that had held up relatively well against the elements. The only thing out of place, other than the empty shelves and fridge cases, was a thin layer of dust. I rummaged through the cabinets beneath what was once the snack counter and found a plastic bag full of hard candy. I'd hit the jackpot. I had no idea how long Jolly Ranchers were good, but I didn't much care. I planned to eat them all. I ripped up the plastic bag they were in and tied it tight around my arm. Finally, I could get a tight enough seal to slow the bleeding.

As soon as the bleeding stopped, I sank to the floor and pulled down the candies, unwrapping them and sucking them as quickly as I could. I searched the room for a sink and found one at the back of the room; I hoped it would still work. I dragged myself to it and turned on the water; after a few sputters it flowed. I drank liberally straight from the tap, then rinsed the wound on my arm. I ripped another piece from my shirt and tapped it over the now "cleaned" wound. I slid back to the floor. I alternated between resting and eating Jolly Ranchers for at least an hour and stood only to drink more water.

The fog was lifting from my mind, and I made a plan that

after finishing the last Jolly Rancher I'd go back to the main road and move as quickly as I could to the highway. I could only hope he'd given up the search for me and gone back to looking for Tammy. Which reminded me that none of this had gotten me any closer to figuring out what had happened to my friend. I reached around to my back and felt the journal.

I pulled it out and moved it under a beam of light that shone in the window from one of the few streetlamps that still worked on the property. I flipped open the book to the cover page. Written in the scrawl of a young child was the declaration, "Propertee of Fern."

Fern, I thought, like from *Charlotte's Web*. Her name made me immediately like her though the only thing I remembered about her was that she liked cats.

I flipped to the back of the book, assuming it would end near the time when the farmer had died, and the family likely moved away, forgetting about the hidden journal. I was stunned to see that the entries in the book ended in 1991, nearly three years after the death of the farmer. The last entry to my dismay said, "Mom used to say growing old was a gift. I guess I didn't get that gift. At least I'll get to see dad again. Que Sera, Sera." I ran my finger over those final words and sang, "Whatever Will be, Will be, Que Sera, Sera. Oh, I'm so sorry Fern." It hurt my heart too much to flip back to find out what happened to her. I set the diary down and decided I couldn't handle the journal in my current situation. "I promise. I'll read you tomorrow, Fern. I'm in a bit of a bind at the moment, and I just can't… Dad, Mom, look out for Fern up there."

The sound of something breaking in the distance broke my calm and I whispered, "And if you could look out for me down here too, that would be great."

I peeked out the corner of the window that I'd crawled through and found my pursuer making his way to the water park. I didn't imagine there was any way he would find me in my hiding spot. All I had to do was stay quiet, and he would move along. That made perfect sense until I looked at my arm and remembered I'd bled all the way to the shack, leaving a nice trail straight to my hiding place.

The urge to curse was great, but the need to survive was greater. I stuffed the journal back in my jeans pocket and stood slowly. Not as firm on my feet as normal but better than I had been an hour ago. I searched the shack and saw that the doors weren't locked from the inside. I'd be able to push a bar and run right out. A plan formed. When and if the Pitbull found my hiding spot, I'd wait for him to get halfway in the wooden window and hit him with whatever I could find before making a run for it out the back door.

"I'm counting on you for the second half of that plan, Dad."

All I could manage for a weapon was a thin metal shelf that probably once held a row of candy bars or chips. I gripped it and waited. To my surprise he didn't try the window first; he kicked at the solid metal doors. I said a silent prayer that I couldn't be killed by a person this stupid. He kicked for far too long, and I so badly wanted to throw open the door and scold him for being such an idiot. The good news was he was kicking way too hard, and unless he had steel-toed shoes, he was going to hurt himself and help me tremendously.

"Ouch, shit, stupid fucking door," he called after a swift kick. I almost laughed. Finally, it went quiet, and he banged around on the sides of the snack shack before he at long last realized the plywood was right there and ripe for the opening. He pushed around the wood until he found the soft corner and pulled up on it. I hid to the side, in the dark part of the room. He reached in with his arm first, holding a Maglite, and I thought that was a way better weapon than a candy rack. I jumped forward, slamming his elbow with the candy rack and knocking the light out of his hand.

"Give that back, you bitch."

"No."

He put his head through the hole this time, and I flashed the light in his eye. He tried to reach in to get it from me, but I kept it just out of his reach and aimed directly in his eyes again, clicking it on and off repeatedly to daze him. He tried to reach out to snatch it, but he was slow. My fear of him was fading a little as I came to realize that he was so very dumb. He switched his tactic to trying to get deeper into the shack, and when he was halfway through the window, I reared back and struck him across the back of his bald head with the Maglite. He was adequately stunned, and I made a dash for the door.

I scanned the property and saw a sign at the top of the waterslide, "Go Big Green." Green was dad's favorite color; Go Green was the war chant for his college, and green was the color of John Deere tractors. It was the clearest message of the whole night. I darted down the cracked sidewalk, past the tattered umbrellas and broken hot dog cart, and headed straight to the stairs at the base of the slide platform.

It creaked with my first step, and the platform swayed. I kept on pushing, darting up the stairs as fast as I could, taking the steps two at a time. He was only just emerging from the snack shack and was stumbling in my direction at a snail's pace. I wondered if I would have been able to outrun him and get back to the main road, but instead I followed a sign to a creaky platform that ended in a slide that emptied into a sludge pond.

The light ahead of me blinked frantically, and I realized I'd stopped. I jumped back to the moment and kept moving up. I made it to the top of the platform and scanned for options. I could feel that he'd reached the platform as it was now swaying wildly though I couldn't see him as he was still too low. I stepped forward toward the opening for the slide and held tight to the bar that would normally be used to propel a person down.

I heard something crack below me and leaned back so that I could look over the edge of the platform. I saw him several floors below me crash through a step. He cried out in pain.

I was still holding onto the bar over the slide opening, I leaned out further and saw that the wood from the step was buried into the flesh of his thigh. He moved to pull his leg out and screamed again. I leaned back up. "Sorry I doubted you, Dad," I whispered.

After several minutes of screaming, it sounded like he was free, but moving slowly. I held tight to the bar, worried that my next move was going to be a ride down the completely black tunnel of terror in front of me, but I held out hope that another rotted piece of wood would take him out completely, leaving me safely at the top of the Big Green to wait for help.

My wish was not granted; he crested the top of the platform, pulling himself with his arms across it slowly. I couldn't bear to look at his leg trailing behind him, leaving a pool of blood in his wake. I couldn't believe he was still coming at me as he clearly couldn't stand, didn't have a weapon, and would be unconscious soon from the loss of blood.

He was closing the distance between us, almost able to reach out to grab me, and I finally made my move; I closed my eyes and jumped into the waterless slide holding my arms crossed over me so my skin wouldn't catch on the plastic and slow me down. It was a steep slide, and I careened quickly to the bottom, but to my horror I was stopped at its base, nearly in complete darkness, with more slide to go. Another incline loomed in front of me. I hadn't gotten enough speed to make it up that hill to the exit of the slide. I could see just a hint of light at the end of the tunnel, and I knew if I could just maneuver enough to prop my legs to the side of the slide, I would be able to push myself up and out. I rolled into a ball and pushed forward, having just enough clearance in the tube to move myself to a face-first position.

As soon as I was in the right spot I jumped. Pressing my hands and legs against the side of the tube, I slid down at first, I didn't have enough traction. I kicked off my shoes and my one remaining sock and leapt again; this time my grip with my feet was spot on. I heard Randy moving down the slide not far behind me, and my adrenaline kicked in; no way was I going to be stuck in a dip with him. I pushed through any pain in my arm and kicked off with my feet, and in a quick motion I was at the flat part of the slide. I army-crawled to the edge of it, looking out over the water below.

A loud thunk sounded behind me, followed by, "Oh, my God, help me."

Then he let out a shrill scream. I felt a little bad knowing he wouldn't be small enough to turn around in that tight space and was likely stuck in a tube, shoulders touching the side, head down, legs up and completely powerless to move.

I steadied myself, preparing to jump into the green water

with the rainbow-colored film of oil over it. I plugged my nose, then stopped, thinking about the journal. I wasn't sure if it would make it through the sludge with me. I clenched the journal in my hand, and with all my might I chucked it to the grass. It landed with a thud on the overgrown grass near the lifeguard chair.

Relief washed over me. All that was left for me to do was to get through the water, and I would be free. I plugged my nose again, squeezed my eyes tight, and leapt into the water. The green muck gave way as I broke through it. The water was thick, almost like slime. Of all the things that had happened that night, unpleasant water was at the bottom of my list of worries.

I crawled out of the water and ran to the side of the pool. I grabbed the journal and hugged it tight. "We did it Fern. We made it."

I walked back through the water park, past the picnic benches and snack shack and back up to the top of the hill. My heartbeat slowed as I walked; it had been beating furiously for hours and at long last was abating. When I got to the apex, I saw a police car pulling up behind Randy's car. It had a Marsh City logo on the side of it. Another car, a luxury sedan, had already parked. I saw the outline of a giant man in the headlights of the police car, and I collapsed.

CHAPTER NINETEEN

WHEN I CAME TO, DOCTOR DAVID was carrying me down the hill. I enjoyed the feel of his arms around me, of knowing someone would take care of me in this situation. He smiled down at me when he realized I was awake.

"Tell the police they'll find a terrified man stuck in a waterslide with a massive leg injury," I said.

"I'll make sure they know," he assured me. "We need to get you to a hospital."

My adrenaline had worn off, and I was very groggy, but I managed to say, "No hospital. I don't have health insurance. I can't afford it."

"You're covered in blood, and you just passed out," he said.

"It's just a puncture, and I've had the night from hell."

He continued to his car and managed to get a blanket out of his trunk while he was still holding me. He wrapped me in it and tucked me into the passenger seat.

"Let me see," he bent down, pulled a flashlight from his glove box, and shined it on my arm. He held it in his mouth as he reached past me to a bottle of water. With a nod from me he poured it over the wound and dabbed away at it with the blanket.

"It's going to need stitches," he said after pulling the flashlight out of his mouth. "I can do that."

"Please, I can't afford a bill for this, and I don't want to put that on my grandparents."

He put his hand on my forehead and shined a light in my eyes. "Nothing else is injured."

"No, the guy in that waterslide is literally going to die. I'm fine."

He handed me what remained of the water, and I drank it in a big gulp.

"I'll go get you more."

He ran off to the police and brought back several bottles

of water.

"I'm taking you home, I have a stitch kit there. Fowler said he'll check in when you are feeling better."

He closed the door to the car, scooted into the driver's seat, and as soon as he hit the lock on the door, I fell into a deep sleep.

I WOKE UP HOURS LATER IN what I can only guess was David's living room. It was a large room that was somehow both expansive and cozy, just like the outside of the house. A blaze roared in the fireplace, and the room had shelves filled with lots of old, leatherbound books. I was nestled into an overstuffed white couch. David was nowhere to be seen. I rolled to my side and looked out the window, able to see a glimpse of the orchard from the light of the porch. David entered through a door that I guessed led to the kitchen. He had a bag slung over his shoulder, a tray in his hands, and a headlamp and magnifier over his eyes. He moved to the floor and set the tray on the ottoman across from me. He pulled items out of his bag and started to work cleaning out my wound.

"What happened?" he asked while looking at my arm.

I recounted the story, telling him about the farm, the long walk back to the water park, even the Jolly Ranchers in the snack shack, and finally my great harrowing moment where I simply ran away, and Randy injured himself.

"Huh," he mused and lifted the magnifier off his eyes to look at me. "What made you think to run up the platform instead of just trying to leave the park?"

That was a secret I only told my closest friends and family. I looked straight into his eyes and told a half-truth, "I had a bad feeling. I didn't realize you were right there on the other side of the hill."

"I'm not sure we would have made it to you in time if you'd run over that hill. We had just arrived. You getting away from him on the tractor, walking that far bleeding all through the night without any light and finding refuge in a waterslide…"

He paused. "That's a damn miracle, Michelle."

He stared at me, and I stared back; finally, he shook his

head and moved the glasses back over his eyes. While working on my arm he said, "I was really worried about you."

"Hey," I said, moving his glasses back up and touching his chin to move his face up to meet mine. "I can't tell you how much it meant to me to find you on the other side of that hill. I…"

We were interrupted by a knock at the door. David moved up from his crouching position and came back with my grandmother, two aunts, and John.

"The patient is in here," he said, walking into the living room and turning up the light.

David stitched me up, my grandmother bathed me in his gigantic spa tub in his master bath, and he opened his home to what ended up as four cousins, two aunts, one uncle, and one grandmother. He had one proper guest room, which he loaned to me, and the rest of my family found air mattresses in the basement, sleeping bags or couches, and treated themselves to a sleepover.

By the time I awoke the next morning, my jeans were cleaned, and the linens from everybody else were in the wash. My family had descended on his kitchen as if it were their own, with a hashbrown casserole in the oven and ham on the stovetop. Grandma was manning the gleaming blue and white kitchen like a general with her wooden spoon held high in the air to give orders to the cousins. My aunts were in the living room folding laundry. My uncle had wandered off with David. I was told they were looking at a problem he was having with his apple tree.

I was wearing pants that were too short, courtesy of my cousin. But at least they weren't soaked in blood. I got a good look at David's work on my arm. He had expertly stitched me up. My bicep now sported a row of six neat stitches. There was no pain and no signs of the trauma from the night before except for my shaken nerves and the jelly in my legs. I felt like I'd run a marathon, and in a thought that did not befit the seriousness of the situation, I wished I'd worn a step counter, so I had some idea how far I'd gone.

Grandma, holding my shoulders delicately, guided me to the table and placed a big glass of chocolate milk in front of me.

"You need the nutrients."

I gladly gulped it down and poured myself a second giant glass. Within a few moments, food was moved to the large kitchen table, which had seating for ten, a bit excessive for a single man and one child. My family packed in around the table and Skeet and David came in to join us.

I couldn't believe how generous he was to let my family descend on his house like we had. He let me bleed all over his lovely white sofa and bright rug, and he let my family sprawl out all over every nook and cranny of his home. When he finally sat, several seats down, and across the table from me, I caught him glancing in my direction every few moments.

My aunt said grace and we all dug in, passing dishes in every direction. The view from the dining room was stunning, David's backyard was as beautiful as the front. There were rolling hills of green, a garden, and a small pond. The room was bright and welcoming just like the rest of the house. It gave me the feeling of my grandparents' farmhouse, welcoming and bright but a little more ordered and modernly decorated.

I couldn't help glance at him also, and the looks from me to him and the smiles from my aunts and grandmother were enough to make me blush.

Grandma finally broke the silence. "We can't thank you enough for all you did for Michelle last night. And for offering to let us all stay here. I mean I know you said we could, but sometimes people offer just to be polite."

"I'm not one of those people. If I offer my home, I mean it," he said. "I'm still amazed that Michelle survived the night with only a scratch."

"It was a pretty big scratch," I added.

"It was a big scratch, but amazing," he was looking right at me. Then he looked around the table, "She needs to tell you all what happened. You won't believe it."

"We know the Cliff's Notes," Skeet said. "How did you trap a guy in a slide?"

I recounted the story in limited detail, not wanting to scare my grandmother more than I'm sure she was, and I left out all the parts about following the advice of my dead parents because that sounded…well…a little crazy.

"How did you know to go up the slide and not out?" John asked. "I would never have gone down some abandoned water slide. I'm scared enough when they aren't abandoned."

"It was a feeling," I answered.

"I get those sometimes too," John said.

"You do!" I was surprised.

My grandmother chuckled.

"What?" John and I asked.

"Well, your grandfather, he always said he got these feelings, well he called them messages, that just gave him hints of where he was supposed to go or what he was supposed to do."

"What kind of hints?" I asked.

"All kinds, like what land to buy. You know we bought our farm for a song. The land was untillable they said, too sandy. But Grandpa had a feeling. I sat by his side with faith in his instincts, and it got us everything we have today. I never doubted his feelings from that day forward."

"But, if…"

I almost asked a question I didn't really want to know the answer to. She anticipated me, and she said, "I know what you want to ask. Did he know your parents were going to pass away; was there a clue or a hint? There was not. He said his instincts led him right up until he had everything he had ever wanted: his farm, his wife, and his kids, and then he never got another clue after that."

"Yup," Skeeter added. "Same with your dad. After your dad had you, he never got another message."

"Do you get them, Skeeter?"

"Shoot yes, I just don't know what I want, so there ain't no way to finish me up."

We went around the table, seeing who else this happened to, having feelings, instincts, or hints to follow, and all of us, every Fry descendent, was privy to clues in life, and it seemed like after kids, marriages, and homes the clues faded away, and they were on their own. I didn't tell them that my visions came as messages from my dead parents. I wanted so badly to ask the nature of their visions, but it was too painful to think my parents might not really be watching over me as I'd thought. I teared up a bit, and my aunt Ida pulled me in and hugged me tight.

"It's okay, honey. I'm so glad that they kept you safe. I'm sorry I've never mentioned it before; I had no idea anybody else in the family felt the same. I thought I'd sound, well, a little crazy."

With that I remembered, my parents weren't the only dead people I had a one-way chat with. I looked around the room frantically and at the ottoman by the couch where I was stitched up. "What happened to Fern?"

CHAPTER TWENTY

AFTER A PAINFUL ROUND OF WHO'S FERN we searched the car, turned over the living room and the walkway up to the house, and we couldn't find the diary anywhere. David insisted he didn't see it when he scooped me up, and I scolded myself for forgetting about it when I was rescued. I made him call the police, and the search was on for the missing diary.

I went home with my grandmother and almost immediately felt bad about leaving David. His work schedule had taken an enormous hit since I'd gotten to town, and I'm sure he wasn't getting his necessary amount of sleep, but I selfishly wanted to spend more time with him anyway.

I thought of calling him and going back but something was nagging at me. There was a piece of the puzzle I was missing, and I felt David fit into it somewhere. He had the best shot at taking the journal from me, but I didn't recall him taking it. He never had a chance to hide it with my family barging in. Then I remembered the trail cam and the missing paper from the ledger. Those pages weren't dusty; somebody had rifled through it recently, and I imagined that was Tammy and Charity. So, they did end up at Cedar Rapids, and they did end up back at the farm, presumably following clues from an old photo. But neither of them had ever been seen again after that night. "So, who do the trail cams belong to?" I wondered.

I was writing my thoughts and clues on a pad of paper with Michigan Milk Producer Association logos on the top and using an MMPA pen when the Coreys pulled in. They brought me a bundle of wildflowers and a quart of fresh strawberries. We sat at Grandma's long dining room table, and I told them what happened after I was kidnapped. Corey kicked himself for not thinking to go back to the waterpark, but he'd let David take that part of the county, everything from Pancakes West, and they took everything from Pancakes East and crisscrossed the whole county, trying to figure out what had happened.

The story of the man stuck in the tube at the bottom of a dark waterslide was enough to make everybody shudder. I hadn't heard if he made it at all, but I assumed he had, or Fowler would have been to see me by now.

"My bigger concern is…"

I stopped myself. I didn't want to accuse David of stealing Fern's diary, but I did want to know what they thought of the missing book. I spoke carefully, "My biggest concern is that we aren't any closer to finding Tammy, and I'm afraid time is almost up."

"I think our timer might have run out too," Corey said. "And now I just want to make sure nobody else ends up missing."

"I think he means you," Neil added, pointing at me.

"We are in sympatico there," I joked. "I also wish not to be abducted again. But there's this other thing that happened, and I don't know what it means."

I told them all about the stolen pictures, the logbook pages that were missing from the farm, the trail cam, and finally about the diary.

"So, the diary was from the farmer's daughter, the one that had the kittens?" Corey asked.

"Yes, and it was hidden. I think there's a clue in there, and maybe it was in the missing ledger pages too, and if you put those together with the photos that Long had, somebody did something that they don't want us to see."

"So Long had photos that he had developed somewhere else; did he have negatives?"

"He said everything was in the car; he had duplicates of the photos, and he gave the first set to Charity for the reunion. I think she saw something in those photos that led her to Cedar Rapids; something about it upset her, so she went to the bar, she saw an old familiar face, Tammy, and they went to investigate."

"I still don't know why Tammy called just you."

"Tammy didn't have a phone plan; she could only call me from Charity's phone. I had to be the only person she knew in Charity's phone, and she wanted somebody to know where she was going. Somebody that she trusted. She knew that guy was after her, and she probably wanted us to look for her in case something happened."

"But Charity also had a jerk of a boyfriend. I don't want to count him out," Corey added.

"I don't think he would stage a crash to look like a murder and be dumb enough to choke her first. He's a professor. I don't know of what, but I think he's smart enough to know that they could still tell that she was choked."

"So, what do we need to find Tammy?" he asked.

"We need to know what was in the missing diary and in the missing logbook that would be bad enough for a coverup today, and we need to find those photos."

We sat around the table taking turns looking at my MMPA pad of paper. By the time we were supposed to clear the table for dinner, Corey and I had filled ten pages completely with our list of clues and suspects. We included the kids on the field trip, only because they were all in town for the reunion though we couldn't figure out what they would have done at age eight worth hiding. We even wrote down Mrs. Perry after her strange reaction though we couldn't figure out what an ageing secretary might have done twenty years before to cause such a response to some fairly innocent questions.

"So," Neil asked, looking it all over, "You think this old woman ruined every picture of the trip and every chaperone on that trip lied to you all for the last twenty years about it."

We nodded.

"I don't think the kids would have done anything worth killing over, but look at the chaperones. Every chaperone on that trip is a suspect. Find out who was on the trip and track them down."

"We aren't going to be able to talk to Mrs. Perry, not after that reaction. But I know somebody who can get this info for us: Grandma. People literally can't say no to her. It's a special gift."

I called her to the dining room; we showed her our list of clues and explained that we needed a chaperone list from the trip. She wiped her hands on her apron and picked up the papers.

"I'll figure it out," she promised. Then she walked over to her purse and pulled out her roll of newspaper clippings. She pulled off a clipping and walked past me to deliver it to Corey.

He flipped it open, read it, and blushed.

"What does it say?" I asked, reaching across the table, and he pulled it back.

"None of your business.

"Grandma, what's it say?"

She shrugged and walked back to the kitchen.

CHAPTER TWENTY-ONE

AFTER DINNER I RECEIVED A CALL from David on the home phone, an old rotary that hung in the hallway next to the kitchen. My phone was still confiscated by police, and I wasn't sure when, if ever, I would get it back.

"I'm working late tonight, but I want to see you again. Will you be my date to the reunion tomorrow?"

In all that had happened I had completely forgotten about the reunion. I hadn't done a thing for the decorating committee, and I wasn't sure if Abby would forgive me even if I had being abducted as an excuse.

"Hello," he interjected.

"Yeah, of course. Sorry, spaced out for a minute there. I just realized I never did any of the duties assigned to me as a decorating committee member."

He agreed to pick me up early for the reunion the next day and help set up the photos.

That meant I still had to actually get the photos. I enlisted Grandma to help me with that task too. She was heading to Charity's house to drop off dessert that evening and planned to bring back the photos that Charity had already collected. I also busied myself with the pictures that Grandma had taken. As wonderful as Grandma was, she was a terrible photographer, and there was no getting around it. Grandma always snapped a picture after the big grand slam, or after the awards were given out. I suppose Grandma liked to live in the moment and capturing it on film was an afterthought.

I enlisted the cousins and spouses who graduated in my year to go through their photo books and get me what they had. By the end of the night, I had a descent sized stack of photos. It was a welcome distraction from all the sleuthing. I'd dedicated almost my whole trip to finding Cedar Rapids, and I wasn't any closer to finding Tammy. Part of me wondered if we should be mourning instead of searching; if Tammy were already lost. I should certainly have been giving Charity some of my thoughts, which reminded me I hadn't heard a thing about her funeral.

Grandma's calendar would have that information. I walked out to the kitchen and scanned the cork board. I found a note for Charity's memorial service on Saturday, but there was no obituary posted. It was probably going in the weekly, which didn't go to print until Friday. At present there were only clippings for other members of her church that had passed from cancer: Doretta Tolbert and Regina Blanch. Blanch, I stopped and reviewed the clipping: Regina Blanch, preceded in death by her husband, Curtis Blanch, and her nephew Andrew Hampton, survived by her son Ronald Blanch, *no wife was listed,* and his children Doctor David Blanch and William Blanch and her grandchildren…

I put my finger over the names of the grandchildren. I didn't want to know David's son's name until he told me. I read on and learned that she travelled in the same circles as my grandmother; they were part of a weekly Wendy's social gathering for women who used to be telephone operators, which solved part of my questions about what she did on Wednesdays. Both women also delivered Meals on Wheels and were in all the same fellowship groups, and they both enjoyed spending their summers at Trident Lakes though I didn't recall ever seeing them there.

I further learned that Regina's grandfather, Theodore Hampton, was one the founding members of the town of Marsh. I thought back to David's road; it was Hampton. He lived on the road named for his family, like me. David and I had been so close to connecting for so many years, yet we never did. Our families were similar; I was surprised my grandmother and David's never conspired to get us together while she was alive.

The most surprising line of all came at the end of the obituary. She passed away peacefully at the family apple orchard where she grew up, surrounded by her friends and family. So, David's house wasn't a house he had selected and decorated; it was his grandmother's house, and somehow, he inherited it, skipping over his father and winning out over his brother.

Grandma came down the hall, pushing Grandpa in front

of her. They saw me reading the clipping.

"Did you know David's grandmother well?" I asked.

"We were acquaintances."

"But how in the same church and at the same campground did you not run into each other more often and become friends?"

"Well, you and David went to the same school and church growing up, and he and John are close; how did you not spend more time with him growing up?"

I opened my mouth to answer, and I realized I didn't have one. *"Touché."* I replied.

Then I turned my attention to Grandpa. I hadn't spent any one-on-one time with him since I'd been to town. "Hey, old man," I called out, and he smiled.

Grandma stepped out from behind the wheelchair. "Would you please move Grandpa to the dining room? I'll bring us some pie."

I moved him with me and helped him into his chair, arranging his oxygen tank behind him. He sat with me as we went through the pictures for the reunion. He couldn't talk much with his oxygen so low, but he could manage to get a word out here and there.

"Did Grandma tell you about my intuition, Grandpa?" he blinked his eyes and nodded. A smile spread across his face.

"Grandma said you used to have it too, but it went away after you bought the farm and had kids."

He nodded slowly.

"You think you passed your intuition down to all us grandkids, Grandpa? Twenty-four people is an awful lot of people to share a little bit of luck."

He shrugged and pointed his thick weathered finger to his heart, and whispered out, "More than luck."

"What do you mean, Grandpa?"

He pointed to the credenza behind me. I turned and ran my hand along it; he stopped me on a black and white picture of him with his parents and brothers. His father was in a dapper suit, and his mother was in a dark, fitted dress and a tiny hat. He and his brothers were a little blurred, but they were smiling.

I pulled the gold-framed photo down and handed it to

him, and he tapped his mother and father and held his hand to his heart again. Tears welled up in me, and it was difficult to find the words. "Your parents guided you?" I asked.

He nodded and tapped his hand to my heart. "Dad guides me, too." He blinked and nodded his head.

"We know," he whispered.

Grandma walked in from the kitchen and put her tiny arms around my shoulders. "We always heard you praying to your father."

"It didn't bother you? Like it was sacrilegious?"

Grandpa shook his head, and Grandma said, "No dear, my ancestors believed that the light of God is in every person, and they can seek it in their own way."

I ran my fingers over the portrait. They were in a grand hall; there were people behind them dancing, but with the slow speed of the camera, those people were just a whir. "Where was this picture taken, Grandpa?"

His hands shook as he turned the frame over. Two pieces of paper fell out onto the table; the first one, which he slid over to me, said it was "The Big Pavilion at Saugatuck, The Brightest Spot on the Great Lakes." I smiled and read about the acts playing that weekend; it was a lot of jazz. The second article he slid over to me and tapped the headline, "Big Pavilion ravaged in fire, May 6, 1960."

"Were you there when it happened, Grandpa?"

He shook his head.

"They moved away long before the big fire," Grandma replied. "They had settled here in Marsh, which was lucky for me, or we never would have met."

My grandmother stepped away from me and put her hand on Grandpa's shoulder. He reached up and touched it, and they looked deep into each other's eyes.

"The best of luck," I said.

WE LOOKED THROUGH OLD FAMILY photos late into the night, and finally I sent Grandma and Grandpa off to bed. I went out to the porch and grabbed an old milk crate to pack up the photos that I owed to the decorating committee. I leafed through them one more time as I placed them in the container, paying special attention to the pictures with Charity and Tammy. I found myself setting them aside. There were pictures of Tammy making faces at me, her tongue ring on display in some. She was so proud of it as the only person in our high school who was allowed to get one. There were pictures of her jumping off of things, skateboarding. There were photos of her at the lake with Missy and Jen for my birthday. The rest of us were standing still for the photo, and she was stepping forward with both hands in the air and her tongue out. She had a wild energy about her, but always a smile.

Next, I looked at pictures of Charity; she looked so demure back then. Her hair was dark before she'd found highlights. She looked so serious and studious; I tried to remember her moniker. It might have been "Best Dancer" or maybe "Best Artist." She was a drama kid like the rest of us; well, she was actually talented, unlike the rest of us. She got the starring roles. There were pictures of her belting out songs for *Hello Dolly* for the community theater and singing as Belle in our high school production of *Beauty and the Beast*. She shrugged off her introverted persona when she hit the stage and became another person entirely. I'd only talked to her on a handful of occasions, but I wished I had taken the time to get to know her better.

I placed all of the photos in the crate, tucking in my two lost friends at the top. Noticeably absent were any of the photos from Hannah Farms.

CHAPTER TWENTY-TWO

THE DAY OF THE REUNION was upon me, and instead of being filled with the excitement of seeing my old classmates and spending another evening with David, a feeling of dread washed over me. I wasn't sure if it was that we still hadn't found Tammy, the reality of what happened to Charity finally hitting me, or that I was selfishly thinking about how I would soon be back in Chicago—lonely.

Tomorrow I would be on my journey back to my empty, colorless, cubicle existence.

I descended the narrow steps slowly, listening to the sounds of my family laughing on the other side of the door. The smell of maple syrup seemed to be searching for me. The thought of leaving the warmth of my family made my heart ache.

Slowly, I cracked open the door which led directly to the dining room. "There she is." Skeet called out. "Rise and shine."

I nodded and walked into the room quietly. Grandma patted a seat next to her and beckoned me over. My place setting was already there, juice was poured, a coffee cup was turned over, and my cousin Jan was up to fill it before I sat down.

My grandmother took notice of my sour mood, "It's been a rough week, hasn't it?"

It had been a rough week, but the worst part of all was I couldn't imagine going through any of it without my family and friends, and none of them would be with me in Chicago.

"I suppose," I said. "I should probably start packing up today."

"If that's what you want, dear. You will have plenty of time tomorrow."

"Unless you stay at David's house tonight," John poked.

My grandmother told him to hush as she stood up from the table and walked out of the room. I ignored him, reaching out for a plate of pancakes.

Skeeter nudged me. "I'm going out for a trail ride, Shell

Bell, want to ride-along? That might cheer you up."

"That reminds me," I said, scanning the room to make sure all the children were on the porch. "I had to run out to The Alpine the other day and your," I made quote marks in the air, "'Booby Bouncer' was the only vehicle I could find." The room erupted in laughter.

"It's not funny; that decal is horrible, and sexist and..."

"Shoot, calm down. It came with that sticker, courtesy of the Cancer Society ladies from the raffle. It's just a sticker. Comes right off. You didn't leave it on there, did you?"

I sank in my seat, "I didn't know it came off."

"Shoot, you drove around town in that. That is embarrassing."

My cousins couldn't contain their chuckles.

"Let's take it off and go for a drive, talk about things."

I looked at my grandma and said, "Things huh."

She didn't look up from her breakfast.

WE PEELED OFF THE STICKER from the side-by-side and drove it through our woods and to the state DNR dirt trails. We couldn't talk on the drive; the engine was too loud, so I just took in the beauty of our surroundings. Picturesque green maple and pine trees flanked us at every part of our journey. We drove for at least a few miles before we finally stopped by a pond surrounded by a green meadow filled with wildflowers. Skeeter pulled open the storage box on the back of the vehicle and pulled out bags of chips and water bottles. We walked over to the edge of the pond and sat on the bank while we munched. It was quiet for a few beats before Skeeter finally got down to business.

"We're all a little worried about you going back to Chicago all by yourself. Grandma is worried most of all."

He waited for me to say something, but all I could muster was, "I'm a little worried about me too." I didn't want to say it as I couldn't come to a solution that didn't make me a burden to everybody else.

"Well, Grandma thinks maybe it's best if you come back. Stay with her and Grandpa for a while until you find something that pays some money, and then we get you back on your feet, a little closer to home."

That was a nonstarter. "I'm not moving back in with Grandma and Grandpa. Grandpa is having a lot of medical problems, and I know the bills have to be stacking up. Grandma says they are doing okay, but I know it's bad. Everybody chips in on the food at the farm, brings a dish to pass, helps split the farm costs. I contribute nothing, and I don't know how long it will be before I can chip in. The recession is hitting pretty hard here."

"Grandma had a fix for that, and she didn't want to say it in front of everybody, could create some hard feelings and all so…"

"I don't like where this is going."

"She's going to give up her spot out at the lake and sell the camper."

"No," I shouted, coming to my feet. "I won't be responsible for that. The lake means so much to everybody."

"It's already in motion. She's calling the campground while we are out here. She's planning to go out tomorrow morning after church to take pictures of the camper to get it sold."

"She should have asked me. I would have told her not to do it. I'm not going to be the reason she sells the camper."

"Grandma didn't want it to be a decision for you, kiddo; it's a decision for her and Grandpa, and they already made it."

I stomped over to the side-by-side.

"We're going back; we have to stop her."

He reluctantly trudged back to the vehicle.

"Come on Shell, I think it's for the best. too. Things seem to be getting on well with you and David. You know before you came to town he ain't barely been seen out of the house since his grandma died. And there's Corey and Missy. Grandma thinks you all need each other, and I think there's something to that. Well, and I don't know if you know about Corey…"

"What about Corey?"

"His mom called up and said to Grandma that he's been up and out of bed this week more than he's been up in months. Truth be told, he's been terrible depressed for a long time, and him and Tammy were getting close again on account of she wasn't doing too good with loneliness herself."

I remembered when I called Corey after hearing from Tammy; it wasn't very early, and he sounded like he was sound asleep.

"His mom is afraid if Tammy ain't found alive and you leave well… he just won't be okay."

That hit me hard and was the most convincing reason to stay that I'd heard yet.

"I just can't let Grandma give up the camper for me, Skeet; she'll never get her spot back. It means so much to her."

"You mean more to her than that spot. Corey means more to her than that spot."

"What if I can save some of my own money? I just need some time. I can figure it out."

"Well, how much you saved so far?"

I thought about my direct deposit that would have hit yesterday. "I have about $200."

"That ain't much after a year working, kiddo."

"If I wait a few months for my three-paycheck month and put in notice on my lease, I can get my deposit back and an extra check and come back with about $1,000; that could situate me for a few months."

He stepped into the side-by-side, "I think a few more months could be a few months too long."

I reached over and turned over the key to start the engine.

When we got back to the house, just as Skeeter had said, Grandma and Grandpa were gone, and everybody else had gone back to their chores. Skeeter left me to head down to the milk barn. That left me alone with nothing to do except sulk or get ready for the reunion.

I managed to get most of my laundry sorted and packed. I tidied up the guest room and put away dishes, then finally pulled out my dress. It was a one-shoulder blue and silver cocktail dress. I bought it for my graduation years ago, and it was still the nicest item of clothing I owned. I swept a layer of metallic eye shadow over my lids and lined my eyes in navy blue. I stepped into a pair of sparkly wedge heals.

Then I searched my grandmother's closet and picked out

a small, beaded pouch from her assortment. I slung it over my shoulder and exited to the front porch to collect the photos I'd gathered the night before. I placed the crate of photos at my feet while I waited on the back steps for David. I watched the sheep run around in the back yard and played brick on my phone while I waited.

He arrived early, just as he promised, to help me get the photos to the hall in time to decorate. My heart melted when I saw him step out of his car. He was sharply dressed in a crisp white shirt and pressed navy suit. It looked brand new, and I imagine his dress clothes weren't five years old. I should have been more excited, but I was full of guilt thinking about what my grandparents were off doing for me. His smile brightened my mood, and I pushed the guilt out of my mind. *I'll have time to try to stop them tomorrow*, I thought.

I hefted the crate, and he ran over, collecting it from me.

"This is a lot of photos you got in one night."

"I called in my family; I get to take no credit."

He popped open his trunk and placed the pictures inside, then made his way over to me and slid his arms around my waist.

"You have no idea how much I've missed you," he held me tightly, and I tilted my head up to him. He bent down and kissed me softly, then his big hands came up to the nape of my neck, pulling me closer into a firm kiss.

He let out a moan and then lifted his head away from me, still staring into my eyes. "We could skip the reunion."

I motioned for him to bend down and whispered in his ear, "No."

CHAPTER TWENTY-THREE

OUR CLASS HAD RENTED OUT THE NICESt bar in town, the one attached to the bowling alley on the edge of the city. It was mostly unchanged in the ten years since I'd left, dark carpeting with a yellow and black confetti print, dark green walls, and a big bar that served both the restaurant and the bowling alley. Abby was easy to find, right by the door giving us all marching orders. She sent David and me out to place photos in frames she'd set on the tables, asking us to prioritize sanctioned school activities. Any photos that were left were supposed to be tacked up to cork boards to make photo collages. She had set them up near the shuffleboard tables.

We were sliding photos into their frames when a group of the old Marsh football players came through carrying bag after bag of balloons in our school colors, black and gold. They put together archways near the entrance to the bar, over the stage that was normally used for karaoke, and put up a wall of balloons to obscure the view of the bowling alley that was easily accessed through an arched pass-through. Not long after the balloons were in place, blown up photos of the homecoming court from our year were trotted out and placed by the entry way door as if they were a receiving line. Of course, David was among the signs, and I insisted I get a picture of him next to his younger self.

"I didn't remember you having pimples," I said. He ran over to a neighboring table and picked up a star sticker, placing it over a giant zit on his chin.

"Much better," I said. And I ran over to a table and put a matching sticker on his face. As soon as I put it on him, he bent down and planted another kiss on me. After he pulled back, I stepped back so I could get him in the frame of my camera.

"Make the intimidating face you made in the picture, no smile," I ordered, and he mugged for one shot.

"Now, a real one," I demanded. He peeled away the stickers and made a genuine smile while pretending to pat the shoulder of his younger self.

We had completed our jobs with just moments to spare. As people started walking through, Abby pulled all of us back to the table to get our name tags. Mine was emblazoned with "Michelle Fry, Tallest Girl in School."

Abby wore her pin, bedazzled in all of its glory to proclaim her, "Most Organized." She passed out other pins with other interesting achievements. I was in the company of "Best Hair" and "Best Bench Press," among many others. I had an idea at that moment and began searching through the name tags. I made little piles, sorting those I had looked at and those that I hadn't until I found the name tags that I was looking for, "Tammy Davis, Life of the Party" and "Charity Stein, Most Likely to End up on Broadway."

I pulled their tags and walked up to the bar, "Can I get two empty glasses?"

The bar tender handed me two pint glasses, and I set them at the edge of the bar, placing a tag next to each glass. "Saving you a spot, Ladies," I whispered.

I felt the familiar hand of Corey touch my shoulder. I reached up and held his hand.

"Good work," he said. He ordered two shots, and we toasted Charity and Tammy and placed empty glasses next to theirs. We started a trend; before long everybody was clamoring to the end of the bar to do shots with the empty glasses.

I'd lost track of David somewhere while I was making my improvised tribute. Corey told me that Anna Doherty, nee Shepherd, also known as "Best Smile" had pulled David away for a surprise. He was gone for so long the reunion opened with Will Smith's 1998 jam, "Getting Jiggy With It," and he was nowhere in sight. The dance floor wasn't filled yet, and there weren't enough people there for him to be hidden. I peeked outside the balloon wall into the bowling alley and didn't see him out there either.

I claimed a round table not far from the stage with Corey, and we were joined shortly by Missy, "Most Likely to be a Dallas Cowboy's Cheerleader" and Corey II or Neil as we were going to call him, who snuck in as her date. Several 90s' jams played before an old favorite of ours came on. A gentle hum at the karaoke station beckoned us to Cranberries' "Linger." I heard it and started to well up. Cranberries was a concert we'd gone to with Tammy when we were young. Corey saw my face and reached out a hand to pull me to the dance floor. Missy and Neil followed, and soon most of the class of '99 was up and swaying to the gentle rhythm of the song. I rested my head on Corey's shoulder, and he patted the back of my head.

I remembered, in our nosebleed seats at Pine Knob, swaying together to the song and my heart fluttering as I laid my head on Corey's chest. A part of me, even then, knew he wouldn't ever reciprocate, but I still hoped one day he would. I hummed the lyrics about being a fool in love, and I noticed the words no longer stung as they once had.

As the music faded, Missy came to us, and the three of us embraced, leaving Neil an outsider in a memory that we shared. With teary eyes we looked to Neil with his hands buried in his pockets. I held my arms out to him and pulled him in with us.

"We are going to make you an honorary inductee in the Cranberries concert club," I said.

Then a slow Jewel song came on, something sweet and melodic, and he asked if he could have my hand for a dance. I scanned the room for David and again failed to find him.

Neil had the rhythm I lacked and knew actual dance moves. I stayed in rhythm with him, and I'm sure he made me look like a better dancer than I was. He gave me a gentle spin, then pulled me back in close. When I twirled back into him, I could smell the sweet cedar aroma from before. His big brown eyes stared down at me, reminiscent of his cousin's "Best Eyes." Somehow, I had never looked into Corey's eyes quite as deeply. As the music faded away, I found myself wanting to stay in an embrace with him. He swayed with me even though the music was gone, and a fast tempo song was just starting. I reluctantly took a step away when he grabbed my hand and spun me back into him, then into a dip.

I felt my heart flutter, and he bent down like he was going to kiss me but instead said, "I've wanted to do that for ten years."

I stared up at him and stammered, "Ten years," just before

I saw David over his shoulder. He had a serious look on his face. Neil looked behind him, pulled me back up to standing, and gave me a kiss on the hand before bowing out behind David.

"What's wrong?" I asked, concerned about the expression on his face.

"Nothing, Anna really ticked me off."

"What did she say?"

"It doesn't matter' let's get a drink."

We walked to the bar, and I showed him the glasses I had set out for Tammy and Charity. Tammy's had been filled with a drink, and somebody had placed a rose in Charity's glass. David ordered a Jack and Coke and another White Russian for me. With drinks in hand, we toasted, "To Tammy and Charity."

I took a sip of my White Russian and shouted, "I did it."

"Did what?" he asked.

"Finally, got to drink a drink that you bought for me!"

"Oh, that's good, I guess. I hadn't noticed you didn't drink the other ones," he shouted back. We tried to yell back and forth a few times before we agreed it was too noisy by the bar and moved to the back of the room. We huddled together at a table closer to the bowling alley. The noise from the lanes was still better than the speaker with the bass turned up on the dance floor. He seemed agitated.

"So, what's going on?" I asked. "You seem a little off."

"I know," he said. "I know you said you were only here for a week, and it hit me today that you're leaving tomorrow and…"

"It hit me today, too," I said.

"I want you to stay; it's not even right to ask, but I don't want you to go."

"I know. I wish we hadn't been so stubborn in high school. I mean look at that handsome guy." I pointed to his cutout. "What was I thinking not to date the guy with that handsome face?"

"I really regret that I didn't get to know you better when we were in school."

"This is going to sound so crazy, but my grandma and I were just talking about how our families were always at these same places, like, the same church and the same social groups. My grandma and your grandma were telephone operators together. Can you believe it? And we both spent our summers at the same campground, and it's kind of crazy that we just didn't spend more time together."

"Campground," he scrunched his face. "We never went to a campground."

"Yeah, you did; your grandmother's obituary said she spent her summers at Trident Lake."

"Oh," he gave me a knowing look. "Trident Lake. That was not..."

He was interrupted by a high-pitched voice emanating from the loudspeaker, "Will David Blanch come to the stage please?"

"Now what?" I asked.

"David Blanch," the words trilled over the speaker. It was Anna's high-pitched squeal.

He gave me a kiss on the forehead and walked reluctantly to the stage; everybody clapped as he made his slow approach. He was nearly up to the stage, and before he could walk up the steps Anna stopped him and placed a big golden crown on his head. He closed his eyes as if it filled him with physical pain to be bestowed a crown. She handed him a tiara and gestured at him to put it on her head. He did so absent mindedly, and it sat crooked on her tousled hair.

"You're king and queen," Abby, "Most Organized," announced to a cacophony of applause.

Suddenly, "You're Still the One," by Shania Twain, blared from the speakers. I had a flash back to high school, David and Anna locked in an embrace singing the very same song to one another in the center of our high school gymnasium. It struck me now how silly those lyrics about still being in love were for two 18-year-olds to be singing. I recalled standing in the gymnasium with Corey and Jen making barfing gestures as they danced.

When my mind came back to the present, I saw her singing the lyrics up to him, but he was in a different world, staring at me and completely ignoring her.

John came over to me and set a basket of popcorn between us. I read his name tag, "Best Leg Press?" I asked.

"Yeah, I wanted that. I did have the best leg press."

"Wouldn't you want to be remembered for something else more about who you are as a person?"

He looked at my tag. "Like being tall?"

"Point made," I said.

"Does it tick you off, your man dancing with Anna Banana? Her face didn't hold up so well, did it? Looks like she's all jowls now."

"Not ticked off in the least, and her face looks fine."

"If you say so. I think she looks like a mastiff," he said, reaching for another fistful of popcorn.

The music ended, and the crowd erupted into cheers. Anna pulled her arms up to David's neck, and she made a tiny leap trying to pull him down to her, but he backed away just as she jumped and waved to the crowd. She took the cue and turned away from him, waving as well. Her face was awash with defeat.

He stepped away and walked over to the DJ.

"He's sweet on you something fierce, Cousin," John said. "Haven't seen him like this since back when he met his wife."

"Did you know her?" I asked.

"I know her."

"What's she like?" I inquired, my tone not as casual as I intended.

"Oh, green eyed monster of jealousy coming outta you," he said.

I rolled my eyes, "I'm not jealous."

"Oh, sure," he teased.

I snapped back at him, "And furthermore, green-eyed monster means jealous, so you could say that the green-eyed monster is coming out or that I am jealous, but to use both together is like saying I'm jealous jealous, which doesn't make any sense at all."

"You are jealous jealous. Look at you."

I stood up and walked away from the table, searching for any other recognizable faces, when I noticed the dance floor filling with a billowing fog. I scanned the bar and was stopped in my tracks, by the sound of creaking, followed by a howling wolf emanating from the speaker. I turned back to the dance floor to find David in the center of the room beckoning me as the intro to "Thriller" rang out from the amplifier.

"Go get him, Michael Jackson girl," a voice called behind me. I felt a gentle nudge at my back as several former classmates pushed me to the dance floor and into David.

I looked up at him and found he had a big grin splashed across his face. Within seconds the fog engulfed us. I shook my head and looked down, "I'm so embarrassed," I said. "I didn't know that I made my Michael Jackson obsession quite this noticeable."

"I told you," he said, gently pushing my chin up so that we were face to face. Then he put his lips to my ear and whispered, "I always knew how much you liked this song, and I know you don't like people to see you dance; that's why I called the DJ and paid for him to bring in a fog machine, so you could go all in."

He swept his hand through the dense fog; we could see only each other through it and nobody else in the room.

As soon as I realized we were under the cover of fog, my heart skipped a beat, and I danced. I let every guard down and let my insecurity about my terrible dancing melt away as I moved without a care. We danced together, wildly, ridiculously, spinning, jumping, jerking our shoulders like the zombies from the music video, and clapping in the air like MJ himself. We danced every insane move that came to our minds. We were wildly dancing out of rhythm and perfectly in time with each other. It was perfectly imperfect, and when the music stopped, we were left staring at each other. I didn't let him catch his breath before I jumped on him, wrapping my legs around his hips and locking my lips to his. I clenched my eyes tight and felt his big hands, holding me tight to him. I felt his heart beating hard against my chest as I intertwined my arms under his, holding on to keep him close. I couldn't catch my breath with his tongue sliding between my lips, and I had to pull away. When I leaned back to catch my breath, I noticed the room had grown quiet. I opened my eyes and found the haze had thinned. David opened his eyes to look at me and realized that we were now exposed. He quickly let go, dropping me back to the floor.

"Woohoo!" my cousin hollered from his dance floor adjacent seat. He was quickly joined in his chant by the rest of the party goers, but not by Anna, who stomped out the door, with streaks of mascara sliding down her jowls.

CHAPTER TWENTY-FOUR

I COULDN'T STOP LOOKING AT HIM from that moment forward. I held his hand tightly as we moved from group to group. We talked to the jocks, many of whom were now salesmen, the artists who were now teachers, and the old friends who were now parents. I listened to their stories and looked at their baby pictures and their wedding pictures. I looked at those things and nodded and smiled, but I didn't process any of it. Because the only thing on my mind was David.

He didn't want to release his grip on me either, and while he dutifully looked through the pictures of our classmates showing off new houses and babies, his eyes kept moving to me.

We danced together again, but only to slow songs, and they were nothing like our dance in the fog. They were nice but not electric. Those dances were a reason to be close and to touch, but they felt like a placeholder for more.

As the reunion was settling down, the drama kids, the ones who knew how to sing and dance, crooned a tribute from *Beauty and the Beast* in honor of Charity. It was followed by a shot of Jack Daniels for Tammy and a moment of silence for both. I noticed Officer Fowler's sister looking down during the moment of silence and edged myself over to her, keeping David with me.

When the moment was over, she looked up and was startled to see me directly in front of her.

"I'm sorry about your friend," she said.

"Thank you. I've been trying to look for her, but I think I ticked your brother off when I went rogue. I haven't heard from him in days."

She nodded. "I know it's been hard not to have more information about her. He's not mad at you though. He's been busy looking for her. I promise you that."

"I just haven't heard anything in days."

She pulled my free hand to her and held it tightly,

"Michelle, I've never seen him work so hard on a case. Late nights, no sleep. He is doing everything he can to figure out what happened to her."

She was genuine in what she said. She looked directly into my eyes as she spoke, and I knew she meant it. That was a relief; I was worried that the police weren't taking her disappearance seriously and I was going to have to find her myself.

I thanked her and stepped away.

CHAPTER TWENTY-FIVE

DAVID AND I STROLLED SLOWLY through the bar on our way out. Just before we got to the door, I paused. The question of your place or mine was hanging between us, unasked and unanswered. I was going back to Chicago the next day either way, but the question was would I be going home after a night with David or not. We were standing near the balloon arch, and he was staring at me. I assumed he was about to ask me where to go, but we were interrupted by the Coreys and Missy, coming up to say their goodbyes. I hugged each one of them, and David shook hands, even with Missy, though she came in for a hug, so he ended up poking her in the chest as she leaned in.

Just as we were about to move outside, John ran to catch up to us with an envelope in his hand. "Hey, wait up," he shouted. "Grandma wanted me to give you this. She said it's for your investigation."

He passed over a sealed Michigan Milk Producers Association envelope. Everybody stood watching me as I opened it. I unfolded the piece of paper inside and found Grandma's familiar shaky chicken scratch. After reading it I looked up at David, scrutinizing his face.

"What?" he asked.

"Did you know your dad was on the trip to Pendleton Farms?" I passed over the paper in my hand. It was the chaperone list that Grandma had assembled. He looked it over. He looked up at me with a distressed expression, "I swear I didn't know."

I scanned the names of the chaperones; among the parents were Ronald Blanch, Tom Perry, Andrew Fowler, Maria Sheldon, John Martin, Bill Packard, and teachers Mrs. Smith, Ms. Abel, and Mrs. Harper.

I looked around the room, the children of several of the people on the list were in the room.

"Let's go outside," I said.

We moved to the edge of the parking lot, where we could

see the list by the light of the bowling alley sign. I held up the paper looking it over again.

"This is weird," I said. "Why were most of the chaperones men?"

I passed it around to the group.

Missy read it out loud, "Blanch, Perry, Fowler, Sheldon, Martin, Packard…"

"Wait," Corey said. "Fowler Avenue, Packard Highway, Sheldon Street, Perry Street, Martin Pass."

"There's no Blanch Street," Missy said.

"No, but there's a Hampton," David said. "Named after my great-grandfather, Theodore Hampton."

"You have a street named after your family too, Michelle, but they aren't on this list."

Neil reached into his pocket and pulled out a pencil, underlining the last names, adding the street names associated with each name. At the bottom he wrote Fry with a question mark.

"Why do all of these people have street names associated with them? Why does your family have a street name, Michelle?" Neil asked.

"My grandparents lived on that road for a long time, and when they were naming the street and putting down new gravel, they just named it for themselves because so many Fry's lived there."

"And David, you live on Hampton?"

"I do, and my family has for a long time."

"What about Fowler and Packard?" Neil asked. "Do they live on their own street?"

"No, Packard is a highway, and Fowler is where City Hall is," I added.

"Shit," David swore. The first time I'd ever heard him curse. "I know what these names are."

He grabbed the paper back from Corey, snatching the pencil in the process. He wrote something at the bottom of the list and underlined it, passing it back to me; it read Hannah Blvd.

"There is a Hannah Boulevard!" I exclaimed, following his train of thought. "The farm, it was called Hannah Farms and there is a Hannah Boulevard here in town. So, the farmer's name is on this town too?"

"He is, and I know exactly why; these are all the names of the people that signed the town charter for Marsh. It's hanging in my grandmother's office."

"So, all of the descendants of Marsh's founding fathers were getting together at our third-grade farm field trip?" Corey asked. "Why?"

"There's a bigger question that you are completely missing, Corey," Missy interjected. "Why did they get together and one of them, the only one who no longer lived in Marsh, end up dead, and why did they try to convince us that we never went there in the first place, even swiping our photos of that day?"

"I remember the accident, Missy," David said. "None of the people on this list were in the field with Hannah. There's no way that somebody killed him. He was alone in the field."

John chimed in, "I had a baler like that one. It had a faulty safety relay on it. A couple of years back I climbed under it, thinking I had turned it off, and it kicked right back on. The damn thing nearly took my arm off. If you knew what you were doing, you could take a safety relay out of a baler and cause somebody a lot of trouble. You'd have to really know what you were doing to do that though."

"You would have to be an engineer," I said, looking at David.

"Like my dad," he said, not meeting my eyes.

"So, the missing pictures could have tied everybody to this accident, and when Missy and Tammy went to the farm and looked at the pictures, maybe they realized that. Then they went to tell somebody, somebody like Fowler. Somebody who was on the trip, and they didn't realize it. So maybe he didn't want them telling anybody, and he just got rid of them."

"But why would Charity show up dead and not Tammy?" Missy asked.

"And," Corey said, "remember back when Mickey Fowler came out to the camper to talk to you? He didn't' seem to know about the farm. Maybe Mickey Fowler doesn't know anything about this, but his dad might."

"Wait, go back," Neil said. "Why did you call the police in the first place?"

"Oh, I forgot you don't know. We called because somebody tried to break into my grandparent's camper the night before."

"You didn't tell me about that," David said, irritated. "Did you find out who it was?"

"I…"

Corey and I exchanged a glance. "No, we never did."

David looked at me with his eyes starting to well with tears.

"I was fine," I tried to comfort him, thinking that he was upset to hear that I had been in danger. "They couldn't get the door open, and when they couldn't get in, they tried the crawl space, but I kicked it closed. I guarantee they walked away in worse shape than me because I kicked it very hard. I felt contact on the other side of that door, so they probably had a good many bruises. I was okay, except for my nerves. And my cousin Andy was one camper away and came over to calm me down. It was no big deal."

He almost whispered as he asked, "Was it last Saturday, the night before I went to The Alpine with you and John?"

"Yeah," I said.

"And your camper is at Trident Lake Campground?" he asked.

"Yes," I answered reluctantly.

"My family owns a cabin on Lake Trident. It's in the woods."

I felt my heart drop. I thought about the height of the dent in the door and looked down at David's hands.

"I know who tried to break in." We all stared at him, expectantly waiting for his reply. He looked stunned as he said, "It was my dad."

CHAPTER TWENTY-SIX

AFTER HE SAID IT WAS HIS FATHER who tried to break into my camper, so many clues clicked into place.

It made sense in some ways; his dad was tall, and he could have made the dent, and he had access to Lake Trident, but there were still so many unanswered questions, like why.

"How do you know it was him?" I asked.

"He was supposed to come to dinner with me that night and never showed up. Then I didn't hear from him for a full day, and he stumbled up to my doorstep a complete wreck, covered in day old bruises. It was that morning I was supposed to meet you to go to the library. I couldn't get a straight answer out of him about what happened."

"You told me somebody had an appendectomy that morning."

"That was also true. I had to move an appointment because my dad showed up at my house needing help. He does that sometimes after he's had too much to drink. Which is a lot more often these days. That's not exactly something I was ready to share."

"Why would your dad try to break into my camper?" I asked.

"I don't know," he said.

"Well, call him," I insisted.

He looked around the parking lot. We were all still congregating under the sign by the road. "I'm not going to call him out here; we need to go someplace more private."

"Go to your car," I prodded.

He pulled out his phone and walked over to his car. We all shamelessly moved closer to the car and craned our necks trying to hear what was said. The call went on for a long time. After more than ten minutes I bent over and looked into his window. I found him staring in the distance, completely still, with the phone turned off in his hand.

I opened the door and poked my head in, "What did he say?"

"He lied."

"Are you sure he lied?"

"Yeah, he said it wasn't him, and the way he said it had this little hitch in his voice. It's his tell. He was lying."

David was silent. I looked down and noticed his hands were shaking.

"Are you okay?"

"I think," he said, "I think my dad knows what happened to Tammy."

"Why?" I asked.

"Because I asked him if he knew what happened to Tammy, and he told me it was none of my business. He didn't say no."

Corey, who was standing behind me, tapped my shoulder, and I opened the door a crack more so he could look in.

"Can you see if you can get your dad to tell us where she is? We can't go to the police in Marsh if the Fowlers are part of this. We're going to have to find her ourselves."

"Oh," Missy jumped into the conversation, and I stood back. "We need to call the State Police. Does anybody know any State Police officers?"

We all shook our heads.

"David," she said, snapping her finger in his direction. "Give me your phone."

Without turning his head or paying any attention to her, he held out his phone. She reached into the car and snatched it from his hand.

"Hi, information lady, can you put me through to the State Police for Michigan?...Hmm...Yeah...I have no idea...just the general line."

She waited and tapped in a bunch of numbers, then left a message.

"I don't think they're going to get that message tonight," she said.

"Well, we need to do something," I replied. "Let's go talk to him."

David was still sitting in stunned silence.

"David, you have to snap out of it," I shouted. "Let me drive to your dad's place while you process whatever it is you are going through." It was probably all hitting him at once. His father might have killed a farmer, his father might have tried to break into my camper. I wanted to tell him it would all be okay. But, if his father really did those things, it would be lying.

After a long silence he finally came around and gave me his father's address. Then he slid over so I could take the wheel. He sat in silence as John, Corey, and I formed a convoy heading through town. We travelled past Packard Highway, and I couldn't help but think of the connection to the list. David's dad lived in the same part of town as the Steins in an old Craftsman house, the kind that you could once order as a kit from the Sears Catalog.

The lights were out, and there were no cars in the driveway.

"He's not home," David said in a monotone voice.

"David, you have to snap out of this funk. I know it seems like your dad is a bad guy here, but we don't know the story. You need to get it together. We need to see if he knows where Tammy is."

He was about to answer when his phone rang; it was sitting in his cup holder. I turned it over and read the caller name. "It's Mickey Fowler," I said, passing it over to him.

He looked at me in surprise and hit the answer button.

"Hey… Yeah… Just in town right now…"

Missy ran up to my window, and I held my hand up and gestured for her to stay quiet, to keep her from knocking.

David continued, "Where? … Why? … I'll be there."

He hung up, and I opened the door. I couldn't keep it closed any longer as Missy was about to jump through the window, unable to keep her curiosity at bay.

"Mickey Fowler just called; he said he needs me to come out to the lake, to my family cabin."

"So did he find her?" Missy asked.

"He didn't say why he needed me. He just told me to hurry."

"Well, if they had something to do with it, they are going

to try to get you in on the cover-up," Missy said. "Like in CSI, they're going to have you do doctor stuff to mess with timelines and all of that."

"I wouldn't agree to any of that, Missy."

"I'm going to call the police again," Missy said. "I swear I'm going to hit zero until I get a person. Also, I need the address to your cabin."

He gave her the address, and she ran back to Corey's truck.

"Could Tammy be with your dad?" I asked. "Could she be in that cabin?"

"She could be."

"Where would they keep her if they took her?"

"There is a cellar there, but I don't know why they would keep her. If it's about pictures they could have destroyed those, and then why keep her at all? And why did they find Charity and not Tammy? They were together, right?"

"I don't know, but I have to look. I have to know. How do I get to your place from the campground?"

He explained where I would find the path, then the clearing, and how I would get into the cellar.

He was coming around a little, but was still in a bit of a daze.

"Can you do this? Can you help us?" I asked.

"I think so," he said.

"David, is your dad dangerous?" I asked.

"Yes."

"Is he a danger to you?"

He didn't answer.

CHAPTER TWENTY-SEVEN

WE LEFT DAVID TO GO TO HIS CABIN ALONE. Missy, the Coreys, John, and I formed a plan to go to the camper, get the golf cart, find the path to the cabin, and look around while David kept his dad and Mickey occupied. Missy had already called the State Police and begged a receptionist to get a patrol car out to Trident Lake and was assured somebody would be there within 24 hours.

We made it to the campground and woke Ernie up from his slumber. He checked us in, and we found our way to my grandparents' camper, parking John's pickup truck next to our site.

John and I darted into the camper, and looked for anything we could use to aid us in our rescue operation. We grabbed the heavy Maglite and plastic kid's flashlights out of the cabinet. In one of the drawers, I found a carabiner and showed it to John.

"What would we do with that?" he asked.

"I have no idea. I feel like people have these in rescue kits."

I put it back and grabbed a bungee cord and scissors. I packed them into my shower bag and searched the room again. I looked down at the crawl space, and John stopped opening drawers to watch me looking at it.

"What is it?" he asked.

"I'm getting a weird vibe like I need something else."

"Like a weird vibe, how?"

I bent down and felt the outside of the cabinet that I had kicked nights ago. I could feel the dents from where I had battered it.

Looking around the room, I tried to figure out what I was supposed to grab. My eyes settled on a wind-up toy tractor. I picked it up and tucked it into the bag.

"Why?" John asked.

"I have no idea."

I looked back down at the crawl space, and the hair on the back of my neck stood up. John looked down at it and shrugged, then stepped out of the camper. I followed him out. After I closed the door, I put my fist up to the hole; it was high above me. John stepped behind me and put his fist up to the dent too. "It was definitely somebody big, like David."

"Something isn't sitting right with this," I said.

He shrugged.

The Coreys had pulled the tarp off the golf cart, and Missy was in the driver's seat.

"We can't all fit on this," I said. "Missy, I think you should stay behind in case something happens, and we need help."

"I don't think my weight is what's going to slow this cart down," she pointed at the rest of us, each about the size of two Missys.

"She's right. Neil, can you stay with her? If we aren't back in an hour call somebody... I don't know, maybe the Dairy police; see if you can get them here."

"We'll figure it out," he said.

The rest of us jumped onto the golf cart and rode it in the dark down the path to the marina and up into the woods. We followed the trail that David told us about. It was overgrown. We rode along it until the trees were too thick for us to traverse with the cart. We turned it around so it was facing the path; that way we could make a quick getaway, quick being about fifteen miles per hour.

We all flicked on our flashlights; I had the big metal one, and Corey and John were holding plastic ones with superhero patterns on them. We walked through the woods, finding the clearing just where David said it would be. We flicked off our lights as soon as we saw the house. The lamps were on inside, and there was enough moonlight for us to see at least a bit of a path.

The home was a log-cabin style with a dark, shingled roof covered in moss with a stone chimney. It was rough around the edges, overgrown, with ivy that wrapped around the windows and doors. The closer we got the worse it looked; many of the logs were chipped, and there were gaps between them.

We quietly made our way around the front porch, crouching under the windows. There were several cars in the driveway: David's, the police cruiser for Officer Fowler, and two other trucks that I hadn't seen before. We kept moving past them until we found the cellar door. The handles were wrapped in a thick chain, bound together by a heavy lock.

John gave it a tug, but it wouldn't budge.

We stayed low and moved to a thicket of shrubs. There was a slight opening between two of the bushes that led to a small basement window.

I saw a spider creeping through the foliage and suddenly wished we had brought Missy with us.

"It's going to be on you to fit in there, Cuz," John said, pointing to the window.

"Kill the spider first," I whispered.

"I'm not allowed to kill spiders outside; that's Grandma's rule."

"Not in life-or-death situations."

"Rules are rules," he replied.

Corey rolled his eyes, stepped forward, and scooped the spider into his palm, moving it away from the window. "Thank you," I mouthed.

I moved to the ground and crawled forward on my hands and knees. Still in my tight dress, I wiggled into the space between the shrubs. I reached back searching for a light, and one was placed in my hand. I shined it into the window and swept it across the floor. All I found was an old Michigan basement, dirt floors and crude stone walls. I was about to flick off the light and get off the ground when I saw a small form step into the light; she was bright white, with dark hair, a dark punk rock tank top, and a silver studded belt over tight jeans. It was Tammy.

I waved at her, then realized the light would be blinding her, so she wouldn't know it was me waving. I turned the flashlight back to light my face. When I shined it back on her she was smiling and jumping. I backed out of the hole, staying low to the ground, "She's here, she's alive."

"No frickin' way." John exclaimed. "Let's get her out."

"We could break the glass, but I think they'll hear us. Maybe we should try to get the window open," Corey said.

"Let me see what I can do."

I bent back into the space and ran the flashlight along the window. I noticed two fresh-looking nails on either side of the opening. I turned and said, "Give me those scissors."

I popped the scissors under the nails and wiggled them until they came out. When both nails were free, the window opened.

"Yes!" Tammy exclaimed.

I held my hands up to my lips in a shushing gesture and motioned for her to come forward. She walked under the window. As she stepped closer, I noticed her hair was matted to her head, and her face was crusted around the eyes and mouth.

"What happened?" I asked.

"Girl, hell if I know. I've been down here forever."

"I mean how did you get down here?"

She shook her head, "It's a long ass story. How did you find me?"

"That's a long ass story, too. Let's get you out of here. Anything you can use to climb out?" I asked.

"Ain't shit down here but me and some jars of peaches."

"Can you give me your belt?"

She pulled it off and tossed it up to me. I looped it around my hand and lowered it back to her, "can you hold on to this, and I'll pull you out?"

She gripped it, and I moved John into position to hold it. Corey got behind him and gripped John. They both pulled at the same time, and both went flying in different directions.

I stepped in front of them and whispered, "I'm going in. Somebody needs to push her out."

I moved feet first toward the window, and John and Corey held my arms to lower me down. Corey followed me into the bush, but he couldn't get all the way in. I had to drop the last foot on my own. I landed easily and quickly turned and embraced Tammy. She rested her head on my shoulder and let out a long sigh. She was thin, too thin.

"We're in some shit, now aren't we, Girl?" she said.

I rested my head on hers. "Not anymore, we've got plenty of help. I'm going to get you out of here."

Tammy said, "You know, I pushed Charity out that window about a week ago, and she took off. Never came back."

"She was in this basement with you a week ago?"

"She was."

"Why did they put you down here?" I asked.

"We found some crazy papers at that old farmhouse, and those shitheads upstairs chased us down and stole them from us, then dragged us out here to the middle of nowhere and locked us in this basement."

"If they took the papers from you, why are you still down here?" I asked.

"Well, they took them, but Charity took them right back. She's super smart. She said that stuff was incriminatin' for a lot of people in Marsh, and they were probably fixing to kill us for them. She said if we didn't move quick and get them back, we were dead. So, we pried open that window, I pushed her out, and she stole all of them back. I told her the best way to get help was to find your place."

"How did she know where to find me?"

"Because I knew where we were. And I remembered the camper. I told her how to find it, and I told her about how we used to sneak in if it was locked."

"Up through the crawl space," I stuttered.

She nodded, and my heart dropped. I thought of the space, tight even for me, and realized that David's father would never have fit in it. The person I was kicking all those nights ago was not an intruder; it was Charity. I thought of the church women saying that when her body was found, she looked like she'd been beaten. My mind raced, remembering how I'd kicked the door so hard, thinking it was somebody trying to hurt me and then the loud bang on the door outside just as I screamed. The sounds were almost at the same time, and I realized it was David's dad punching the door and Charity trying to get away from him.

"So, did she ever find you?" Tammy asked, her head still on my shoulder.

"She found the camper," I hoarsely whispered.

"I knew it," Tammy said. "You got the papers then, so these guys are toast."

"I didn't find any papers."

"Well, then Charity has to have them."

"Tammy," I choked on the words. I couldn't tell her that Charity was dead. Not like this. "She must have them," I lied.

She started shaking, like she was cold, but it was warm.

I had to get back on track and get us out of the basement.

"Is there anything we can use to get us out of here?" I asked.

"Like I said. It's just me and the peaches."

"Where are the peaches? Maybe there's a shelf or something I can stand on."

Tammy stepped over toward a darkened wall and came back with a jar of peaches. "There ain't no shelf. And I don't think he knew these were down here. I found them like the second day; there was this shining spot on the wall, and I picked at it, because shit, what else did I have to do, and I found this little hole, full of canned peaches. They're damn good. Kept me going anyway."

I walked over to the hole in the wall and flashed my light in it.

"Like I said, nothing else," she said, and she was right.

"I'll figure out another way. Let's just worry about you. The guys can get you back to Corey's cousin and Missy and come back for me."

"Hey, I won't leave you behind like Charity did," she said.

"She didn't…well, we'll talk about it when we are all safe."

I held out my hand to give her a boost. She pushed her way up the wall, and when she was to the top a strong set of hands reached through the window and pulled her up.

"I'll be back with a way to get you out," John promised.

Corey stayed with me, searching the area for something to help me out.

I moved away from the wall and examined the room,

looking for another way out; there was just a set of steps and the window. I slowly crept up the steps and realized I could see through the slats in the door to the living room above me.

I pushed the door, but it didn't budge.

David stepped into view over the door above me, and I could see two older men standing across from him; one was Mr. Perry, and the taller man next to him I assumed was David's father.

When I put my ear up to the ceiling, I could just make out the conversation.

"Nobody meant to kill Mr. Hannah, David. We only meant to scare him."

"But why would you even want to scare him?"

"Because he needed to learn," Captain Fowler said stepping into view.

"Needed to learn what?" David asked skeptically.

"That you can't walk away from your responsibility. His family took an oath to protect our town no matter what," Ronald Blanch said, his voice a deep bass. "It's the same oath I took, and it's an oath you will take, too when the time is right."

My hand prickled as I felt something touch me, something with too many legs skittering across the back of my hand. I had to suck in a deep breath to keep from screaming. I closed my eyes and took a moment to control my breathing, willing the horrible thing to get off me.

Corey must have sensed something was wrong and flashed his light in my direction. In trying not to look at what was crawling on me, I gazed up at the ceiling of the basement and found it teeming with spider webs; the shine of the light glistened on the webs, and the inhabitants of the basement began to stir. I motioned for him to turn it back off. I was far better off not knowing those were up there.

I shook my hand and heard a plink on the floor below, then steadied myself and pushed my ear back up to the ceiling.

"You don't understand what we were protecting you from," Mr. Perry said. "If all of it ever got out, it would ruin you just as much as us."

"What would ruin us?"

"Your duty to protect prosperity," he said.

"I don't even know what that means!" David shouted.

"David, Mickey, listen," Captain Fowler said. "When our town was founded, we all pledged to be a Town of Prosperity, and with that came a duty."

"A duty to what?" David asked.

"To protect the prosperity of our city. We built something special in Marsh. We don't have crime and poverty like our neighbors. Do you want us to turn into Dairy? All bars and mobile homes? Our town is special. Everybody has us to thank for what they have. But they wouldn't understand what we had to do to get it."

Corey shined a light on me, flashing it on and off. I gestured for him to turn the light off so I could continue to listen, but he flashed me again.

I held up one finger to make him wait.

Fowler continued. "Hannah left and abandoned his duty to the town; there are explicit instructions for what we do to those who abandon their duty."

Corey flashed the light at me again, and I crept down the stairs.

"What?" I whispered.

"We got a ladder."

He passed it through the window; it was a small ladder like one that would be used on a bunk bed. I pushed it up against the wall and had just started to ascend it, when it slid out from under me and crashed to the ground, taking me with it. I fell with my fingers wrapped around the highest rung, smashing my knuckles and my knees into the concrete. I scrambled back up to my feet, and the door at the top of the stairs flung open, spilling light onto the other side of the room. A flurry of steps descended, and I scrambled to push the ladder back up against the wall.

"Who the hell is that?" Ronald shouted.

Corey's hands pushed through the window frame and reached down to me. I only managed to get two steps up the ladder and jumped up, hoping he would catch me. I heard him let out an "oof" as he gripped my forearms, digging his fingers into my skin hard. He pulled up and at the same time a strong pair of hands wrapped around my ankles trying to pull me back down.

"You can't let her out," Captain Fowler shouted.

I turned to see that Fowler's attention was on Blanch and landed a kick on his face, hearing a crack as his head spun. He was stunned for a moment, and Corey tried to pull me up again, but the angle wasn't right; my shoulder was caught in the window.

Fowler regained his senses, and I tried my best to kick him off of me again, losing both shoes in the process. He started landing blows on the backs of my legs, pulling and punching at the same time. A particularly bad blow hit me behind the knee.

I screamed, and David jumped forward, wrapping Captain Fowler in a headlock. It only took a moment for Fowler to lose his grip on me, but Corey still couldn't pull me out. To my surprise Mickey Fowler jumped forward, and just when I thought he was going to pull me back down, he grabbed both of my feet and pushed me up with force, sending me up and out the window. Corey, who still had a tight grip on me, fell backwards, and we both tumbled into the bush, breaking it under us. The limbs cut into me as I landed on Corey. I took a second to catch my breath, but the sounds of footsteps at the front of the house kicked me back into gear.

"Get up, Corey!" I shouted, pulling on him. He screamed; his arm was bent in an unnatural direction. I grabbed his good arm and pulled him up.

"We've gotta run!" I said, shaking him.

He snapped to attention and put one foot in front of the other. I pulled him away from the opening that led to the path toward the woods.

"We'll go around and find another way," I said.

A shot rang out, and a bullet hit a tree just feet away from us.

We darted into the tree line. Corey found a burst of adrenaline to get him away from the danger, but within moments the injury to his arm registered again, and I looked back to find him cradling his injured limb.

We scurried into the woods, but it was so dark without the light of the moon that it was hard to know which way to go.

We couldn't turn on our flashlights or we would give away our positions.

"Give me a sign, Dad." I whispered.

"Go north," Corey said.

"I don't know what north is without a compass."

"Seriously," he said. "Grab my shirt so we can stay together. We're going left."

I reached out and grabbed the hem of his flannel, and he took off quickly, dodging trees by mere inches. The sound of footsteps was getting closer behind us.

"We have to go faster," I whispered.

"We can't without light," he said.

"I'm taking the lead," I jumped in front of him, still holding his shirt. I flicked on the light, found a clear path, and turned it back off. I ran fast and hard, flicking the light on again when I'd run out of clear path. I did this again and again until we were deep into the woods, and the sounds of footsteps fell away.

We stood quietly for a moment, listening to see if they were still in pursuit.

Something in me was tugging, telling me to get back to the camper.

"Where are we going?" he asked.

"I need you, Dad; something's happening," I whispered, closing my eyes tight.

There was a new sound ahead of us, like a grunt, then rustling.

I took a step toward it, and Corey reached out, holding me back.

"What if it's them?"

"It's not."

There was more rustling behind us, then, hurried steps.

I grabbed Corey again and pulled him with me, following the sound. A shot rang out, and we picked up our pace, but Corey kept hesitating, slowing me down.

"We're going to hit a tree," he whispered.

"We won't; remember I told you my Dad is guiding us; it's a thing."

I knew he didn't want to trust it, but he had no choice. He

gripped the fabric of my dress and said, "Go."

The sound picked up again, and I darted as fast as I could, my bare feet crunching the earth and sticks below me. The sound ahead would turn and move, and I would bob and turn with it, feeling trees whiz past me. After just a few turns I heard a scream behind me as our pursuers crashed into the trees that we missed. We were moving rapidly, the sound guiding me in and out of thick patches of trees, then suddenly all was quiet.

We stopped to catch our breath. I turned in a circle trying to figure out where we were.

"What do we do?" he asked.

"This is where we're supposed to be. I guess."

I flicked on my light and swept it in a half circle. I caught a glimpse of a deer, who stopped when my light hit him and realized that was what we were following. He stared directly at me and twitched his ears, then jumped away. I caught a glimpse of something shining in the distance in the direction he ran. I clicked the light back off, grabbed Corey's good hand and pulled him with me. It didn't take long for me to figure out the shine was a reflector on a boat ramp. We were back at the marina.

Rather than step out into the open we stayed close to the woods. The quarter moon shone better without the trees obscuring its light, and after running in the dark so long, we could see our way clearly in the open green of the marina.

We slowed as we approached the camper. We found the golf cart parked off to the side, near the woods, but nobody was on it. I looked it over and found the keys still in the ignition.

"Something's wrong," I said to Corey. We tucked into the woods, walking slowly toward the camper.

WE FOUND MISSY HIDDEN among the trees. She had crouched low and was looking out to the clearing for the campground. I pointed her out to Corey. We snuck up on her, and I jumped forward, putting my hand over her mouth before she could scream. She tensed up and thrashed under my grip. Corey stepped in front of her and waved his hand. She stopped resisting, and I lowered her back to the ground.

"What happened?" I whispered.

Missy pointed to the camper, now surrounded by cop cars and trucks.

She said, "John came back with Tammy, and they were about to get in his car and go to Dairy; then, all these cops pulled up."

"Where did Tammy and John go?"

"In the camper. I heard the cops say to shoot Tammy as soon as they see her. And he said if they don't come out soon, he's going to smoke them out."

I noticed a fire had been started in the ring next to the RV.

"Is that why they started a fire?" I asked.

"That, and they are looking for something. They said when they find it, they want to burn it."

A zing ran up my spine. "I know what it is."

They both looked at me.

"I know what they are looking for. They are incriminating documents," I clarified. "The reason all of this is happening. It's the reason they took Tammy and Charity. And I think Charity hid those documents in the crawl space."

"Why do you think that?" Corey asked.

"I had a feeling there was something in there earlier tonight, and Tammy told me that Charity was trying to find me the night she died. That same night I thought somebody was trying to break into the camper. It wasn't an intruder; it was Charity," I said. "She was looking for help."

"So, the person you kicked," Corey trailed off.

"It was Charity," I said apologetically. "She was in the crawl space, and Mr. Blanch was at the door, and I gave away her position when I screamed and kicked her."

They were both quiet. I took a deep breath and said, "I have to make this right. Charity trusted me with this."

Corey and Missy nodded at me.

I tamped down my guilt and focused on the problem at hand.

"How did you get away from the police?" I asked Missy.

"John sent me with a ladder to get you out, and on my way back I heard all this craziness, and I just went in the woods and hid."

"So, they don't know you're here?"

"Nope."

"Missy, I'm going to need you to get that package."

"You are sure it's in there?" she asked.

"I'm ninety-nine percent sure. We need to get it and somehow get it to the State Police before these guys can stop us, so they can't kill Tammy."

"I know what to do with it." She pulled a piece of paper out of her bra and passed it to me. "I wrote down every number I could find for the State Police: I have the fax at the bottom." She passed it over to me.

"There's a fax machine at the guard shack. You need to get those documents, get to the guard shack, and tell Ernie I sent you. Tell him you have to send those documents tonight."

"How?" she pointed back to the camper. It was surrounded.

"I have a plan."

CHAPTER TWENTY-EIGHT

I WOUND UP THE TRACTOR TOY I had stashed in my bag and gave it to Corey. He was in no shape to do anything other than to be a distraction and make a run for it. I sent him to the front of the camper with the toy wound up, and Missy and I moved to the bushes as close to the rear side of the trailer as we could get. Missy had kicked off her shoes and dress and was down to just her bralette and spanks. She was shaking her hands in preparation for her task, just like she did back in her old gymnast days.

She took a deep breath, and we waited for Corey's signal, a whistle.

I whispered to her, "Remember, jump in, grab whatever you can, three count, and I'm pulling you right back out. Then hoof it to the golf cart, straight to the guard shack. I'll be a distraction if we need it."

She nodded.

We heard the whistle, and the men standing guard at the back of the camper moved away, checking on our distraction just as I had planned. I took off running for the storage compartment; I snapped the latches and quietly lowered the gate. I threw out a beachball blocking the crawl space. Missy was hot on my heels and jumped up, right into the space. I mentally counted one, two, and three. I grabbed her foot and pulled her out; she emerged with a big manilla envelope in hand and smiled at me.

I placed her on the ground, and we turned to run back to the golf cart. "Hey," a voice shouted.

"Go, Missy!" I barked and turned, running in the opposite direction of the cart.

Without taking any stock of who was chasing me, I ran along the lane turning left for the shower barn, leaving the path free for Missy to make a right for the guard shack.

"Stop, or I'll shoot," I heard behind me and kept on pressing, taking my chances. From what I'd seen that night, nobody on that squad was a crack shot. I ran as fast as I could, rushing into the women's bathroom. I flung open the door, and the motion lights clicked on, blinding me momentarily. I pushed a chair up to the door, jamming it closed, and searched for another way out. The only thing I could think of was to crawl up into the rafters and move to the men's side, which had a separate entrance.

I jumped up on the bench in a shower stall and pulled myself up to stand on the cinder block walls that separated the showers. I balanced myself on the high, narrow wall, and for the second time in one night, I found myself in a literal spiders' nest. I cursed the spiders and vowed that, if I survived, I would risk the wrath of every person in that campground and kill the barn spiders. You never knew when somebody would need to use those rafters for their safety, and here I was in eminent danger of being killed, and to add insult to injury, I was going to have to touch arachnids.

The door to the bathroom jiggled, followed by pounding. I was cautiously moving along the wall, but the urgency of the person at the door prodded me to move more quickly. I had to bite the bullet and reach up to grab the rafters, chanting to myself, "They are more afraid of you than you are of them." But after a few chants it came out as, "I'm more afraid of them than they are of me."

Before I knew it, I was on the men's side of the bathroom, and I ducked down just as the ladies' room door burst open. As I maneuvered into the nearest stall, I heard Captain Fowler on the other side calling for me to show myself. He was making a slow search, kicking open the stalls in the women's room. Quietly, I tiptoed to the door and hesitated to open it, waiting to time it with one of his kicks to a stall. Just as he smashed one, I slammed open the door and took off for the guard shack.

Within moments, I saw Missy driving away from the guard shack on the golf cart. She had a piece of paper in her hand, and she was waving it over her head. She barely slowed as she came to me, shouting for me to hop on.

I jumped in and she sped up, back down the lane towards the camper.

"What is it?" I asked, looking at the paper.

She passed it back to me and it read: "Fax successful. Recipient: Michigan State Police, Pages: 32 Sent by: Trident Campgrounds, Life's Better at the Lake. Delivery Successful.

"And it turns out Ernie used to be a state trooper. He knew just who to call. They are on their way."

"What was in the envelope?" I asked.

"A picture of David's dad holding a part; Ernie said it was a safety relay. Then there was a bunch of documents about the town founders of Marsh signing up as a Town of Prosperity. The document said stuff like no Black people, or Asians, or Catholics, or Irish people, and it had all this stuff they were supposed to do to get them out of town, and if they didn't leave, they were supposed to, well you know...."

"So, these guys are trying to hide that their ancestors pledged loyalty to this Town of Prosperity thing?"

"Oh, it's way more than that," she said, still with her pedal to the floor. "They weren't just doing things in the past. They vowed to be members, past, present, and future. They pledged to kill dissenters who left and any undesirables who stayed."

She handed me the envelope, and I looked inside, shining my flashlight on the first set of papers. The top document said *members Rogers Family lynching.*

"Whoa!" I said looking to her. "They committed hate crimes and took attendance?"

"Yup, and those documents go right up to the 1980's, and they have the names of all sorts of people we know on it, Blanch, Fowler, half of the police force."

Missy and I turned off the cart lights and parked it in a ditch two lanes away from my grandparents' place. The envelope was clutched tightly in my hands. We tucked ourselves up against the RV at a neighboring camp site, the Miller's place. We realized we couldn't get any closer without giving away our position.

"The Miller's camper is probably unlocked," I whispered. I grabbed Missy's hand and pulled her with me. We gently pried open the door, unlocked as I suspected, and tiptoed into their trailer, walking past the kitchen nook to the living room sofa at the back of the trailer. We left the lights off and peeked out through the back window.

We had a full view of the fire burning in the pit at the Fry family site. Standing around the fire were both the Fowlers, the Blanchs, the Shepherds, Mr. Perry and his nephew, and more people who looked familiar, but not familiar enough that I could name them.

David and Mickey Fowler were hanging back from the crowd, close enough that I thought we might be able to get their attention. I searched the window and found a turn crank. It squeaked as I twisted it. Each turn made me wince, afraid that it was going to draw attention to us. Missy kept her eyes on the men as I cranked, and as soon as we had it open just a crack, we started to whisper, "Hey."

We could hear Captain Fowler near the fire, "If we can't find it, we're going to have to burn the whole place down."

A murmur of agreement passed among the men standing around the fire.

With that comment, my panic rose, "Hey," I said, finally loud enough to get David's attention. He turned around and scanned the camper, clearly not noticing me. I stuck my fingers through the slats of the open window and wiggled them. He turned, without catching the attention of Fowler Junior, and walked slowly toward the camper, crouching down to look in the window.

"Don't let them set the camper on fire," I whispered. He leaned in and whispered, "Michelle?"

"I have what they are looking for," I whispered back.

I passed the folder through the window, and he reached up to take it from me. Just before he got it, Missy smacked my shoulder.

"What?" I asked.

"He's going to burn it."

"The cops already have it," I said. "He needs it, to keep them from hurting Tammy or John."

Missy tugged my arm back and said, "We need to stop them. We need to make sure nobody else gets hurt before the police get here."

"What do you think we should do?" I asked.

"We need to wake this place up."

She ran out of the camper. I looked at the envelope in my hand and clutched it. Then, I turned back to David and whispered, "Don't let them burn the camper."

"I won't," he promised.

I darted out after Missy. She was back at the cart. She motioned for me to hurry. As soon as I jumped in, she pushed her foot to the floor. "Turn on the radio and flash the lights," she said.

I cranked up the radio, and John Denver's "Thank God I'm a Country Boy" bellowed out. I turned the volume to full blast and flicked the lights of the cart on and off. Then Missy slammed her hand onto the horn button, and it emitted a high-pitched beep. Lights started to flick on all through the campground as we whizzed by.

She slowed just enough at each light to shout, "Trouble at the Fry place."

When we turned down the final lane back to site 001, people were ambling down the pavement in their night clothes with flashlights. We flew past them, Missy knowing time was of the essence. We got to the police blockade, where they had guns fixed on the door to the camper. We broke their concentration, and they held their guns down and turned around. It only took a moment for them to realize it was me and Missy, and they didn't notice the crowd coming behind us.

"They came back," Captain Fowler shouted. "Get them."

Just as they turned their weapons back on us, Missy and I took off at a run, heading back towards the oncoming crowd. We pushed as fast as we could. Within seconds we heard a gun cock, and I moved into a faster gear, one that I didn't know I had. Before I knew it, I was immersed in a crowd of family, friends, and neighbors curious to know what was going on. When I turned, the men chasing us had put their guns back down and were staring into the crowd. There was no way they were going to shoot with all the witnesses we managed to attract.

In the safety of the crowd, I pulled the fax sheet out of the envelope I was still carrying. I knew I needed to end it. I took a deep breath and stepped out of the crowd. I moved forward until I was standing nose to nose with Captain Fowler.

"It's over," I said, handing him the sheet. He read it and looked up. He chewed on his own lip for a moment. His hand was hovering over his gun. Finally, he took a deep breath and said, "Weapons down, boys."

Within a moment, the sounds of sirens could be heard, as police cruisers came flying down the lane.

It only took an hour before every state trooper in the area had descended on our little campground, and most of the prominent citizens of Marsh found themselves in cuffs. Crimes ranged from concealment, to aiding and abetting, kidnapping, and sadly even murder. We knew for sure now that it was Charity that I had kicked out of the camper, and she met her gruesome fate only moments later, though not before one last heroic act: storing the documents with me, trusting me to get her justice.

I felt terrible guilt thinking about kicking her away that night, wondering if I'd let her in if she would have survived, or if we both would have died.

The pictures did hold incriminating evidence as we suspected. Farmer Hannah didn't merely suffer an accident; he was killed for refusing to pledge fealty to the founders of Marsh. He'd left after he fell in love with a woman from Muskegon and could no longer support, even silently, the founders' ideals.

Captain Fowler begged Tammy to tell him where she found the documents, something that the group had been seeking for nearly twenty years. She refused to give him the satisfaction of an answer. Tammy was tough as nails; for an entire week she had resisted telling Captain Fowler or Mr. Blanch the secret of the camper crawl space. As soon as Fowler was carted away, she revealed her secrets to me and Missy.

"For a bunch of town founders they were sure a bunch of dip shits," she said. "The farmer's wife must have helped the farmer with his notes because he wrote things in code. It would say something like "Marsh Meeting" in the book, and for each meeting he wrote a recipe under that date. Charity and me, we saw that old *Better Homes and Gardens Cookbook* up on the shelf. You know, the one with the red checker pattern that everybody has. I recognized a couple of the recipes, the one for Snickerdoodles and the one for stuffed peppers."

"They wrote recipes down and nobody could crack that code?" I asked.

"Yup. That's not even half of it. The damn fools took roll calls before hate crimes and kept the roll call right next to the list of crimes."

"I can't get over it. The Marsh town founders were keeping a list of hate crimes in a cookbook?"

"Well, Farmer Hannah or his wife did. We saw the notes and we knew what they were. We saw the cookbook, pulled it down, and all these papers fell out. Charity and I scooped them up, and when we saw what we had, we were like, this is some major conspiracy shit."

"So, you got the documents, but how did they figure out that you had them?" I asked.

"Well, first we went out for pancakes up at Paradise, and we met this farmer dude who told us about the safety thing for the hay baler in these pictures. We were like oh, man, the farmer died in the baler that day. So, we called the police in Marsh to tell them. Charity was talking to Captain Fowler; she told him everything. We didn't realize then that he was part of everything. We hadn't read all the papers. The captain tells us to meet him out at the lake, which was sort of the closest place in Marsh to Paradise Pancakes, so we didn't think anything of it. We go there, and the next thing we knew some cars came roaring up to meet us and they dragged us into that cabin.

Well, you know what happened after that. Charity was brave as hell, got out the cellar window, snuck around to the front of the cabin and got the papers back, but before she could open the cellar door for me, she heard someone coming back to the cabin. She had to make a run for it without me. I'd already told her all about your family camper by then."

Missy asked, "How did you and Charity end up together in the first place?"

She smiled. "So let me tell you how it all started. Charity came into the bar last week, didn't know I worked there, just heading to her parent's place, and she stops in, and we like recognize each other. There was this creep following me around, and I was telling her about it, and she's like, 'I'll stay with you while you close up, in case he comes back.' So, she cleans the bar with me, and we help ourselves to a couple of drinks, and I talk about how shitty my life was going, and she tells me her life isn't going so hot either. She tells me this douche she's been dating had decked her that night. She was going back to her parents' house, trying to get away from him.

"Then we both talked about how things were when we were kids and things were simple, just reminiscing and shit. And she says 'Hey, remember that farm trip,' and I was like yeah, and she says the Asian kid that moved away had pictures from it. I say 'no shit;' then, she shows me these pictures, we see Hannah Farms, and we were like, grab a Yellow Pages and go. That was that."

"Well, I have a bit of good news for you. That creep you talked about chasing after you. I don't think he's looking for you anymore."

"No shit?" she shivered.

"Yeah, I took care of him. But that's a story for another day. Let's get you home."

I didn't see David again that night; he wasn't arrested, but he was questioned. I told the State Police what David and Mickey Fowler had done for us, trying to protect us. Corey was taken away by ambulance, the angle of his dislocated elbow making even the police officers queasy.

The sun was nearly up by the time I rolled back into my grandparents' house, and there was a mighty welcoming party, more than just my family, waiting around the circle drive to greet us. John stepped out of the car first to a cacophony of cheers, and his very pregnant wife looked ready to slap him, or hug him, or both. In the end, she went for a hug and then a good cry. I crawled out, the injuries from the night before finally setting in, scratches, bumps, and bruises, and possibly a few broken fingers from my tumble on the ladder.

I moved to my grandparents first, my grandmother jumping up to hug me and my grandfather tapping his heart as he looked at me.

"Good kid," he managed. I bent down and hugged him; he couldn't lift his arms high enough to reciprocate, instead tapping my arm.

My aunts all came in for hugs, and everybody wanted to hear me and John recount what happened and how we found the missing girl and solved a murder. We were too tired and gave the abbreviated version. As much as I wanted to bask in the warmth of my family, I needed a shower and a minute to sit down. I was going to have to move my train ticket out a day and break the news to my boss that I'd need to take another day off. I was sure it would be fine. After all, I'd solved a murder and saved a woman.

As I moved toward the house, Skeet called me over, pleading that he had to show me one last thing before I took my shower. He pulled me to the barn and opened his arms pointing to an old Winnebago Brave.

"You win another one?" I asked.

"Nope," he said. "This one's for you. Sold the Booby Bouncer. Figured out maybe that's why I won it in the first place. Grandma is keeping her spot at the lake, and you can have this and a little cash to boot, enough for a season at the campground if you want. It's a car and a house all in one. Needs a little TLC, but I figure with you leaving your job and all you are going to have time to do that."

If it weren't for the exhaustion, I would have been jumping up and down, but I was beat, so I merely cried and stammered out a thank you.

Skeeter hugged me and leaned in. "I killed all the spiders in it and everything, certified spider free."

I sputtered, laughing through the tears.

CHAPTER TWENTY-NINE

I MADE MY WAY BACK TO CHICAGO on Tuesday, and my boss Bill was an absolute wreck, not over what I told him had happened to me but over the missed deadlines that were sure to follow my extra day off.

I was scarce on details but brought a newspaper clipping from the daily paper in Lansing back with me, hoping he would understand the gravity of my situation and offer some condolences or sympathy, especially as he indicated a write up for calling out on short notice might be in order. He read the clipping talking about the kidnapping, murder and my traumatic experience at the waterpark and said, "Yup, all this news is Michigan-based. This doesn't have anything to do with our work, and it's no excuse for calling out on short notice. What I need is for you to focus, get over it, and get your city council story finished."

What I had planned prior to that moment was a very professional meeting where I would give my two weeks' notice and thank Bill for giving me the opportunity to work at the paper, but what happened instead was I picked up his cup of coffee and turned it over onto his keyboard and tossed his tumbler full of pencils off of his desk, sending them flying all over the floor. I stormed out of his office, threw my name badge on the empty reception counter, and walked out.

That night I packed the last of my belongings in suitcases and garbage bags, threw away the small amount of food from my pantry, and placed my furniture, which I had gotten from the curb, back where it came from.

I called my grandmother and told her I'd be back the next day, much to her delight. I gave my building manager notice, and to my surprise he said he needed the apartment for a nephew who was in desperate need of a place and wouldn't be charging me a break-lease fee.

With one last night in the city, I had not thought through my bed situation and had to camp out on the living room floor, using an old Michigan State sweatshirt as a blanket. Even in those circumstances, just like the nights at the camper with my family, I felt at ease. A weight was off me, a weight I hadn't noticed I was carrying. It occurred to me that perhaps I had been fighting my destiny. Writing at a tiny newspaper in Chicago, living all alone, that wasn't what I was meant to do. I didn't realize until I quit trying to fight it; I'd been trying to fit a square peg in a round hole. Only now, with a plan to move back home, was I doing what I was meant to do, and I could feel the rightness in every cell of my body.

It was late, dark, and the sounds of the city were quieter than normal, an almost perfect scenario for me to fall asleep. I couldn't help but think about David and our trip to Singapore. He hadn't called, hadn't seen me off at the train station. My mind went back to the date, and the story of the man who refused to leave his town. He crawled in and out of my mind just like he had crawled in and out of that window in the sand dunes, and I couldn't shake the image. I scrambled out from under my sweatshirt and grabbed a notepad and pen from my bag and started to write:

In the early 1800s, the small town of Singapore had a beautiful shoreline and a strong economy anchored by several sawmills, a successful bank, and a first-rate hotel. The bustling port town attracted people who dreamed of success and saw opportunity.

It was a city on the rise, built to rival the metropolis across the water, Chicago.

For years, the inhabitants of Singapore were uncommonly lucky, enjoying a meteoric ascent that brought its citizens excellent health and wealth. When the Chicago fire nearly destroyed their sister city, the citizens of Singapore gave their resources to help rebuild. The sawmills were ordered to work at a pace never before seen.

But what the citizens of Singapore gave away in good faith tore at the very foundations of their town. Within just a few short years, Chicago was again standing strong, with the timber of Singapore holding it up, and Singapore was a husk, buried and gone forever...

ACKNOWLEDGEMENTS

A hearty thanks to the authors and editors who have helped me along the way. To Erin, who always had faith in me. Mindy, who gave me inspiration. Karen, who wouldn't let me quit. Melissa and Kate, who brought the fun. Janet, who could see what I could not. And my newest team member, Cheryl, for keeping an eye on my commas. I've met so many more along the way. I'm not letting any of them edit this, so forgive them my errors as I forgive the errors that Microsoft Word has introduced to my work over the years.

ABOUT THE AUTHOR

Nicole is an award-winning journalist and author. The Michigan Press Association recognized her as a top feature writer. In 2014, she won an honorable mention in genre fiction from in the Writer's Digest Self-Publishing Competition. She wrote for two daily newspapers in the greater Philadelphia area before producing a best-selling book series. She now writes from her home in Michigan, where she lives with her husband and her two children.

Milton Keynes UK
Ingram Content Group UK Ltd.
UKHW021118030524
442090UK00005BA/79